To protect her daughter from the fast life and bad influence of London, her mother sends her to school in rural Ghana.

THE MOVE IS FOR THE GIRL'S OWN GOOD, IN HER MOTHER'S MIND, but for the daughter, the reality of being the new girl, the foreigner-among-your-own-people, is even worse than the idea.

During her time at school, she would learn that Ghana was much more complicated than her fellow expats had ever told her, including how much a London-raised child takes something like water for granted. In Ghana, "water becomes a symbol of who had and who didn't. If you didn't have water . . . you were poor because no one had sent you some."

After six months in Ghana—which felt like six years—her mother summons her home to London to meet the new man in her mother's life—and his daughter. The reunion is bittersweet and short-lived as her parents decide it's time for her to get to know her father. So once again, she's sent off, this time to live with her father and his new wife, and their young children in New York—but not before a family trip to Disney World.

Powder
Necklace

A Novel

NANA EKUA BREW-HAMMOND

WASHINGTON SQUARE PRESS
New York • London • Toronto • Sydney

Washington Square Press
A Division of Simon & Schuster, Inc.
1230 Avenue of the Americas
New York, NY 10020

First Washington Square Press trade paperback edition April 2010

WASHINGTON SQUARE PRESS and colophon are registered trademarks
of Simon & Schuster, Inc.

For information about special discounts for bulk purchases,
please contact Simon & Schuster Special Sales at
1-866-506-1949 or business@simonandschuster.com.

The Simon & Schuster Speakers Bureau can bring authors
to your live event. For more information or to book an
event contact the Simon & Schuster Speakers Bureau at
1-866-248-3049 or visit our website at www.simonspeakers.com.

Designed by Julie Adams

Manufactured in the United States of America

10 9 8 7 6 5 4 3 2 1

Library of Congress Cataloging-in-Publication Data
Brew-Hammond, Nana Ekua.
  Powder necklace : a novel / Nana Ekua Brew-Hammond.
    p. cm.
  1. Children of divorced parents—Fiction. 2. English—United States—
Fiction. 3. New York (N.Y.)—Fiction. I. Title.
  PS3602.R4588P69 2010
  813'.6—dc22   2009020992

ISBN 978-1-4391-2610-3
ISBN 978-1-4391-4911-9 (ebook)

For anyone who's ever felt
she couldn't hold her head up high—
but mostly for my family
who raised me to hold up mine . . .
no matter what.

1

Everything happens for God's good reason is the cliché my mother has drilled in my head since I was old enough to ask "Why?"—but too young to question why she really didn't seem to believe this was true regarding her and my father. She would go off on these paranoid rants about him and how he had left us. These tirades were always followed with a lecture on how I should let that be a lesson to me about boys, how they only wanted to spoil me ("spoil" being her euphemism for sex), and how much she had sacrificed for my benefit.

She usually got this way after her typically long day at work, a glass of sherry, or a love scene in a television movie. I was smart enough—even at ages four, five, and six—to know I couldn't help her. So I tuned her out. But when I got older, her tirades sent me into hiccupping, snotty hysterics.

My tears seemed to work like rain in those moments, extinguishing the flames of her bitter outbursts. She'd use the velvety back of her hand, like the windshield wiper on our Opel, to stop each sliding drop until I was calm.

Everything I do is for your good, she'd say.

On those nights, after she turned out the light in my room, I'd pray to God that my mother would be happy. Truly happy. That she would forget about my father. That

I would be enough for her. I wanted to be good for her, never disappoint her, never leave her the way my father had.

Every time Mum would rant, I wished my father could be there since it was he who was really her target audience. Mum didn't mean it when she said to me—practically foaming at the mouth—"Go on. Ask him. Ask him why you only hear from him on your birthday, on Christmas and New Year's." I ignored her reverse psychology and went to Auntie Flora to take Mum up on her suggestion to call him.

"It's complicated, Lila," Auntie Flora said when I worked up the courage to ask her what had happened between Mum and my father to make her so bitter. She added, not unlike my Mum, "Maybe he can explain to you himself."

My father's voice boomed on the other end of the line. I wanted to ask him what he was so happy about. He answered before I could ask.

"Lila! You're a big sister. Your mother just had twins!" I listened, confused, until I realized he meant his wife, my stepmother, had just had twins.

Tears suddenly seared my eyes like meat in a saucepan of oil and onions. I had called to . . . now I didn't know what I had called to hear or say. I wasn't expecting the jealousy, the outrage.

I handed Auntie Flora the phone, choking on hiccups. My armpits started itching the way they inexplicably do whenever I get freaked out or excited. Auntie Flora's eyes got big with panic.

We both knew she didn't want Mum to find me this way. We both knew Mum was always waiting for something bad to happen to me when I was with Auntie Flora. She'd ask, "What happened?" whenever Auntie Flora dropped me off at home, instead of "Did you have fun?"

Of course Mum clapped the knocker on Auntie Flora's door just at that moment when I had my meltdown. I was relieved to see her even though I knew she'd be furious that I had spoken to my father in her absence. When Mum saw me, she flew to my side and cleared my tears. She looked up at Auntie Flora. "What happened?" When Auntie Flora answered, she led me out of Auntie Flora's flat to the Opel parked several blocks away without so much as a word.

I didn't see Auntie Flora again until three years later.

My father still called me on my birthdays, for Christmas and New Year's, but I got off the phone as quickly as I could from then on.

"We just got on the phone, Lila," he once said, the boom in his voice slightly diminished.

"I know," I said cruelly, glancing over at Mum, hoping she was pleased with me for icing my father out.

I lived to please Mum then—even when it stopped being as simple as being mean to my father. That's why I still don't understand how she could so abruptly have sent me away.

2

I'd seen the boys before; they represented everything Mum had warned me about. They were often at the bus stop near the Off License shop, a gang of friends trying to chat up any of the girls from school who would stop and listen. I always rushed past them, succeeding in making myself invisible to them as I walked home, but one day, I made the mistake of making eye contact with one of them . . .

"You! In the blue coat," he shouted after me. My armpits started to itch. "You! I'm talking to you!"

"Please leave me alone," I said, which he took as an invitation to do the opposite, because the next thing I knew he was running up to me.

"Why you walking so fast?"

My armpits pumped wildly as I took off running. I could hear his friends laughing at me and him. When I got around the corner, I checked to see that he wasn't following me before I started walking again.

The following day, I told my friend from school Everton about Bus Stop Boy, and he offered to walk me home. Everton was the sort of boy who had more girl than guy friends. Not because he was gay, though there was something girlish about his quiet obedience, but because he wasn't one of the boys at the back of the classroom laughing or loudly clearing his throat to throw Mrs. McGovern off—nothing like the boy who harassed me at the bus stop. He was smart and respectful, and he was a good listener—the kind of guy who would grow up to be a player and/or a politician.

"That's him," I whispered to Ev, rubbing the itch out of my underarm as we passed the guy who had tried to chat me up.

Ev tried to look more mannish when I pointed him out, but next to Bus Stop Boy and his gang of tossers—chains glinting at their throats and wrists, fuzz blackening their upper lips, Nike trainers sparkling on their feet—he looked like the pre-teen zygote that he was. One of them pointed at Ev's rubber-soled school shoes and the whole group had a chuckle at his expense. I felt if Ev walked back past them alone right away they might try to take a pop at him, so I invited him into our flat. Thus, we established our ritual. He would walk me home past the boys who lived to spoil me, and we would do our homework together. Afterward, we'd play video games. I made sure he left before Mum came home.

We had a laugh on those afternoons about the full beard that sprouted from Mrs. McGovern's chin and posed reasons why our classmate Roma couldn't speak without globules of saliva collecting at the corners of her mouth. (We decided Roma's braces were the culprit.) We pooled our allowance together and took turns treating each other to crisps and döner kebabs. That sort of thing.

Ev had no intention of spoiling me. In fact, he was completely oblivious to my immense crush on him. *I* was the one who wanted to kiss him. But nothing happened.

The day Mum caught us in the living room, granted, we were lying on our stomachs, close, in front of the television. I was waiting my turn as Ev's thumbs defied blisters, flying between the buttons on his video game controller, and the next thing I knew, Mum was clapping Ev's head back and forth between her hands and screaming, "You! You! You want to spoil my daughter!" The television had been on so loud, we hadn't heard her come in.

I started shouting and running behind Mum as she chased him out. "Mum, stop it! Ev, I'm so sorry!"

There wasn't too far to run in our cramped flat, so just after Ev smacked into the side table next to the couch, sending a vase of silk wildflowers crashing to the carpet in his race to our door, he was gone. And then it was just us, the television still blaring in the background.

Mum slumped against the door she'd just slammed behind Ev, suddenly drained of her rage and color.

"Lila, haven't you been hearing me?" she asked me. "You think these boys mean you any good?"

"Mum, we weren't doing anything! We were just—"

"You were just *what*? Are you allowed to have boys in this house? Eh? Eh? *Eh?*" Before I could answer, she started the Tirade. Boys were walking penises—*pen-usses,* as she pronounced it in the lilting accent of a Ghanaian woman who had lived in London for fifteen years. When they were through spoiling me, they would move on and spoil some other girl. *"Don't ever think you are different or special to them."*

I looked at Mum anew that day and wondered if her rants had anything to do with why my father was in New York and she was here.

I started to get up. I wanted to leave Ev a message before he got home and reiterate how sorry I was that Mum had gone senseless on him, but she snatched my moving leg like the leash of an errant dog. I tumbled to the carpet, shocked. My purple polished toenails painfully curled under my feet. Mum had spanked me before, but that day she proceeded to *beat* me. Her hands came down like lightning, clapping like thunder as they rained on my arms, back, bum, and thighs.

I cried enough tears to just about fill the Thames, but my tears didn't put out Mum's fire this time. She continued to beat me as she kept repeating, "Haven't you been hearing me?"

When she finished, she left me in hiccups, mucus streaming past my lips to my chin and down to the hollow in my throat, and disappeared behind her bedroom door. I pulled myself from the carpet to the washroom and took a shower. I was careful to be quick because Mum was always going on about how my long steamy showers would make the wallpaper pucker. "Father . . . ," I prayed in the shower. My prayer started and ended there. I couldn't speak, guilt battling defiant outrage at Mum. I knew I had disappointed her by letting Ev into the house, but we hadn't done anything. I needed her to know nothing had happened, but she wouldn't hear anything.

"Lila, I'm sending you to your Auntie Flora's for a bit," Mum announced the next day when she got home from work. "I just . . . need . . . a break." She wheezed out each word. "Start packing. Now."

Looking back, I should have known something really wrong was in the works if Mum was reintroducing Auntie Flora into our lives. I packed a suitcase of sweaters and jeans that rainy September Friday, figuring I'd be at Auntie Flora's just for the weekend. By Sunday, Mum would have cooled down enough that I could let her know unequivocally that I had not let Ev spoil me.

I followed her into the Opel and watched my power lock come down. Sinking back in my seat as the streetlamps and traffic lights reflected off the narrow, rain-slick roads, I noticed more and more signs directing us to Heathrow Airport.

This wasn't the way to Auntie Flora's. I turned to her, confused.

"Mum, where are we going?"

I'll never forget the cut of her profile against her rain-splattered window as she answered me. Like something out of a horror film, her honey-brown skin was silhouette-black and her small flat nose tilted upward as she kept her eyes fixed on the road. The curtain of skinny braids covering the side of her face vibrated with the motion of the car. Her voice shook a little too. "You're going to Ghana," she said.

3

I felt numb, still too shocked to process what had just happened as I sat on the connecting flight from Accra to Kumasi. I was starting to feel a chill on the inside, like I was coming down with a cold—except the sickness I felt wasn't in my body.

I fixated on who was picking me up as the small plane landed in the middle of the pitch-black airport runway, the Kumasi Airport sign glowing in the distance. Mum's sister Auntie Irene could be the one, but then it could be any one of the aunties and uncles whose voices crackled in the bad phone connection between Ghana and England. (In Ghanaian culture, every adult is an "auntie" or "uncle" whether they're related to you or not.)

I marveled at my gross underestimation of Mum's anti-boys stance. I knew what a live wire the matter was for Mum and I'd stupidly stepped on it with wet feet. I still couldn't understand why she had reacted so violently though. At some point in my transition from little girl to woman, Mum had to know I would meet a guy and like him.

Equally baffling to me was when Mum had bought the ticket. She was always complaining there was no money for extras. *Ah! There is no money—you're embarrassing me!* she would sharply reprimand me if I asked for brand-name anything at the shops.

A black-skinned man with golden-yellow teeth broke into my thoughts. Grinning his ears off and clapping like a seal, he separated his hands to make the sign of the cross before he started applauding again.

"We tank God, oh. We tank God for safe landing," he sang.

I wanted to laugh—at "tank" and the thought of applauding a plane landing—but I knew if I started laughing, tears would follow. I had cried on and off since I passed the "Only Passengers Beyond This Point" threshold at Heathrow.

Helen, the lanky, scarlet-lipped air hostess who had been minding me on the flight, gave me several sheets of paper when I told her why I was crying. "Write everything you're feeling right now, then read it again a week from now. You'll be surprised how different you feel then."

I did as she said, surprised how quickly I filled each sheet, front and back, with my confusion, shock, panic, disappointment, anger, and feelings of loss and betrayal. I folded the sheets into a thick square and pushed them into my back pocket.

"Helen, do you know who's coming to pick me up?" I asked, pulling my UNACCOMPANIED MINOR tag over my head now that the plane had come to a full stop.

"I don't, love, but we'll figure it out once we get to the arrivals hall."

The seat belt sign went dim and the captain made an announcement over the loudspeaker as I watched Helen's fellow hostesses take their places at the plane doors. Not everyone had been tricked into coming to Ghana, it occurred to me. For some it was their job.

All I knew of my parents' homeland, and Africa in general, was what Mum had told me (*Everyone is a crook, Lila, hustling for that almighty cedi*), what I had seen in pictures (miles of dirt where sidewalks and streets were supposed to be), on the news (bloated-bellied kids too weak to swat away buzzing flies), at the Ghana market (stinky foodstuffs), and what I had heard from all the aunties and uncles in London (most of whom weren't actually related to me, but I had to call them "Auntie" and "Uncle" out of respect). They all claimed to love Ghana but contradicted themselves by threatening to send their kids there when they misbehaved. They themselves had left decades ago, and while they always spoke about going back, none of them had.

I'd always felt lucky to have been born in London—the place they'd all escaped to. But now I was where they had been.

I followed Helen past the curtain, now drawn back, that had separated the World Traveler section from the combined Club World and first-class cabins. The moment Helen and I trod down the steep and narrow metal steps at the plane door, we got kissed by a thick, wet heat. The hairs at my temple sprang away from my ponytail. My two-week-old perm had become a frizz ball by the time I got to the bottom of the stairs. Two dimly lit Ghana Airways buses waited for us.

When our bus pulled up to the airport terminal, we emptied into an airless building. I sniffed around, trying to place the source of the garlicky, boiled-egg, sulphur-hair-pomade smell in the room. I even peeled off the cardigan I'd worn on the plane and snuck a whiff of my armpits. But it wasn't me. Helen nodded blame in the direction of one of the men in the orange reflector vests. "These guys don't wear deodorant," she whispered to me. The man passed by as if on cue. The power of his rank odor made me nearly throw up my roasted chicken, mixed vegetables, and clotted cream supper.

I followed Helen around a corner where two men in swamp-green uniforms sat behind elevated desks under an IMMIGRA-TION sign and a welcome banner that read AKWAABA. I didn't feel welcome as I stood on the "Other Nationals" queue behind the all-white cabin crew and another white man complaining about the heat.

I looked over at the longer "Ghanaians" queue, which could have been called the Ugly Queue: long and lined with short sweaty men and women wearing bad wigs fussing over fidgeting children.

"Your passport."

I turned my attention to the man at the immigration desk and pulled my passport from my back pocket.

The officer looked from my baby picture to me to Helen before stamping it. "*Ewura, akwaaba,*" he said. *Welcome home, girl.* This was not my home.

The body odor attacked me afresh when we walked into the baggage claim area as men in coveralls stamped PORTER rushed us with baggage trolleys. More men in jumpsuits started hauling in the luggage from our flight and stacking the bags in the middle of the room.

"*Onuanu yɛ medie!*" *That one is mine,* the We Tank God Oh! Clapper from the plane shouted as he wrestled his battered suitcase from the mess of plaid plastic bags and bloated cases that were Magic Markered with names or whose handles were wrapped with identifying bits of twine and string.

"Lila, wait right here while I figure out who's coming to collect you," Helen said.

As soon as Helen's navy, red-and-white-flecked uniform swished behind the door of a corner office, I heard "*Tsss! Tsss!*" From across the terminal, a porter hissed again, coming my way. Every porter in the room seemed to be charging at me with their trolleys. "*Tsssssss! Broni, mamin kitanu ma wo!*" *White girl, let me carry that for you!* They made their service offering sound like a demand. "*Broni!*" I was sure I had heard the white-person part wrong.

My pits itched like mad as the *tsss*ing porter came closer. I looked around for Helen, for an exit sign. Someone tapped me on the shoulder and that intensely awful garlic-egg-sulphur smell floated through my nose to my mouth. I wanted to gag as I scraped my armpits. Then the room went completely black.

"*Ho!* Lights off? *Ah!*" A man shouted. I screamed as the lights flickered on. Now two porters surrounded me.

"*You for disappear!*" The porter who had hissed at me roared at the other. He locked his hand around my wrist. "*You no dey see I dey help 'em?*"

"Let me go!" I flailed his hand off.

"Lila!"

I crumpled into relieved tears at the sight of Auntie Irene. Helen was with her, wheeling the small navy suitcase I had packed with sweaters and jeans for what was supposed to be a weekend stay at Auntie Flora's.

"I'll leave you two alone then. Lila, have a wonderful visit." Helen waved her chalk-white arm at us before turning to disappear into the crush of black passengers.

"Auntie Irene!" I fell into her fleshy arms and wouldn't let go. I filled my chest with quick, deep gulps of her fresh powder scent as my tears splashed on her blouse and spread to form a huge wet spot. When we separated, I was shaking so much I couldn't even have a giggle at the gold rings and gaudily long nails that crowded Auntie Irene's fingers or the high heels and tight jeans that made her legs look like drumsticks.

She looked awful. Parted in the middle, her coarse hair was gelled down in an unsuccessful attempt to match the silky black and blond-highlighted weave that waved around her face. I'd always thought—and thanked God—that she looked nothing like Mum.

"What have you done to her?" Auntie Irene asked the porter

roughly, a cold English accent frosting her tone as she stroked my face the way Mum did, trying to calm me down.

"Oh, madam, I was only trying to help my small sister find her bag." His tone had dropped a few octaves. He wasn't *tsss*ing now.

"You don't see that you are frightening her? What is your name? I will see that Uncle Fifi deals with you."

"Oh, madam, *ɛnyɛ Uncle Fifi asɛm. W'oa wo nim, kakra yɛ be di nti.*" *This isn't something Uncle Fifi needs to know about. You know we work for the little that we eat.*

"Take the suitcase," she ordered.

Auntie Irene squeezed her fingers around mine, her long nail tips softly digging into my palm, and led me out of baggage claim.

"When they hear the English accent, they know they are not on your level," she explained as we followed close behind the porter. "Give me your passport."

She showed it to the customs agent, he tipped his hat to Auntie Irene, and then we were in the hot, pitch-black night again. My shirt was soaked. My hair might as well have been natural at this point, no longer honoring the chemicals I used to control its curl pattern.

I untied my cardigan from my waist—the hem of my shirt beneath it was now ringed with sweat—and tossed it onto the trolley as the porter pushed it through the car park. When we got to Auntie Irene's truck, she pushed a few folded cedi notes into the porter's hand through the window after he had packed my suitcase into the backseat. He bowed his head in thanks and skipped off in the direction of the arrivals terminal, pulling his trolley behind him.

4

"Welcome to Ghana, my dear." Auntie Irene turned to hand me her handbag as she started the engine. The radio delivered the news. "So, you got the lights-off greeting, eh?" Auntie Irene asked.

I yanked the stiff lever at my side to roll my window down, taking my frustration out on the handle. "Auntie Irene, how long am I going to be here?"

"*Mhm.*" She twisted her head. "Keep the window up or the mosquitoes will eat you for supper." She turned on the air conditioner before she answered me. "Lila, your mum needs a break."

A break? This was the second time I'd heard that. "I didn't know mothers were allowed 'breaks' from their kids."

"Well, we learn something new every day, don't we?"

"How long is this break supposed to be?"

"As long as she needs it to be." Auntie Irene pulled up to the gatehouse in front of us. "Lila, look in my bag and take out two hundred cedis, eh."

I bent to pick up the handbag resting between my legs and held up the rubber-banded wad of limp paper inside. "This?"

Auntie Irene took one of the bills from me and leaned over to hand it to the graying man in the gatehouse. "Uncle Fifi, *me-dasi, ai.*" She thanked him —for what, I wasn't sure.

"*Ei!* Madam Seamstress!" A smirk stretched across his face as he hid the money in his shirt pocket.

"My sister's child," Auntie Irene introduced me. "*Ofrɛ nu* Lila."

"*Ei! Ewura, ɛtisɛn?*"

"I'm fine."

His eyes lit up. "*Ei!* Your sister has done well! These Abrokye kids come here and wrinkle their faces like they've smelled something bad when you speak Twi to them." He squeezed his face to demonstrate. "But you should have answered me back in our language."

"Right," I mumbled, looking out the window.

"Her mother has sent her to stay for a while."

Uncle Fifi let out a throaty chuckle. "Ah, okay." He reached into the car to clap me on the back. "By the time you leave this place, you will love it, eh. Ghana is your *home.*"

I bristled at the word as Auntie Irene started the car again. "Home" was 14 Benjamin Road, SE 15, Peckham, London.

A bony girl with her hair cut low like a boy's scurried to greet us when we arrived at Auntie Irene's place. She took my bag.

"Lila, this is Enyo. You two are the same age, so you should get on nicely."

"*Wezo,*" Enyo said, shyly raising her eyes to mine.

My Twi was limited to what I'd heard Mum speak so it didn't surprise me that Enyo's greeting didn't sound familiar.

"Enyo is from the Volta region, so she speaks Ewe," Auntie Irene explained.

"I said, 'Welcome.'" Enyo smirked.

I wondered why Enyo was here if she wasn't from where we were, but I let the question go for the time being as I followed her into the small bungalow.

I could tell that, once upon a time, the room's walls had been white, but now, under the twitching fluorescent light, they were a dingy ash color that got dirtier toward the floor. I jumped when I saw a lizard slither up the wall and rest in a corner of the ceiling.

Enyo giggled at me.

"*Ho!* It's just a wall gecko." Auntie Irene rolled her eyes.

A giant freezer hummed a dirge against the longest wall. Enyo opened the door at the end of this wall and led the way into a dark room. The smell of incense was thick; a glowing tip burned on the floor. She flipped on the light and quickly closed the door behind her. The incense, a dark green swirl, didn't look anything like what they sold in the shops on Peckham Rye.

"Mosquito coil," Enyo said, answering the question mark on my face. "If the mosquitoes bite you, you will get malaria and have to take chloroquine, which will make you *itch.*" She pretended to scratch herself to show how bad this itch would be. I scratched my armpits at the thought. "They don't have that in Abrokye?" Enyo marveled.

She laid my suitcase on the full-size bed and started to unpack it.

"I can do that." I was embarrassed by the heavy clothing inside that proved I hadn't planned this trip.

"*Ei,* this is nice!" She held up my cardigan. "Can I have it?"

It was like 30° C and she wanted a cardigan? I remembered Mum saying how Ghanaians were always stretching their hands out for something. *Always asking me to send them this or that— expecting it—as if I am a rich woman here.*

"Sure," I said. I was exhausted and just wanted to sleep—and wake up in London shaking my head at how real this dream had been. Besides, if Enyo wanted to unpack for me, she should get something for the work.

I turned into a corner and had started to take off my jeans and T-shirt when Auntie Irene walked into the room with a phone identical to the one we had in London. I remembered the day Mum bought it and packed it in a suitcase full of things she told me Auntie Irene couldn't get in Ghana.

"It's your mother."

I started to cry before the phone was on my ear. "Mum, when can I come home?"

Mum's voice crackled in the bad connection. "Not for a bit, Lila."

"How long is 'a bit'? Mum, *please.*" Why weren't my tears working their magic anymore?

"Lila, this will be good for you. You'll learn about Ghana and—"

"Mum, nothing happened. *Okay?*" *Father, please.* I petitioned Mum and God for an immediate about-face of this horrible misunderstanding, but no response. The connection seemed to be bad all around.

Auntie Irene took the phone from my ear. "*Obɛ* get used to it," Auntie Irene assured Mum as she walked out of the room. Enyo ran after Auntie Irene to close the door. "We don't want any mosquitoes to come inside," she explained.

I will never get used to this, I thought as I pulled out the sheets of paper I'd poured out my feelings to on the plane and tucked them in the side pocket of my suitcase.

5

I woke up to a radio deejay announcing it was 25° C outside. I cried my now magicless tears. My prayer—that it had all been a nightmare, that Mum hadn't gotten the wrong idea about me and Ev—hadn't gotten past the ceiling, where, by the way, another gecko was resting. I was in Ghana; the man on the radio had a fake British accent; and Enyo was walking into the room with a bucket of water.

"Oh! Why are you weeping?" She put the bucket down at the edge of the bed we had shared.

"I want to go home."

She sucked her teeth and picked up the bucket with an "Is that all?" look on her face. "I fetched this for you to have your bath."

"To have my *bath*?" I wiped my tears with the bedsheet. "In a bucket?"

She went to the bureau and handed me a handkerchief for my tears from one of the drawers. "Come, I'll show you the washroom."

I followed her past a small toilet room to the bigger washroom with a tub and a waterless toilet bowl.

"It's a bidet—to clean your *pipi* and buttocks," Enyo explained, giggling at the confusion on my face. She squatted over it to show me how it worked.

When I coiled my ponytail up, Enyo rushed to touch my hair. "Your hair is long, oh!"

I looked over at her close crop. "If you like long hair, why don't you grow yours out?"

"*Bɛ* we have to cut our hair for school."

"Really? Why?" I shook my head, hoping Mum's break would be over before I'd have to worry about the answer. "Never mind."

When Enyo left, I took off my nightie, pulled my bucket into the tub, and scooped a little water to wet the bar of soap. The water was ice cold! I twisted the handle labeled HOT, but cold water flowed from it even after I let it run for a while.

"*Auntie Irene! Auntie Irene!*" I put my nightie on and went to find her.

Enyo was in the toilet room, crouching to clean the dirt behind the bowl, as I marched past. "What is it?"

"The hot water's not working!"

"Oh." Enyo continued scrubbing. "I can heat it for you when I am finished cleaning, or you can put some water on the stove."

"Hot water doesn't flow from the tap?" I started to cry again, mourning for the steamy shower I had taken just the day before. Auntie Irene appeared at the door.

"Lila, what is it?" she asked, alarmed.

"I want to take a *hot* shower."

Auntie Irene sucked her teeth. "Ah! Are you a baby? Go and heat the water then. Ah!" She added as an afterthought, "The cool water will even make you feel fresh in this heat."

Tears slid down my cheeks and dropped from my chin onto Enyo's work. Enyo got up. "I'll heat your water for you."

Auntie Irene stopped her. "Listen to me, Lila. You are here, and, I'm sorry to say, all the crying in the world won't change that. Take this opportunity to learn a new way of doing things. Now, *mun freho*." *Get out.* She dismissed both Enyo and me. "I want to use the toilet."

I brushed back my tears and went to the kitchen to heat my water, but each burner on the stovetop was covered. I sighed and marched back to the washroom, grimacing as I splashed my face and arms the way I would at the beach. It was the fastest bath I'd ever taken.

When I got back to the room, my clothes were laid out on the bed along with a comb, a canister of powder, and a small jar of skin pomade. I twisted open the jar to find oil sitting on a lard-like substance, then closed it right back up. There was no way I was putting that on my skin. I put on my clothes and walked out into the living room.

"Auntie Irene?"

"I'm in the kitchen."

I followed Auntie Irene's voice to find her sitting behind a sewing machine. Her gold-streaked weave was pulled away from her face in a loose ponytail. Her foot worked the machine's pedal as her fingers guided a piece of fabric under the needle. A shaggy mushroom-colored mutt spied me through the screen door and ran up to yelp at me. In the distance behind him I could see a black dog sleeping in the shade of a small shed.

"You have dogs?!" For the first time since I'd left London, I smiled. I'd always wanted a pet, but Mum didn't believe in having animals in the house. She thought every last domesticated one of them had it in them to return to their wild roots and attack without warning. *Didn't you read that story about the dog who killed his owner?* she'd always ask. *Hey! Not me.*

I ran to the door to let him in. He hesitated before running inside, then circled me until he decided it was okay to lick my feet.

Auntie Irene sprang to her slippers and scooped him up. "That's Bits," she told me, opening the screen door and gently pushing him out. "Bits, *wo nim sɛ,* you are not allowed inside."

I followed Bits out the door.

"Lila, aren't you hot in that sweater?" Auntie Irene called after me.

"I only have sweaters."

"Didn't Enyo give you a top?"

"Auntie, if I have to stay here, I want Mum to send *my* things."

Auntie Irene sighed and closed the door. I made kissing sounds at Bits and he ran to lick my chipped purple toenails again as I noticed the other dog covered in dirty, nappy black curls opening one eye at me. I went to stroke the other dog but it whipped its head around quicker than lightning, not to bite, but to let me know it could and would.

I jumped back. "Auntie Irene, what's the other dog's name?"

"Moko." "Pepper," the name meant in Twi. She shouted through the doorway as the door slammed against its frame, "She's such a rude girl."

I turned to see Enyo walking toward us with a saucepan full of slop. Bits jumped headfirst into the pan before she could finish putting it down. Moko sniffed at the food and turned away.

"Moko doesn't like anything but meat," she explained with a shrug.

"Can't we give her some?"

Enyo started chuckling. "You want to give a *dog* meat?" She shook her head at the thought as she walked back into the house.

6

"Enyo, take money for a chicken for supper tonight," Auntie Irene told her as the screen door slammed behind me. "Uncle Fifi is coming tonight with the headmistress of Dadaba Girls' Secondary School." She turned to me. "That's where you will be going, Lila. God willing."

You're going to be here for a whole school year. You're going to have to cut your hair. I took a deep breath as these truths hit me in the head.

"School here is not like in London," Auntie Irene continued. "There are limited spots open. They admit students at form one and sixth form, and then by special permission for the other forms.

"They've just started a new system—JSS and SSS, junior and senior secondary school—so it may be harder to get you into form two. The system hasn't been proven, so many people have jumped their children one and two years to get them into the last class of the old system." Auntie Irene sighed as she started up the sewing machine again. "Anyway, we'll see. Uncle Fifi went to Tech with the headmistress at Dadaba, so he was able to get us an interview."

"Fine."

Auntie Irene stopped the machine to look at me. "Lila,

you can't give any attitude when she comes here. Dadaba is a *very* prestigious Cape Coast school. One of *the* best in Ghana. Kwame Nkrumah founded it."

"Who's Kwame Nkrumah?"

"*Ei!* Lila, Kwame Nkrumah was Ghana's first president. He led Ghana to independence from the British."

"Oh."

"Don't ask that when she is here, oh. *Please.* Just be *sweet*, okay?"

"What happens if I'm not 'sweet'? What if she doesn't accept me into the school?"

"You won't go back to London, Lila," Auntie Irene said, seeing where I was going with the question. "If you don't get into Dadaba, you'll go to some other school—or Sito with Enyo." She didn't say "Sito" with the same enunciated respect she gave Dadaba.

I glanced over at Enyo, who was washing the dog's slop pot.

"What's Sito?"

"Trust me, you don't want to go there, *broni*." Auntie Irene called me a white person, laughing to herself.

"Why does everyone keep calling me a *broni*?"

"Because like a white person, you don't know anything about Ghana, and you ask too many questions—now come, let me see something." She held up the cloth she had been sewing. It was loosely formed into a *kaba* blouse, like the ones Mum used to wear to Ghanaian funerals in London.

"Try it on. We don't have much time to get it right before they come."

"I can't wear jeans?"

"Lila, *please.* You're giving me a headache with all these silly questions." She shook the *kaba* at me and I took it from her. If

I was going to be in Ghana for a whole school year, I couldn't afford to piss Auntie Irene off. There was no telling where Mum would send me if Auntie Irene needed a break.

Auntie Irene admired me for a second. "Look at you, looking like your mother." She turned to Enyo. "It fits her nicely, doesn't it?" She put a few pins between her lips and took them out one by one to pin the *kaba* tighter to my bust and waist.

Enyo nodded without looking and left to sweep the compound.

7

I woke up from my nap to the sounds: *Slap! Squawk! "Ah!"* I scratched the crust from my eyes and adjusted to the lights. The clock radio blinked 4:19 P.M.

Slap! Squawk! "Ah!"

I followed the sounds through Auntie Irene's living room to the screen door. Through the door's net, I watched Enyo chase a chicken that wanted to live as Bits yelped at Enyo's heels and Moko lay, mouth over paw, with a scowl on her face, clearly pissed that Enyo, Bits, and the marked hen were disturbing her peace.

Slap! Squawk! "Ah!" Feathers slipped through Enyo's fingers. I stepped out into the early evening, the sun just beginning to disappear in the distance, the screen door slamming against its wooden frame.

"You are awake," Enyo acknowledged, her eyes still following the fowl.

"What are you doing?"

She ignored me, sidle-hopping after the fowl with the stumble of a winded boxer as Bits barked behind her. I dropped to the hard, cool red earth, hugging my thighs to my chest, and watched in amazement this girl my age who was about to kill a chicken for our supper. Enyo stopped moving. She had cornered the bawling hen between Auntie Irene's backyard wall and the dog shed.

Enyo snapped her fingers. "Lila, hand me the knife."

As soon as she asked, I saw the steak knife at my feet. The hen must have understood, because she let out a shriek that pierced the air with a chilling appeal. Enyo dipped to twist the hen's head until I heard a faint crack that silenced her forever.

I almost dropped the knife as I shrank back from where I stood over Enyo's shoulder. Bits was disgusted as well. He ran into the shed. Moko yawned and made room for Bits.

Enyo took the knife from me and with a grunt separated the chicken's head from its still-twitching body. I was horrified and transfixed as dark pink, watery blood gurgled over her hand.

"Come, let's pluck," she directed, walking past me with the dead bird.

Auntie Irene stood at the fridge downing a glass of ice water when we walked into the kitchen.

"While Enyo prepares the chicken, go and have your bath and get dressed. Uncle Fifi and Madam will be here at seven," Auntie Irene said, setting her empty glass on the counter near a downy feather. She dug her long nails through the armpit of her T-shirt to scratch under her breast as she handed me the *kaba* and *slit* skirt she had sewn.

"Quickly, Lila, I want to have time to make alterations if the dress doesn't fit you well."

"*Ko ko ko!*" Uncle Fifi shouted through the screen door, using his voice instead of his hands to knock.

"Go and answer it," Auntie Irene said to me, stopping Enyo. I rustled to the door in my new outfit and the sandals Auntie Irene had loaned me.

Just before I opened the door, she said, "You look like a *sweet*

Ghanaian girl." I think she was more reminding me how she expected me to behave than commenting on how I looked.

"*Ei!* Lila, *etisɛn?*" Uncle Fifi greeted me and came in followed by a tall, hefty woman in a peacock-printed cloth. Her hair looked like she had just taken the rollers out but hadn't bothered to comb the curls into a style. Auntie Irene shuffled to welcome them.

"Hello, Madam." Auntie Irene curtsied slightly in front of the woman. "Girls, get Madam and Uncle Fifi some water."

"*Ei!* Madam Seamstress!" Uncle Fifi said as he and the headmistress followed Auntie Irene to the living room.

In the kitchen, Enyo filled two glasses. I started to take the water out to them, but she stopped me. "You need to put it on saucers, on a tray."

I watched her gingerly place the glasses on teacup saucers and take them to the living room on a rusted but clean silver platter.

"Lila, go in my room and get me the cloth on my bed," Auntie said.

I went to get the fold of blue and white fabric sitting on Auntie Irene's bed. A brick of cedis fell from it as Auntie Irene came in behind me.

"What's taking you so long?" She took the money, folded the cloth back over it, and brought it to the headmistress.

"Thank you, my dear," Madam said. "Fifi tells me all the Tech girls come to you for their dresses and pretend they bought them in Abrokye during the summer long-vac."

Auntie Irene giggled at the compliment. "I'll have to take your measurements before you go."

Madam tilted her head in my direction as she set the gift on her lap. "So you want to attend Dadaba, eh?" Her beady eyes swept over me, resting on my toenails. "You won't be allowed to wear nail polish if I accept you at Dadaba," she said finally. "And you'll have to cut your hair. At Dadaba we keep the girls too busy with their schoolwork to waste time on their hair."

"She knows her hair can grow back," Auntie Irene said quickly.

"Can she do form two work?" The light caught a stray hair on her chin. I thought about Mrs. McGovern's beard and Ev with sadness. "Can you?"

"Yes." I nodded, frosting my English the way Auntie Irene had for the porter. I wished I could tell Madam I wasn't in Ghana because I couldn't keep up with my schoolwork.

Madam sneered at my voice's dip in temperature. "Do you know anything about the legacy of Dadaba Girls' Secondary School?"

Auntie Irene rushed to answer for me. "Madam, Lila is new to Ghana, but I've told her Dadaba is one of the best schools in the country."

"*The* best," Madam corrected, her eyes still locked with mine. "Why should I allow you to come from Abrokye and become part of a legacy my girls—my duchesses—have struggled all through primary and now JSS to get to? Why?"

I couldn't give her the answer I wanted—*I don't want to be in Ghana and I don't want to come to your bloody school.* So I stood silent, annoyed.

"Madam, Lila is a very bright girl," Auntie Irene assured her. "She was top of her class in London—"

"Then why is she here?" Madam tilted her head up at Auntie Irene, suspicion cocking her left eyebrow.

"Her mother wants her to know Ghana."

"Are you sure her mother didn't send her here because she's a bad girl? I won't have these bad Abrokye children come and spoil my girls."

Why were adults so afraid of us getting "spoiled"? We were

girls, not milk. Auntie Irene chuckled, looking from me to Uncle Fifi for help. He was only half-listening, his eyes fixed on the news. "Look at this *sweet* girl."

"Leave us alone, Lila," Madam said.

I walked out of the living room and joined Enyo, who had been watching us through the kitchen's louvered window. Madam unfolded the material Auntie Irene had given her and stuffed the money in her bag. They all moved to the dining table in the corner of the living room.

"Lila. Enyo. Come, let's eat," Auntie Irene called to us.

Madam produced a thin stack of stapled papers and handed them to me as I took my seat.

"This is the syllabus. You are to abide by *every* rule documented on these pages. You are to have *every* item required on this list." She turned to Auntie Irene. "We'll see her on Sunday."

"Thank you, Madam!" Auntie Irene gushed as dread dripped slowly into my stomach.

After supper and all the cleaning, Madam, Uncle Fifi, and Auntie Irene talked into the night while Enyo and I retreated to our room. Enyo took the syllabus from me and started to study it.

" 'Required: one bucket for bathing and laundering,' " she read aloud in the newscasters' fake British accent.

"*Laundering?*"

Enyo laughed at me. "*Bε* you will have to wash your clothes by hand." She giggled at my horrified eyes.

"I don't know how to wash clothes by hand."

"You'll learn." She shrugged, continuing. " 'Towels—three recommended.' *Ei*, what do you need three towels for?"

Maybe I wouldn't need to wash my towels. The first term was three months long; I could use one towel per month.

" 'Key soap—three bars recommended . . . Three plates—

plastic is recommended as opposed to glass . . . Talcum powder . . .' " By the end of the list, Enyo was bored. Her tone had lost its mirth and British accent. "This is a lot of *required* provisions." She sounded a little annoyed.

"I don't want to go away to school. Why can't I just go to school with you?"

"Because I go to Sito," she answered flatly.

I remembered Auntie Irene saying I wouldn't want to go to Sito. "Well, what's it like? Is it so bad?"

"Auntie is kind to let me go to school at all."

"Why wouldn't she let you go to school? Everyone has the right to an education."

"Where I was before, the madam wasn't sending me."

"Why not?"

"She said she didn't have money to send the maid to school," she told me.

When she called herself a maid, I realized I didn't know who Enyo was or how she had even come to live in Auntie Irene's house. All I knew was that she fetched water for me and Auntie Irene in the mornings, made us breakfast and lunch, killed chickens for supper, and fed the dogs. "Where are your parents?" I asked, expecting her to say they were dead.

"In the village. In Alloy. In Volta Region. I haven't met a *broni* before but you do ask a lot of questions," she said, ending the conversation.

Since I didn't know Alloy from Cape Coast, where Dadaba was supposed to be, I stopped talking. Plus, she had gotten quiet and sullen all of a sudden. From where Enyo sat, I was lucky, I realized. I knew she thought I was a brat, but I wanted to explain to her that I wasn't lucky at all. Just like her, I was away from my home and my family. She tossed the syllabus onto the bureau and turned off the light.

8

"London girl! Come!"
 "American girl, make you come see my provisions."
"Jeans dey for inside my kiosk!"
"*Obroni!* I have *niiiiice* cloth for you!"
"*Broni! Broni! Broni!*"
We were in Kumasi Market buying school supplies, and the sellers called to me from their stalls and from behind wooden tables, cartons, baskets, and piles of fabric spread on the ground. They wanted to show me their bright printed cloths, their palm oil poured into recycled bottles, their peeled oranges, their math sets . . .

I wanted to drag my feet. I was so depressed to think that tomorrow I would be even farther away from home, but it was too chaotic, crowded, and treacherous to feel sorry for myself. Between the hawking sellers, the boys squeezing alerts from their bike horns as they zigzagged through the foot traffic screaming, "Fan Ice! Fan Yogo!" and the odd one-armed/wheelchair-bound/ blind person begging for money, I could barely keep up with Auntie Irene and Enyo. They were walking so fast, sidestepping stagnant pools of sewage like they were playing hopscotch.

I wondered how the young girls balanced on their heads bowls full of individually packaged, breast-shaped sacks of water, or display cases of fried dough, or whatever else they were selling. Enyo was doing the same, navigating the glutted walkway steadily and surely, barely looking down as she carried a big tub full of my provisions on her head.

I had offered to help, but I was just being polite. I couldn't carry all those things and walk through that madness. I just wasn't used to it. Besides, they all fit so neatly in the container on her head, even the "skoo mattress" that the seller had folded lengthwise in half, then rolled into a tight curl before tying some twine around it. (It was called a school mattress because it wasn't the thick slab of foam we slept on at home, but a much thinner one encased in a sack printed with a flour mill's logo.)

"Lila! Hurry up!" Auntie Irene turned around to make sure I was still there. "We still need to get you a trunk, one of those wooden chop boxes for your provisions, a hymnbook, and the fabric for your uniforms."

We stopped at a man surrounded by black metal rectangular boxes with rows of red hearts spray-painted all over them. Behind him stood a proper English chest.

"Oh! That one's really cool."

"Ahen?" Auntie Irene asked how much the chest was, her tone coarsening as she prepared to bargain. I wondered at her change of tone. At the airport, she had all but let the porters believe she couldn't speak Twi, and now there was no trace of the English accent she had affected. She told me later, "You don't speak English—especially *your* kind of English—when you're at the market, else they'll rob you blind!"

"Fifty thousand," the man said, matching her tone and looking at me, not Auntie Irene.

"Ei! Na wei yɛ sɛn?" She pointed to a black tin box spray-painted with red hearts. *How much is this one?*

"Ten thousand."

My eyes widened at the price difference.

"*Ebei!* You think we're white?" she asked in Twi. Auntie Irene sucked her teeth and counted ten ¢500 notes into his hands. "My friend, I don't have time for this. This trunk is five thousand." She nodded me over to help her carry the Ghana trunk away as the man shook his head but pocketed the cash. When we got to the car, Enyo started to pack the backseat neatly with the things we'd bought.

"Lila, go and help her. You won't be getting this kind of service at Dadaba," Auntie Irene warned.

"Auntie, it's okay," Enyo said.

"Spoiled girl!" Auntie Irene swatted me as I ducked and smiled. She started the car and moved us through the darkening streets, her headlights spotlighting the scripted proverbs painted on passing lorries and roadside businesses. ONLY JESUS, one lorry evangelized. JEHOVAH JIREH read another. In Him We Live Provisions. Thy Will Be Done Hair Salon. God's Way Chop Bar.

In England, religion was confined to church and the odd person preaching outside the tube station. In Ghana it spilled into every crevice of life like a soft drink that had been shaken before its cap was twisted off. Its contents had sprayed liquid-sugar glue everywhere.

This wasn't even religion, I decided. It was faith. Only faith could see God in the shoe- and car-eating red dirt roads, the bothersome flies, the malaria-carrying mosquitoes, the bare-foot toddlers playing in and around sewage-choked gutters, the kids not much older than the toddlers selling provisions from the tops of their heads . . . Only faith could wake up early to go to church and praise God amid all that.

In London, Mum and I had gone to church most Sundays when she wasn't tired from work. The congregants were mostly Ghanaian, as was the minister, and I remembered thinking it was so different from the church services I'd seen on television. In our church we sang hymns too, but they had a beat, and the organ was accompanied by drums, bass guitars, rhythmic clapping, crying babies, and harsh rebukes to misbehaving children.

My favorite time was prayer time. I welcomed the silence of those moments after the loud singing, when the smallest children had gone to Children's Church. With my eyes closed and my hands clasped together, I felt like I did when I was in bed, in those moments right before I fell into sleep, when my thoughts were so random yet so focused they only made sense to me. In those moments, I could *feel* God. I knew he was listening. But like my tears, my prayers had seemed to lose their power the day Mum had come home to find me with Ev.

We stopped at the row of sellers in front of God's Way Chop Bar, kerosene wicks illuminating their display cases of oily *chofi* (deep-fried turkey tails), bubbling vats of deep-frying *kele wele* (bite-sized cubes of spiced plantains), and orange and tinfoil packets of gum. Auntie Irene bought much more than she, Enyo, and I, combined, could eat.

"Who's all that for?" I asked her.

"It's for you to take to school," Auntie Irene said.

"But I already have so much stuff!" I pointed to the stacks of canned fish, powdered drinks, and *gari* bags spilling over in the backseat next to Enyo.

"Believe me, you'll need it."

When we got home, Bits yelped and ran to us. Moko frowned at the headlight and retreated deeper into the darkness of her shed. After Enyo and I had brought everything inside and started to pack, Auntie Irene came into our room and sat on the bed.

"Lila, your schoolmates will be jealous of you because you're from London. They may try to *homo* you—"

"*Homo?*" I stopped her.

"Make you do foolish things for no reason to initiate you," Auntie Irene clarified.

"What kind of 'foolish things'?" I asked her. I was stuck on the word "homo."

"They could make you walk on your knees from one end of the campus to another, silly things like that."

"No way." I shook my head.

"Lila, just listen to me. Don't go and be *too known*."

" 'Too known'?"

Auntie Irene pretended to be me. "*Why do you do things this way? Eww, what's that?*" She shook her head. "If you want to be happy there, just try not to stand out too much. Wake up when they tell you to wake up. Go to bed when they tell you to. Eat when they tell you to. Respect your mates and elders. Call anyone in a form higher than you 'sister' . . . You see the *chofi* and *kele wele* we bought? Share it with your roommates so they'll be too busy swallowing to resent you because you are from Abrokye.

"And study, Lila," she went on. "You're smart, but the academics here are much harder. We don't have the facilities and resources you do in London. The teachers here are underpaid. They have a vested interest in students not understanding so those who need extra help pay them double and triple their school fees for remedial tutoring over the Christmas, Easter, and long vacs."

I sighed. If things were this bad, why would Mum send me here?

Auntie Irene squeezed my arm softly. "It's been a long time since I was in secondary school. Maybe things have changed. I just want you to be prepared. If you do everything I'm telling you, it won't be bad. You will survive. Your mum and I went through school in Ghana and we turned out fine.

"Anyway, it's time you acquainted yourself with who you are. No matter where you were born, *broni,* and how long you stay away, you are a Ghanaian. Ghana is your home."

I shook my head. "I'm *English.*"

Auntie Irene shook her head at me as she let out a long sigh punctuated by dry laughter. "Oh, Lila, I don't have the time to tell you how many ways you are wrong about that. We leave at dawn tomorrow so I'll leave you and Enyo to finish packing." She rose to her feet and started to walk out of our room, turning to add as an afterthought, "Don't forget you need to wipe your nail polish off. Enyo will cut your hair after you pack."

"Cut my hair?" I looked over at Enyo's boy cut. Did Mum know they made girls cut their hair? Mum wouldn't want this. She loved my hair. "Can we call Mum?"

Auntie Irene rolled her eyes. "About what? Your hair? Lila, if we don't cut it for you here, they'll cut it at school. I can guarantee you won't like the way they cut it."

"Then let them cut it," I said.

Auntie Irene sighed. "Ah! I am tired. Braid her hair for her then, Enyo."

When we were done packing, I sat between Enyo's thighs. I watched in front of the full-length mirror she had taken from Auntie Irene's room as she combed and parted my hair, then dipped her finger in the jar of Blue Magic to slick my scalp with the pomade.

"Your hair is so nice," she said as she dipped, slicked, and twisted my hair into shining rows of plaits. "I hope they let you keep it." I fell asleep the moment we tumbled into bed, almost an hour later.

The next day Enyo woke me up when it was still dark. "I prepared hot water for you."

"Thanks, Enyo," I muttered groggily, and rolled out of bed.

By the time I was dressed in my newly sewn red and white hibiscus-print uniform, Enyo had finished packing Auntie Irene's Rover with my things. We got in the car as the sun was beginning to burn away the night's fog. A rooster crowed in the distance and a pissed-off Moko growled back at the rooster's rude awakening. I waved good-bye to Enyo and Bits. Auntie Irene switched gears and we jerked out of her dirt driveway, leaving Enyo, the dogs, and the bungalow lost in the smoke of Ghana's red dust.

9

By the time we reached Dadaba Girls' Secondary School, my head hurt from squinting and my arms ached from covering my eyes. The sun had come up quickly, blazing and blinding through the dashboard's tinted glass and our down-turned visors. But it wasn't just the sun that had my head hurting. I was scared. At Auntie Irene's, at least I was with family. But at Dadaba, I would be farther away from home. And alone.

I read the sign outside the tall black gate. Under the school's name it said OBRA WOTO BOBO—*Life takes time to live.* What was that supposed to mean?

"Ah! Where is the gate man?" Auntie Irene pumped the horn on her wheel. The watchman emerged from the gate looking annoyed. He rubbed his bloodshot eyes and moved the chewing stick that dangled from the left side of his mouth to the other side before slowly bending to lift the metal that locked the gate into the red dirt.

Auntie Irene lowered her window. "Uncle, *pokyo,* can you show us how to get to Addo House?"

The watchman returned the chewing stick to the left as he peered across Auntie Irene to look at me. After a pause, he waved us in and directed us to Addo in some funny-sounding Twi.

"He was speaking Fanti. Dadaba is a proper Fanti school, one of the best in Ghana," she explained.

I turned to look out the window as crumbling buildings badly in need of a fresh coat of paint and tufts of unkempt grass flew past. *This* was "one of the best schools in Ghana"? I wondered what Enyo's Sito school was like.

Girls walked around in blue, yellow, and green versions of the red print dress I was wearing, some stopping to watch Auntie Irene and me. We parked in front of a dingy building next to a clump of bush with a faded red plaque that identified it as Addo House.

The small circle of onlookers grew as Auntie Irene and I got down. A tall, skinny girl parted the pack to approach us. Her short reddish-brown hair blended into her clay-colored skin.

"No one here has hair," I whispered to Auntie Irene.

"Didn't I tell you?" Auntie Irene sighed and put on a smile as the girl stopped at the truck.

"Hello, Auntie. *Wo frɛm* Penny—Penelope Fordjour," she said, introducing herself.

"*Onu yɛ* Lila—Lila Adjei. She's coming to start form two."

"*Nyew.*" She nodded. "Madam told me you were coming."

Auntie Irene and I trailed Penny up the stairs, past the girls who stepped aside to make way for us, and onto a veranda that a line of torn, dust-caked mosquito nets and louvers looked out onto.

"*Hwɛ ne tiri.*" *Look at her hair,* someone whispered from behind the louvers.

"*Broni wei yɛ tuntum, oh!*" *That white girl is blaaack!*

Penny spun around. "Back to your rooms!"

We stopped at a warped wooden door with rusted hinges just as I heard someone inside complain with a sigh, "*Ebei! Broni furfro?*" *Another white girl? Ugh!*

"This is your room," Penny announced.

I looked inside, still hoping this had all been a dream, but it was all very real. I was in Ghana and one of the thirty-two bunk beds crammed into the tight space, with a very narrow passageway down the middle, was mine.

Laundry lines hung above the bunks, and my new roommates had clipped knickers, towels, bathing sponges, nightgowns, and uniforms to them. A lightbulb dangled at the end of a wire from the water-soiled ceiling. On the floor, cracked pieces of tile clung to the corners and random spots in the middle of the room—the only proof that tiles had once covered the hard concrete.

Thin mattresses like the one Auntie Irene had bought me in the market covered all but one cot with small chains crisscrossing to form a sagging support under them.

"This will be your bed." Penny patted the chains above a fair-skinned girl who slit her eyes at me and Auntie Irene. "Ivy, come and help us with Lila's things. Hari, *wo su*, get up." Penny turned to snap her fingers at the tiny dark-skinned girl who slept on the top bunk next to my bed.

Ivy dropped to her feet and stepped into a pair of slippers. Hari covered her forehead with the back of her hand. "*Pokyo*, S'ter Penny, my head hurts. I have my period," she croaked in Twi.

"As for you, you always have your period," S'ter Penny muttered.

"You are from Britain, eh?" Ivy asked me as we walked back to the car.

"From London." I nodded.

"What brings you *here*?" She looked around and held her hands out as if she were serving the school on Enyo's rusted silver platter.

Before I could tell Ivy I certainly wasn't at Dadaba by choice, Auntie Irene turned to silence me with her eyes.

"My mother is in America, in *New* Jersey," Ivy continued proudly. She said "new" as if there was a "y" in it. "Neyoo" Jersey. "I'm going there after I write my O-level exams."

"Really?" I asked. "My father lives in America as well. In New York."

"You are from London and your father lives in America? I hear that many people are divorced in Abrokye." I wondered why she hadn't remarked about the fact that I was here and my family wasn't.

"Well, why are you here if your parents live in New Jersey?"

"Just my mother is there. My father is here."

"So they're also divorced."

"No!" She was offended. "My mother is just working there. She's only been there a year."

I didn't see much difference between her parents' separation and my parents' divorce, but this wasn't the time to say so. When we had carried the last of my things between the Rover and my new room, we walked Auntie Irene out.

Auntie Irene slipped a few cedi notes into S'ter Penny's hand. "Look after her for me, okay?"

S'ter Penny nodded. "Lila, when your Auntie leaves, come to my room."

S'ter Penny started to go but stopped when she noticed Ivy was still standing with us. "Heh! Ivy Abankwah, *jai* foreskinning!" She told her to stop doing something—I wasn't sure what "foreskinning" meant.

Ivy reluctantly walked away as Auntie Irene pulled me close. Tears sprang to my eyes. She handed me a thick wad of rubber-banded bills. "That's ₵50,000, Lila. You saw how far Kumasi is. Petrol is too expensive for me to be driving back and forth to visit you. You have to make this money last until you break for

Christmas. Do you hear me? Don't let anyone know how much I've given you.

"And remember what I told you at home: Don't try to stand out. You already do. Just blend in as much as you can and you'll be fine. Okay?"

Auntie Irene hugged me to her sweaty breasts and kissed my forehead. "Write to me, okay? Share the *chofi* and *kele wele* I packed for you the moment you get back to your room."

I tried to hang on to her, but Auntie Irene gently pushed me away and got in the Rover. The gold on her fingers reflected metallic streaks onto her skin as she set her hands on the steering wheel.

"I'll see you in December." She raised one arm to wave, exposing deodorant crumbs.

I broke down.

10

Hari—the girl who had excused herself from helping me with my things because she had her period—was looking through my trunk when I walked into my new dorm room. Ivy and a few other girls surrounded her.

I brushed my tears away and rushed over, expecting them to scatter, but none of them did. "What do you think you're doing?!"

"What do you *fink*?" One of my new roommates made fun of my accent, sending bubbles of laughter floating through the room.

Hari sucked her teeth and slammed the trunk door shut. "Ah! Check your precious things."

I opened my trunk and looked inside. Aside from the fact that the things Enyo had neatly folded were all over the place, it looked like everything was there. But I was wrong.

"You have some *nice* cutlery." One roommate held up my wood-handled fork and spoon. "I've never seen some like this before." I checked my trunk again. Now I noticed my cutlery was missing.

"I have to go to Abrokye, oh. You can't find pens like these here," said the slit-eyed girl who slept on the bunk under mine. She was holding the fountain pen Ev had given me.

"Give it back!" I screamed at her.

She looked me in the eye, fingering my pen as she spoke. "*Broni*, watch how you talk to me."

"Are you serious?"

She turned to the girl lying on the only single bed in the room. "Ashiaki, tell this girl who I am."

Ashiaki was ignoring the drama, her face hidden behind a biology textbook. She chuckled and lowered the book slightly to reveal her eyes. "*Ebei*, Josie." In her accent it sounded like her name was *Joe-See*. "You are wicked. Does Madam know her daughter is so wicked?"

I looked at Joe-See again. Now that I knew they were related, S'ter Joe-See was a clone of her mother. Both of them were thick and tall as tree trunks.

"*Broni*, didn't you read the syllabus? You must cut your hair," Ashiaki continued. A short, busty girl marched into the room as my hands flew to my plaits.

"Where is the *broni*?"

"Can't you tell?" Hari pointed at me.

"I'm Patience," the busty girl said, introducing herself, "but you can call me Pay-Shee. S'ter Penny wants to see you in her room."

"*Broni*, lock your trunk, eh," Ashiaki advised. I quickly rummaged through my trunk to find the padlock we'd bought at the market before following Pay-Shee to the room next door.

The sixth formers' room was less cramped, with only eight single beds on each side. Most of the tiles were on the floor too, which made the room feel cleaner and bigger. S'ter Penny sat under a filmy mosquito net that stretched tall from her bed to its knotted loops on the laundry lines above.

A yellow-skinned girl with a short and spiky blond perm stood beside S'ter Penny's bed. Her eyes were so light, so clear, they seemed see-through, like you could see straight into her mind if you stared long enough. I couldn't stop looking at her.

I knew before S'ter Penny introduced us—"Lila, this is Brempomaa. She's from London too"—that she wasn't from Ghana. Like the people on the international line at the airport, she looked better. Like she was used to better, expected better, knew better. I smiled at her, let her know with my eyes that I also knew better.

"S'ter Penny, I'm from Brooklyn," Brempomaa corrected in a sharp American accent.

S'ter Penny shrugged. "London. America. They're all Abrokye." Brempomaa's glassy eyes flashed with irritation at S'ter Penny's dismissal.

"Brempomaa has been here for a week. She's one of your roommates, so she can look after you.

"I won't lie to you," S'ter Penny continued. "It's going to be very hard for you *bronis* here. Brempomaa has had a little taste; she can tell you herself. These girls will test you because you don't look like them, act like them, speak like them, or understand the language. They will try to prey on your ignorance, but don't worry," she assured us, "I'll sort out anyone who worries you."

I started to let her know Mum had actually made sure I understood Twi, refusing to speak English to me when I was younger until Auntie Flora told her she was doing me more harm than good. *You're setting her up to fail, Felicia! We're in England, not Ghana.*

I knew I should tell S'ter Penny that I could speak Twi and even knew a few Ewe words I'd picked up from Enyo, but it sounded like her sorting people out was dependent upon us not understanding, so I kept my mouth shut.

"Now, Lila, you have to cut your hair. I've told Ashiaki to do it for you. When you're done, bring your chop box in here."

I started to protest, but I knew it was over. When Brempomaa and I got back to the room, S'ter Ashiaki had an overturned bucket by her bed with a pillow on top of it and a pair of sewing scissors in her hand.

"Anybody want any *chofi*?" I asked, trying to stall.

"*Ei!* Me!" Ivy sang. I bypassed S'ter Ashiaki and unlocked my chop box to share the plastic bag of fried turkey tail snacks. Ivy tore it open and shared it with the roommates.

"Won't you eat any?" Ivy asked me.

I shook my head and uncurled my mattress. I laid the large fold of cloth Auntie Irene had given me on my bed and climbed to my top cot. The metal links immediately sank under me. I thought I would fall through—right on top of slit-eyed S'ter Joe-See, who obviously hated me.

I started to unravel each braid. S'ter Ashiaki and the rest of my roommates watched, many of them smirking as I lovingly detangled hair that would be chopped off.

"Oh! This thick hair has to be cut." Ivy mourned with me.

When I was done, I shook out my hair like the *broni* everybody kept calling me, the crimped waves brushing my shoulders. I wanted them to see—I wanted them to *know*—that even when my hair was short like theirs, I was a *broni* or whatever else they wanted to call me. I was different from them. I was better.

I took my seat on the bucket and sat with my back straight, my head high as S'ter Ashiaki started to cut. But when I heard the first heavy slice of the scissors and saw my hair float to the floor, I started to cry for more than the hair I was losing. I *would* look like a maid. I would look like *them*.

The next morning a loud clanging bell joined at least two roosters cock-a-doodle-dooing from afar to wake me up. It was pitch-black outside, but the light in our room was on and the clatter of buckets was all around me.

"Let's go get some water." Holding a bucket in one hand, Brempomaa tapped my foot with the other.

I moved out from under my clumsily erected mosquito net and almost stumbled. My head had never felt so weightless, even when my hair was freshly permed. It felt like if I turned around too quickly, it would roll off my neck to the floor. I touched my newly bald head. It was shorter on the sides and at the back, with a little more height on the top.

"It doesn't look that bad," Brempomaa assured me. "S'ter Ashiaki gave you a punk cut. Just be careful Madam Afisiafi doesn't catch you. That woman walks around with scissors in her pocket ready to cut anyone's hair that's not one inch all around like it says in the syllabus."

Tears started to come, but I fought them back. Like Auntie Irene had said, all the crying in the world wouldn't change the fact that I was here.

"Why are you in Ghana?" I asked Brempomaa as we took our place at the back of the line of girls waiting their turn at the tap.

"My parents moved back to save Ghana." She seemed doubtful that it could be done. "Daddy's an economist and Mommy's a doctor, so they think together they can solve Ghana's economic and health problems all by themselves." She shook her head.

We moved up a space in the line as two girls moved from the tap balancing a full bucket between them. "We've been here almost two years trying to fix a problem that goes back thirty-three years, and probably longer than that." She turned to the slowly dripping tap. "Know why the tap's flowing so slow? Cape Coast has water pressure problems. It doesn't help that we're on a hill. And it's only going to get worse when Harmattan kicks in."

"What's Harmattan?"

"The dry season—it starts in December and ends in Febru-ary. Everything gets even dustier and the wind blows so dry you have to grease your skin like three times a day."

"I thought you just got here last week," I said, impressed that Brempomaa knew how many years Ghana had been having problems and that Cape Coast had water pressure issues.

"I did. I was at GIS—Ghana International School—but my parents couldn't afford the tuition anymore. Now *that* was a good school. Better than the one I went to in Brooklyn even," she said. I found it hard to believe that any school in Ghana could be better than the ones abroad, but maybe America was different. "But every spoiled, rich, half-caste diplomat's kid in Accra went there," she continued. "The way some of them used to talk to the custodial staff was just insane. And lots of them didn't even believe in God." She shook her head and arched her eyebrows at me. "Are you a Christian?"

I nodded. I had been baptized, had my first communion, and I prayed all the time.

"Are you *born again*?" she probed. "You're not a Christian if you're not born again."

"What's 'born again'?"

"You let Jesus into your heart, which means you pray the Sinners' Prayer and read the Bible every day to find out what God's good will is. Wanna be born again?"

We moved up in the line. I smiled. She'd said "wanna" in-stead of "want to."

I wondered if it was because I wasn't born again that God had let me end up in Ghana. I hadn't read the Bible in years, but I could do that. "Okay."

"Okay, pray this prayer after me . . ." Brempomaa closed her eyes and started to pray.

I looked around. I wasn't about to pray outside on this line waiting to fetch a bucket of water. "I can do it on my own."

Brempomaa opened her eyes and shook her head. "No, you have to pray this prayer aloud, after me."

I looked over at the tap. Three girls were ahead of us and the water was dripping really slowly. A faraway rooster crowed again as the sun started to rise. "Why can't I just pray on my own?"

Irritation darkened Brempomaa's yellow eyes and stained her butter-colored cheeks red. I saw the small knot in her throat move up and down under her pale skin as she swallowed her disappointment. "Fine," she said. "I just wanted you to get the prayer right."

I hoped Brempomaa wouldn't stop waking me up to get water just because I didn't want to pray the Sinners' Prayer right there with her. I needed her. She was a *broni* and we needed to stick together to survive Dadaba.

11

Brempomaa and I walked slowly, trying not to spill any of the water in our bucket as we carried it between us to Addo. The water we had waited forever for sloshed everywhere and soaked the hems of our nighties, since Brempomaa was taller than me. She sighed watching girls pass us, balancing buckets on their heads the way Enyo had at the market.

"Okay, stop. If we keep going like this we are not gonna have any water left to bathe with." Instead of "going to" she said "gonna," instead of "bath" she said "bathe."

"Whatchu smiling at?"

"You said 'bathe' instead of 'bath.' "

"I said 'bathe' instead of 'baf'? I hope so." She smirked as she knelt to the ground. Before I could explain that her use of the word "bathe" suggested—at least in British English—a dip in a swimming pool, she said, "Help me lift this onto my head."

I couldn't believe what she was asking. "You can do that?"

"We spent a few months in my mother's village. There was no running water so we had to fetch from a well." She shrugged.

A few months? In a village? Kumasi was far from what I was used to in London, but it was nothing like the villages we'd passed through on the drive to Dadaba.

I watched in awe as Brempomaa rose slowly to her feet, the

bucket wobbling slightly but staying put. She looked so tall to me with that bucket crowning her head, her long, thick arms rising to hold its brim steady as she took careful steps. She did it. We made it to the bathhouse without any of the water spilling.

The chemical stench of urine covered with disinfectant greeted us at the bathhouse door. An ankle-deep puddle of milk-colored water collected in the valley between the rows of shower cubicles. Naked girls and flies buzzed around us, filling every cubicle.

A bell rang in the distance. "The work bell," Brempomaa explained. "We can't wait for a cubicle or we'll be late for inspection." She bent to lather her net bathing sponge, her bum cheeks in the air.

I turned away, but there were cheeks and breasts and pubic hair there as well. "Inspection?" I asked, slowly bunching my nightie up over my hips, uncomfortable with all these naked bodies around me. Meanwhile, the unself-conscious girls of Addo House chatted freely, lifting their legs to scrub their holes and cracks, splashing pails of water over their suds-covered parts.

"The House Prefects come around and make sure our beds are laid with perfect white sheets and that we did our housework properly," Brempomaa explained.

Now my nightie was at my belly button. I snuck a peek at Brempomaa to see if she was spying on me, but she was shaking her head.

"Oh boy, here comes Ivy."

I sighed and pulled my nightie up past my breasts. When it was off and knotted around the bucket handle like Brempomaa's was, Ivy was in our face holding her sponge out.

"Brempomaa, can I have some of your soap? My mother sent me some liquid soap from *Neyoo* Jersey, but it is finished." She accepted a squeeze from Brempomaa's soap dispenser.

When she walked away, Brempomaa shook her head again. "That girl is such a *broni* foreskinner."

I remembered that S'ter Penny had told Ivy to stop "foreskinning." "What's a *broni* foreskinner?"

"It's like she's the foreskin on an uncircumcised dick—clinging to us *bronis*." Brempomaa giggled at the image I couldn't imagine. I had never seen a dick before. I hadn't even known there was a difference between the way uncircumcised and circumcised penises looked. "You know what a foreskin is, right?" Brempomaa asked me.

"No," I admitted, swatting a fly that landed on and tickled my newly exposed scalp.

"It's like this extra piece of skin covering the top." She tried to show me with her hands what it looked like.

"How do you know all this?" I was realizing Brempomaa knew more than "better."

"My mother's a doctor, remember?"

"Oh," I said, still trying to picture the foreskin of a penis as I rinsed off.

Another bell sounded and Brempomaa and I waded through the body wash to leave the bathhouse. A fly followed me out despite my attempts to shake it. It buzzed off for a second, then settled on my eyebrow. I flailed and smacked myself trying to get it off. "Ugh!" I wailed, hot tears of frustration catching me off guard.

Brempomaa laced her fingers through mine and we walked into our room together. My trunk was wide open. I had forgotten to lock it again.

I quickly looked inside. Again it looked like nothing was missing, but I knew I'd find out soon enough what was. I pulled out a crisp white bedsheet and a fresh uniform and padlocked my trunk. Just when I had made my bed and zipped my uniform on, Pay-Shee walked into the room and stopped in front of my bed.

"S'ter Penny wants to see you."

S'ter Penny was starched and pressed into her uniform, combing out her Afro, when I walked into the sixth formers' room. She patted an empty space on her bed. "How did you find your first night?"

"My roommates stole my things," I tattled, new tears choking my throat.

She frowned. "I'll sort them out later. In the meantime, for your own good, I don't want it to appear that I am playing favorites with you, so I have to give you a work assignment."

I wiped my tears. *Work assignment?*

"I'll give you compound duty. It's a small plot. Just under the lines where you hang your towels to dry outside. All you have to do is sweep; you won't have to scrub on the weekends. Okay?" She didn't wait for me to answer. "Do you know how to use our brooms?"

I remembered bending to sweep my hair away with S'ter Ashiaki's broom. It was uncomfortable and annoying having to adjust and readjust the bunched-up reeds tied together at the top to form a handle. "Yes," I answered. "My broom is in my chop box."

We got up and S'ter Penny helped me pull my chop box out from under her bed. I took out the broom and followed S'ter Penny out onto the compound. She watched me sweep for a second and started to laugh.

"Here, let me show you." With even, deliberate strokes, she created crescent-shaped marks in the red dust. A few girls stopped to point and whisper at what was apparently the unusual sight of the school prefect sweeping. "Now you try."

I tried to match her form, bending only my top half, keeping my knees straight, one hand behind my back as I swiped the

ground. "Good," S'ter Penny said. "When you've finished sweeping, stand by it and wait for the house prefect to inspect it."

My plot was quite big—about the size of a small yard—but
I noticed that other girls were sweeping much larger patches. I
was almost done filling every square inch with crescents when
I heard a *clump*. An orange peel had fallen on my plot, behind
it a trail of garbage. I looked up to see S'ter Joe-See marching
across the compound holding a wad of rubbish wrapped loosely
in newspaper.

"S'ter Joe-See! You're dropping rubbish all over my work," I
yelled after her.

"Watch your tone with me, *broni*. If you think because
S'ter Penny is your dear you're too good to clean up, you are
wrong."

I stared after her, completely confused. What was she talking
about? Wasn't I cleaning up? I started to walk up to her when I
felt an arm on my shoulder.

"Forget her. The inspection bell's about to ring," Brempomaa said. She bent to help me pick up the rubbish. I shivered
with rage as I collected S'ter Joe-See's mess.

The bell rang and the house prefect walked up to and circled
each girl standing by her work before nodding them away. When
she came to my plot, she smiled at me, impressed. "Good job,
broni."

I walked back to my room and joined the girls standing in
front of their beds, each mattress practically shrink-wrapped
into their white sheets, except mine. Another prefect made the
rounds.

"*Broni*, you have to learn to lay your bed properly," she told
me. "Next time, I'll toss your mattress onto the compound."

"I'll show you how," Brempomaa promised when the house
prefect left. Another bell rang.

"What's *that* bell for?" I asked Brempomaa.

"Morning devotion. It's a short service we have every day before classes."

The two of us walked out of Addo and followed the mass exodus of girls as the prefect started locking the rooms. Our red and white prints flowed into the Ofori House girls' blue and white prints until we all merged with the green and white of Danquah House and the yellow and white Lamptey House uniforms, all on our way to devotion. Prefects stood outside the chapel clapping and shouting at us, "Hurry up! *Yɛn tɛm!*"

Next to the prefects I saw Pay-Shee ringing the bell before slipping into the chapel to take her seat.

I thought to myself that the chapel looked like a barn when I walked in for the first time. It was long and squat with massive glassless windows, capped by alternately gleaming and rusted sheets of corrugated iron. Up front there was a stage and on it were a piano and small wooden pulpit that looked down onto new wooden pews in the front and rotting ones in the back. Every pew spilled over with two too many girls.

Brempomaa pulled up one of the ragged two- and three-legged chairs that slumped against the chapel's back wall.

"We don't have a pew?" It just got worse and worse.

She gave me a "You know the answer to that" look.

I dragged one of the crippled chairs next to Brempomaa's. I didn't have to cry. The chair scraping against the concrete floor made the shrieking sound for me.

"Heh! *Broni,* you will be punished for making noise during devotion!" Hari warned me in a sharp whisper, whipping her head around from the pew in front of us.

Onstage, a tiny man with a pinched face took a seat at the piano and cracked his knuckles loudly before commencing to massage a melody out of the keys. The headmistress took her place behind the pulpit and all the girls immediately rose. She was wearing the cloth Auntie Irene had given her.

Brempomaa and I stood up. My chair clapped to the ground. Hari whipped her head around again. I noticed Brempomaa was holding her chair up with one hand, her hymnbook with the other.

Madam announced the hymn and the piano man started playing.

We gather together, to ask the Lord's blessing . . . I flipped to the song in the hymnbook and started singing along.

"Wait. Wait. *Wait.*" Madam shook her head. "Mr. Blankson, stop playing."

The room went silent.

"Some of you don't have your hymnbooks." She squinted her eyes at us. "Everyone hold your hymnbook in the air. If you don't have yours, you know what to do."

Brempomaa and I held ours up as most hands stretched across the room. Then slowly, a few girls pushed their way off their pews and walked outside. It was then that I noticed a few more girls were outside, kneeling on the sharp gravel outside the chapel. They were the ones who hadn't made it to chapel before Pay-Shee had rung the final bell for morning devotion, I figured. The girls without hymnbooks sank to the stones beside them.

"Now we can continue," Madam said.

Mr. Blankson started playing again and as we started singing, Madam closed her eyes, a smile pushing her cheeks up. "Dadaba girls, you sound like little duchesses," she crowed.

12

"There's an extra seat in my classroom," Brempomaa said as we filed out of chapel. I knew by now not to ask whether I was going to be assigned a classroom. I followed Brempomaa into a tight room crammed with about sixty desks. I had to shimmy sideways to the empty desk at the back of the class as flies rose and settled around me.

I noticed Hari and Ivy and silently thanked God my seat was directly opposite their corner of the room.

"*Bronis*, you don't know how to greet?" Hari shouted at us.

"Hari, leave us alone," Brempomaa warned.

"You don't want anyone worrying your dear, eh, *broni*?" Hari retorted.

"Hari, don't call me that," Brempomaa advised her.

"*Ei*, don't show off now that your *broni* dear has come, oh."

I didn't know what a "dear" was, but whatever it meant didn't sound good. I lowered my head to my notebook, letting the cool hard cover take my thoughts away from the heat and the flies and the fact that I had to learn this new vocabulary of slang like "foreskinning" and "dear." I would have given anything to hear someone say "innit."

Ivy came over to my desk. "Is it true she's your dear?"

"What's a 'dear'?" I sighed.

"A *dear* friend," Ivy explained. "A dear is *special* to you. She makes you feel *good*. Like your boyfriend. Do you have a boyfriend?"

"What? No, she's not—"

"Mr. Kisseh is coming, oh!" Hari hissed the warning.

Ivy skittered away, slinking between the tight spaces to her desk just as a big, potbellied man swaggered into the classroom.

Each girl shot up from her desk, the way they had at chapel when Madam took the stage, and chorused in unison, "Good mawning, Mr. Kiss-Say!"

Mr. Kiss-Say waved us down with a smile. The gap between his front teeth was so wide it looked like one of his teeth had been knocked out.

"Good mawning, beautiful Dadaba girls," he sang in reply, leering at us. He paced the room, his eyes settling on my breasts. "And who is this?"

"Another *broni*," Hari told him.

"She's from London," Ivy chimed in.

I put my head on my notebook again, exhausted by this *broni broni* business, until a slam exploded in my ear. When I jumped up, Mr. Kiss-Say was standing over me, a fat biology textbook inches from my head, where he had dropped it.

"I don't know how you behaved at your school in London," he began in an awful attempt at a British accent, "but when I am teaching a crass I require furr attention." He exchanged his "L"s for "R"s. I smiled even as I watched him walk back to the chalkboard through a blur of tears.

At the end of that first week, I wrote Mum begging her to let me come home. "<u>NOTHING HAPPENED BETWEEN EVERTON AND ME!</u>" I hoped to convince her with underlined capital letters and an exclamation point. A month passed before her postcard reply came.

NANA EKUA BREW-HAMMOND 67

"Lila, it doesn't matter what did or didn't happen anymore," she wrote. *What the . . . ?! Now it didn't matter?* "Honestly, I just need some time. Not away from you, but for myself. Please don't be cross with me. I love you, Lila. I wouldn't have sent you to Ghana if I thought it would do you anything but good."

13

Is Ghana doing me good? I wondered as I woke up to the clang of a bell. In the month and a half I'd been away from home, I couldn't see how. Was it a good thing that I had learned to live by a bell? A bell rang, and like a dog, I knew to wake up, clean up, eat, nap, study, pray.

Was it good for me that I now knew how to sit on a three-legged chair without falling and eat fast enough that the surrounding swarm of flies couldn't settle on my food? Was it good that I knew what a "foreskinner" and a "dear" were? That I could sweep with a broom made of dried reeds? That I could make my bed with hospital corners? That I knew how to fetch and bath with a bucket of water? Was it good for me to bath in a filthy bathhouse? Forget good—was it hygienic?

I wrote to ask Mum these questions when I got her postcard and tucked the letter in my trunk to mail to her.

I ignored the bell and pretended to sleep as the sounds of a Dadaba morning rose around me. The sucking of teeth, the shuffling of feet, the clatter of buckets.

"Lila," S'ter Ashiaki called to me, and I let my eyes flutter open. She was setting her bucket down to pull her bathing sponge from the laundry line. "*Wo ko gyare? A ko bo* five thirty."

I pretended not to understand. Only Brempomaa knew I understood Twi.

Hari sucked her teeth. "You people are Ghanaians. You need to know your language. She asked if you've had your bath yet."

I shook my head.

"Well, hurry up! There's a long queue at the tap."

As she spoke, Brempomaa came through the door balancing a half-full bucket on her head. "The tap isn't flowing anymore," she announced breathlessly. "I was the last one to get some water and this was all I could get before the tap stopped flowing completely."

S'ter Joe-See sucked her teeth, shaking our bunk bed's frame as she sat up. "*Broni koko,* give me your water," she demanded.

Brempomaa dropped her knickers into the bucket. "Oh! Sorry, S'ter Joe-See! That was an accident." She pulled out her dirty knickers. "Do you still want some?"

S'ter Joe-See looked around the room, embarrassment staining her face. "*Ɛnyɛ hwee.* I'll just go home," she said with a shrug.

"*Ei,* it must be nice to have the headmistress as your mother," Hari muttered long after S'ter Joe-See was out of earshot.

"Let's go, Lila," Brempomaa said.

I wasn't that excited about bathing with Brempomaa's dirty knicker water either, but it was that or no bath at all. I quickly grabbed my towel and sponge from the line and followed my friend out the door.

Light was starting to dilute the dark sky, spilling through the bathhouse louvers as we walked in. As usual, all the cubicles were taken. I nearly slipped on a piece of soap hidden in the murky pond of body wash as Brempomaa and I found the shallowest spot in the middle and started to lather up. A dissolving clot of menstrual blood bobbed up next to my foot. I kicked it away as S'ter Joe-See walked in, claiming a space directly opposite us.

I guess one good thing had come of the month and a half since I arrived: I wasn't crying all the time anymore. A month ago if I'd seen a blood clot floating past as I was having my bath, I would've burst into tears. I wasn't sure though if it meant I was becoming stronger or just becoming desensitized to the 360-degree filth.

"Let's hurry up and get out of here," I said, nodding in S'ter Joe-See's direction as I lathered up. Like most Dadabans, S'ter Joe-See didn't like us, but her resentment was on another level. Her eyes narrowed every time I came to our shared bunk bed and every time she saw Brempomaa and me in passing on the way to chapel or on the way from class. And she never called us by our names. It was *broni tuntum* (*black white person*) for me and *broni koko* (*red white person*) for Brempomaa.

"She doesn't scare me." Brempomaa shrugged, splashing a pail full of water over her head. I watched the soap stream down her pale skin just as S'ter Joe-See passed us and kicked our bucket over.

Brempomaa and I were too shocked to react as we watched our bath water flow into the chalky body wash. The blood clot found its way back to us, a trail of dark red following it as soap burned my eyes.

Before I could say anything, Brempomaa's long, buttercream-colored arm swiped at S'ter Joe-See, her wet palm clapping the back of S'ter Joe-See's head. All I heard was *fwap!* Now it was S'ter Joe-See's turn to stand speechless.

In fact, the whole bathhouse stopped for a second. The room that had just been shrill with chatting girls, splashing water, clanging buckets, the sucking sound of *chalewote* bathroom slippers sticking and unsticking to the watery floor was so still you could hear people's breath rise and fall. But only for a second.

"Kneel down! Kneel down! Kneel down! *Kneel! Down!*" S'ter Joe-See sputtered like a faulty car, gathering volume and speed each time she shouted the command. Her pale brown skin, as light as Brempomaa's but with more of a sand-colored tint to it, was burning red.

"Let's go." I pulled Brempomaa away, hoping we could hurry up and get dressed before S'ter Joe-See got back to the dorm. We had almost made it when what felt like a brick hit me on the tiny bone that sticks out the back of my neck. I turned to see S'ter Joe-See standing naked at the bathhouse entrance, her pitching arm in the air. At my feet I saw that the brick was actually a block of Key soap.

"*Obronis,* if you don't know how things are done here I will teach you," S'ter Joe-See hissed before stalking past us.

Again Brempomaa's hand snagged her and before I knew it, the two yellow girls were naked on the ground locked in a violent embrace, rolling, grabbing, scraping, poking, punching, kicking, and screaming. Our bathhouse audience had followed us outside and started chanting.

I ignored the throbbing pain at the back of my neck and tried to pull Brempomaa and S'ter Joe-See apart, my hands already dry from the Harmattan wind that blew about us. S'ter Penny and S'ter Ashiaki shouted their way through the mob and separated them. Brempomaa and S'ter Joe-See stood apart, heaving with anger and adrenaline, covered in pink scratches. Then Pay-Shee appeared, shaking the bell.

"All of you get to your work assignments. I will be around to inspect!" S'ter Penny barked at the crowd.

Brempomaa and S'ter Joe-See started to slink back to our room but S'ter Penny stopped them. "The two of you report to my room when you are dressed."

The bell gonged again for chapel when Brempomaa and S'ter Joe-See returned from S'ter Penny's.

"What happened?" I rushed over to Brempomaa.

"Your dear will be moving to Ofori House," S'ter Joe-See sneered.

"I get to go home for a few days, to sew blue and whites," she explained, touching her red and white uniform and trying to downplay the magnitude of her leaving Addo House.

I was going to be alone with S'ter Joe-See and the rest of these awful girls. Each house was its own universe at Dadaba. With Brempomaa in Ofori House, we couldn't sit together at the dining hall because seats were assigned by house. After dining, we couldn't walk back to the house together. In the mornings we couldn't fetch water or bath together or walk to morning devotion together.

"I'll see you in class and chapel," she said, reading my mind. Then she turned to S'ter Joe-See. "You won't always be Madam's daughter."

S'ter Joe-See sucked her teeth. "Then who will I be? Who will I be?"

I thought about how my life had changed. How Brempomaa's existence must have morphed when she left Brooklyn for Ghana. It was true. We all wouldn't always be who we were at that moment.

S'ter Joe-See got in Brempomaa's face. "I said, who will I be?"

Brempomaa sidestepped S'ter Joe-See, completely unimpressed by her posturing. She put her towel and sponge in a plastic bag, pulled down her mosquito net and locked it in her trunk.

The next morning, Ivy lifted my mosquito net and slapped at my feet. She was still breathing heavily from carrying the bucket she had just brought into the room. "I fetched us some water."

I rolled over and groaned at the chain links Brempomaa's mattress had covered just yesterday. Then I got up.

14

It's funny how quickly change becomes the way things are. Now that I only saw Brempomaa in class and chapel—all the places we weren't allowed to talk—we could only catch up as we walked to and from the tuck shop, Dadaba's small group of snack sellers, for the fifteen-minute break we had two periods before lunch.

As our schoolmates waved fists of cash at the headmistress's maid, Auntie Araba, and the other house girls who sold hot and cold snacks for their faculty guardians, we would trade our *broni* miseries over Madam Quainoo's meat pies or Madam Afisiafi's sugar donuts, wiping the grease from our hands with the oil-blotted newspaper the snacks were served in.

But once I was back at Addo, Ivy was my best friend. We bathed together, and when we didn't wake up early enough to get water on the days the taps didn't flow, she showed me how to paint a translucent band of Saturday Evening Shade powder across my neck so no one would know we hadn't bathed and call us dirty girls.

From Ivy I learned to enjoy the *gari* and *shito* I had barely touched in my chop box, and how to prepare the perfect cup of *gari* soakings—two handfuls of *gari* and three tablespoons of sugar swirled together, milk from a tin can to soak every *gari* grain, and half a cup of water—which was a good thing now that I had finished the crisps and Tree Top orange drink Auntie Irene had filled my chop box with.

Aside from the fact that S'ter Joe-See now completely hated me and Hari didn't like the fact that she had to share me with her friend, being in Addo without Brempomaa wasn't as bad as I thought—until Pay-Shee walked into our room and stopped at my bed. "S'ter Penny wants to see you."

S'ter Penny was sitting cross-legged on her bed, frowning into a cup of soakings. Ivy was there too, standing at attention with two buckets stacked one into the other. Something was off.

"Lila, *wo ti* Twi?" *Lila, do you understand Twi?*

I gave S'ter Penny my dumb look, but as she met my eyes while spoon-scraping the last sweet mush of soakings from her cup, I knew she knew.

"Lila, I don't like lies or liars," she told me in Twi. I looked over at Ivy. She was the only one aside from Brempomaa who knew. She avoided my eyes.

"I thought you needed my help." S'ter Penny looked hurt.

"I do!" Hadn't S'ter Penny seen the bruise at the back of my neck from the soap S'ter Joe-See had hurled at me? Wasn't she the one who had made the big production of telling Brempomaa and me to look out for each other?

"Go and help Ivy wash our things. And wash this too," she said finally, handing me her dirty cup.

"You told S'ter Penny!" I accused Ivy when we were out of the sixth formers' room.

"I'm sorry, eh. It just slipped out." She clasped my hands between hers and widened her eyes. "Please, don't be mad with me."

I said nothing, but I let her hold my hands. I couldn't afford to stay angry with Ivy. I needed her. I had no idea how to hand-wash clothes. Up until that day, I'd given S'ter Penny my things and she'd given them to her "small girl" to wash for me. I hadn't even known Ivy was her small girl.

"How are we going to wash S'ter Penny's things? The taps aren't flowing."

She winked at me, dragging me along. "There's a secret well."

We walked past Ofori House, the school block, the tuck shop, the dining hall, the chapel, the field where we had PE, and the teachers' flats until we reached a gate of bushes.

"It's here on the farm," Ivy said, raising the skirt of her dress so she could move more freely through the scratch of shrubs.

"Where?" I asked, hesitant.

She looped her arm through mine. "Just follow me, *broni!*"

We hiked through a couple hundred feet of patchy bush until Ivy stopped at a bald spot of red soil and started to dig. The ground was lumpy with tubers pushing through the surface on the farmed land surrounding us. In between the bumpy rows, tomato vines spiralled up and around rods that speared the ground.

I dropped the laundry bundle and watched Ivy exhume a cloudy one-liter Coke bottle that looked like it was about to burst. She smeared away the mud that covered it and unscrewed the cap gingerly. The corn-colored fluid inside ran down the sides of the bottle, over her hands. She licked her muddy fingers, took a generous swig, and offered me the dirty bottle. The smell of hard liquor cut the hairs in my nose.

"*Heh!*" A voice hissed at us from behind.

My armpits started to itch. I knew, without knowing what was going on, that if any prefect or mistress caught us we would be expelled. Thankfully, it was just Hari holding two cups and her own bundle of clothes. Hari eyed me suspiciously as she approached, dropping her dirty bundle onto the ground. Ivy took a swig.

"*Ei,* leave me some!" Hari held her hand out for the bottle.

Ivy poured a shot of the thick solution into each of the cups and handed one to Hari and one to me.

"Drink," she said.

"What is it?" I put my finger in first and touched my tongue. The drink tasted like it looked—chalky, briny, and sweet at the same time. It was actually quite nice.

"*Wawt* is it?" Hari and Ivy laughed at my accent. "*Ei!* These your slangs. They sound like a mosquito in my ear," Hari said.

"It's *fermɛ,*" Ivy explained. "Do you know *mashké?*" I shook my head. "You take *kenkey,* sugar, and water, bury it for a day or two, and it ferments to become *fermɛ.*"

I swallowed the rest of the cup. Hari refilled it. We sat in silence for a while. I could hear water moving behind me.

"That's the well," Ivy explained.

"No one knows about this well, so don't go and say anything, *broni.*" Hari wagged her finger at me.

"No, I won't." I shook my head furiously, passing Hari the last of the *fermɛ.*

"Let's start washing S'ter Penny's things."

15

I studied Ivy and Hari as they got to work, loosening their belts and knotting them together to form a rope. Hari turned to me. "Your belt." I handed my belt over and watched them lengthen the rope before tying it to the bucket handle. I followed them to a hole hidden by a ring of weeds. Hari knelt so close to it I got scared she would fall inside when she pushed the weeds aside and lowered the bucket.

I heard the metal hit water and watched the muscles in her arms bulge as she pulled the bucket up. Ivy held the empty bucket down as Hari filled it with the murky yellow water she had just fetched. Hari fetched another bucket of water. Ivy opened the bag of dirty clothes S'ter Penny had given us.

"Lila, we are through washing your things," Hari told me as Ivy shook out the prints, blouses, slips, and nighties, some of them with my name Magic Markered at the inside collars.

"Of course," I said, a little scared. As I watched them turn their knuckles and palms into washboards, scrubbing the fabric against itself in the sudsy water, I knew I couldn't do it. I stooped over one of the buckets and sprinkled some blue Omo grains inside.

"Ah! You'll finish the whole box of soap!" Ivy slapped the box of detergent from my hand. She stood over me as I dropped one of my prints into the water and began to massage it, then swish it around the thick suds.

Hari started to laugh. "Is the dress your boyfriend? Look at the way you are caressing it."

I ignored Hari, squeezed the dress free of water, and dumped it on the grass the way I saw Ivy do it.

Ivy came over. "Like *this*. Let me show you."

I stepped aside, grateful that Ivy was a *broni* foreskinner. Hari shook her head when she saw the relieved smirk on my face. "No! Ivy! Let her do it!"

"*Bε* she doesn't know how. She's wasting time."

Hari yanked my bucket out from under Ivy's hand. "No. Let the *broni* learn."

"*A ko bo* lunch," Ivy said with a sigh. *It's about to be lunch-time.*

Hari twisted her head firmly and pointed at the bucket. "Lila, start washing."

I thought I would explode from the humiliation of it. This morning someone had been assigned to wash my things; now I was a "small girl" washer.

"You think we don't know why you pretended not to understand Twi?" Hari stood over me as I bent to wash. "*Wo'n pε sε nipa hu wu tisε o mu hu yεn,*" Hari told me. *You don't want people to look at you the way they look at us.*

"Well, look what happened once S'ter Penny found out I understand Twi. Now I have to wash my own clothes."

"And who should wash them for you, *broni*?" Hari barked at me. If Moko could speak, she would have sounded just like Hari did.

"You think you're better than us, don't you? Because you were born in Britain," Hari continued.

I didn't have to say yes because we all knew the answer. Maybe it was the *fermɛ* in me, but for the first time since I stood on the "Other Nationals" line at the airport, I wondered why I did think I was better than the Ghana-borns—and why most of them thought so as well.

"You're no better than us. You're just like us," Hari insisted, daring me to say the opposite.

I nodded in agreement, but Ivy shook her head.

"No," she said. "She's not like us. She's a *broni*."

16

After hanging the laundry to dry on the lines behind Addo, we snuck our lunch to the farm and polished off another bottle of *fermε*. We stayed there long after the sun had formed a semicircle at the horizon and the bells for supper, then entertainment had rung. The flies had gone to sleep and now the mosquitoes were awake, along with the crickets, which seemed to be chirping along to the beats that blasted from the dining-hall-turned-nightclub for Jams.

Hari read my lips as I absentmindedly sang along. *She was doing the butt!*

"Will you write the words down for me?" I nodded as Ivy's eyes lit up with another question. "Do you know how to do the Butt?"

I nodded again with a tipsy giggle.

"Show us!"

I stood up, teetering a little from the *fermε*, and stuck my bum in the air, shaking it and rubbing it in circular motions.

"Like this?" Ivy stood up and twitched her bum like someone had lit a match to it.

Hari and I burst into giggles.

"What?" Ivy asked, turning suddenly to slap her hands together. She inspected her palms. "Let's get away from these mosquitoes."

I pulled myself up reluctantly, surprised by how much fun I was having with these Ghana-born girls. I realized I hadn't seen Brempomaa all day.

That night I slept better than I ever had since I came to Dadaba—so well that I woke up the following Sunday morning too late to bath before the breakfast bell. I quickly raked a pick through my matted hair, patted some powder across my throat, and headed out the door with Hari and Ivy.

A pot of *agbele* rice water left a ring of sweat on our dining table. The corn-kernel porridge was the Sunday special. I turned my back to the food, which was studded with rice weevils, as usual.

"*Ei!* You won't eat?" Hari held out her bowl to the girl dishing out our food. "Add hers to mine."

I watched the other girls at our table steal jealous looks at Hari as she ate a bigger portion of bug-infested porridge, and I wanted to laugh at the ridiculousness of it—but it wasn't funny.

When the breakfast-over bell rang, Hari, Ivy, and I walked back to Addo. "Let's go to the farm and get water for our baths."

Brempomaa ran up to us. *What are you doing with them?* her eyes asked me as she said, "Where were you all day yesterday?"

"On the farm. Punished. S'ter Penny found out I could speak Twi."

She eyed Hari and Ivy. "How?"

I ignored the question. What did it matter now? "We're going to the farm, for water. Want to come?"

"There's water on the farm?" Brempomaa's eyes widened at the revelation.

Hari sucked her teeth. "Ah, *broni*, why don't you announce it at morning devotion?"

Brempomaa followed us to our room. It being a Sunday morning, there were no compulsory activities on the schedule except Sunday evening service. The room was practically empty. The few girls around lay quietly under their mosquito nets listening to their Walkmen, reading Mills and Boon romance novels, or breathing heavily from deep sleep.

We grabbed two buckets that weren't ours and took the visitors' road to the farm so the only people who would see us with buckets were girls who'd be so busy being happy they had a visitor who'd brought them a loaf of sweet bread and home-cooked food that they wouldn't focus on us.

I giggled at the absurdity of our secret water mission when we were past the visitors' road. "This is fun."

"You never thought you'd be looking for water, eh, *broni*?" Ivy laughed.

"Poor *bronis*," Hari muttered dryly.

When we finally got through the bushes to the well, Hari peered down the black hole. "It's too low to fetch." She sighed, walking away.

"What? Yesterday it was high enough." Hari glared at me. "Did you tell anyone else about this well, *broni*?"

"No!"

"Hmmph." Hari didn't believe me.

"*Bɛ* it's Harmattan," Ivy pointed out. "Everything is drying up."

"Well, let's try at least." Ivy tied the ends of our belts together and dropped the bucket down the hole. Nothing came up, though we heard the bucket's bottom hit water. Ivy tried again, getting on her stomach to be closer. The mouth of the well sank beneath her.

I screamed louder than Ivy did as Hari and Brempomaa

saved her from following the bucket down the narrow blackness.

"*Heh!* Who is there?!" a man's voice called out to us.

"*Ei!*" Hari dropped the bucket in her hands and fled.

"Who's that?" I stood still to find out.

"Let's go!" Brempomaa nearly yanked my arm off my shoulder and we took off running.

17

Weeks passed with no flowing water—no fresh water to drink, no water to bath with, no water to wash our clothes, no water to flush the toilets—and no announcement from the headmistress as to what the school was doing about it. Meanwhile, we were expected to keep our bedsheets pristine white for inspection and those who had work assignments that required scrubbing had to find water to do their work. Meanwhile, it was Harmattan, which meant the dry winds blew a fresh coat of dry red dust over every available surface, from the leaves to the tops of our trunks.

Water became a symbol of who had and who didn't. If you didn't have water to bath with you were poor because no one had sent you some. Those who were lucky enough to be able to bath made sure everyone knew it by painting their throats with chokers of powder. Those of us who didn't took the matter into our own hands.

Before lights-out we were slaves to the bell, rising, working, praying, learning, eating at each rusty clang. But after Pay-Shee rang the lights-out bell, a new day began. And the first order of business was taking a dump.

"Who will go to T?" one of our roommates would ask, and those of us who wanted to go would hop out of bed, grab a wad of T-roll and a plastic bag, and head to the back of the house to shit under the stars. When we were done, we'd hurl our digested supper into the bushes behind the house mistress's bungalow.

After, Hari, Ivy, Brempomaa, and I would join the company of girls who fanned out across campus with cups or pails in one hand and buckets in the other, sneaking into dorms and stealing water from the sleeping girls whose parents had started sending them water. We kept it to cups and pails, but bolder girls stole whole buckets. To protect the water we'd stolen from thieves, we dropped period-stained knickers into our buckets.

To the rage of the girls who had taken to stealing full buckets, their owners started padlocking their buckets to their bedposts. When one girl found her booty locked down, she flipped it over onto the owner's bed in her frustration. The owner woke up soaking wet, her bucket empty. She burst into tears and whispered incantations against the culprit.

When the girls whose parents sent them barrels, bottles, or jerricans filled with water ran out, they joined us thieves or the girls who consulted oracles at dawn, or they offered sex to the male faculty for a full bucket. The Christians fasted and prayed for a water miracle.

"After the flood, you promised you would never again destroy the earth with water," I heard some of them say during all-night vigils by the milk bushes outside Addo.

What an interesting interpretation of the Noah's ark story, I thought as I lay with one eye open, keeping watch over my bucket. On those nights, I prayed along with them. I thought about what Brempomaa had told me about being born again. I never had prayed the Sinners' Prayer.

"Father, I don't know what the Sinners' Prayer is, but if I need to be born again, please make me born again."

A lot of Dadaba girls converted during this time. On Sundays, after lunch, we all powdered our necks down to look as if we had bathed and moved to the chapel with Bibles tucked under our armpits for Scripture Union. We went as a group, Brempomaa, Hari, Ivy, and I.

S'ter Angela was hip-bumping a tambourine at the front of the packed chapel when we walked in.

"Glory be to God in the highest!" S'ter Angela shouted the song.

"Hallelujah!" we shouted back at her, clapping our hands in time.

She repeated the call and we responded. "Everybody, shout 'Hallelujah!'"

"Ha-lay-loo-ya!"

Even though I hadn't wanted to spend my Sunday morning at SU when we'd have to go to chapel again that evening for compulsory service, I must say I enjoyed myself. It felt good to release all the anxiety we'd built up worrying about where our next bath was coming from by singing, dancing, jumping, and shouting.

"It's time to cry out now, Dadaba girls!" S'ter Angela told us as she continued to bump a jingle from her tambourine. "Tell Him you need water. Tell Him you need Him . . ." A hum of prayers rose above my head and I started to pray as well. For water. To get out of Dadaba . . .

S'ter Angela broke into song: "It is well with my soul . . ." The SU regulars hummed along as she began to pitch.

"Salvation is a process," S'ter Angela said. "You might be here today and you have been lying down. *Sorre*. Today is the day to get up. Are you walking? Then run. Are you running? This is your moment to fly. Make the commitment to God and to yourself. Come. Give your life to Jesus."

The front of the chapel swelled with girls who wanted to fly.

I moved where I stood, swaying to the ambient humming as S'ter Angela waited for the girls who were still grappling. As I watched the girls at the front with their arms raised above their heads, I thought to myself that this was private. Why did they have to let everyone know they were born again?

S'ter Angela made one last call, and to my surprise Ivy pushed past us to the altar. Brempomaa raised her arms even higher as she pressed her back against the pew to give Ivy room. S'ter Angela prayed over the new converts, then sent all of us on our way.

We walked toward our houses introspective, humming "It Is Well" to ourselves. Brempomaa left us at Ofori and we continued on to Addo to find just about all of Addo House camped outside our door. S'ter Joe-See came to the doorway, blocking my entry.

She took a deep breath—at least that's what I thought she was doing when she threw her head back—but instead of exhaling she pursed her lips and blew a glob of lathery spit in my face. The warm suds slid down my cheek to my red and white print and dropped to my sandals. "If the bathhouse is so filthy, why don't you clean it? *Hwɛ ne nim. Broni Tuntum. Kai!*" *Look at her face. The black white girl. Disgusting!*

"Oh, Joe-See!" S'ter Ashiaki was shocked by the spit.

S'ter Joe-See ran back into our room to produce the letter I had forgotten to mail to Mum, the letter I had tucked in my trunk weeks ago. I looked over at my black box with the red stenciled hearts. The padlock swung open from the latch. Again, I had forgotten to lock it.

I said nothing as S'ter Joe-See waved the letter in my face. I just moved past her and climbed onto my bed, wishing I could become invisible under my transparent mosquito net. S'ter Joe-See flew to her bed and started kicking at the chain link supporting my mattress. She jerked me around my top bunk until I tumbled into the space between our bed and the one next to it.

"Joe-See, *jai!*" S'ter Ashiaki ran to help me up. *Stop it!*

I got back onto my bed and hugged my knees. Not a tear fell from my eyes. Then S'ter Penny's voice scattered the crowd like a gunshot. "Leave her! *Now!*"

Someone handed S'ter Penny my letter. She scanned it with a shrug. "You people don't know that in Abrokye the washrooms are clean? That they don't have weevils in their food? That they have clear, running water? She's not used to this." She dropped the letter to the ground and moved to console me. "Lila, I'll sort this out."

S'ter Penny looked around the room. "Who found the letter?"

S'ter Joe-See stepped up. "I did."

"Joe-See," S'ter Penny sneered. "I should have known." She turned to me. "Lila, come. Ashiaki, you too." I blinked at her. Shouldn't S'ter Joe-See be coming with us? But as I followed S'ter Ashiaki into S'ter Penny's room, I answered my own question. She was Madam's daughter. Of course she wouldn't be punished.

"Ashiaki, I need you to look after Lila," S'ter Penny said as we stood at her bed. "Now that the whole house is against her she'll need you."

S'ter Ashiaki nodded and took my hand as we returned to our room. The next day, she gave me some of the water her parents had sent her from the barrel she kept padlocked next to her bed. She walked with me to devotion and walked me back to Addo after lunch. It wasn't long before everyone was buzzing that we were dears, but I didn't care.

18

"You ready to go to the farm?" Hari asked me and Ivy after SU the following Sunday.

"For water?" Brempomaa asked.

"For *fermɛ*," Hari explained.

Brempomaa's yellow eyes met mine. "They drink that in the *village*, Lila."

"We're Ghanaians, Brempomaa. If *fermɛ* is good enough for people in the village . . . ," I started to answer defensively.

She sucked her teeth and turned to give Ivy a sideways glance. "You going too?" Ivy shook her head and nodded at the same time.

Hari rolled her eyes. "*Hwɛ*, if this is because you are a born-again *Crifé* now"—she paused to look up at the sky—"I won't drink another drop of *fermɛ* again if the taps flow today."

Ivy and I averted our eyes from Brempomaa and followed Hari to our spot on the farm. Hari unearthed our bottle and tipped it to her mouth.

"Ivy, do the Butt again," Hari said.

I shook with laughter until my chest hurt as Ivy moved her bum like she was going into spasms.

"Let me show you how it is done, *mate!*" Hari winked at me as she dropped her head, stuck out her bum, then slowly rolled her head back as she rubbed her cheeks. A shadow started to cover her face as she continued to dance.

Ivy and I looked up to see a cloud stretching over the sun. The fragrance of rain suddenly filled my nose.

"That was your last taste of *fermɛ*, my friend," I joked with Hari in a thick Ghanaian accent, wiping my mouth as a warm breeze gathered speed around us and the leaves on the bushes started to vibrate. "It's about to rain on your unbelieving arse."

Ivy wasn't laughing with me as I handed her the bottle. She shook her head and lowered herself to lie flat on her back under the cloud. Hari yanked the *fermɛ* from me and took a swig.

The two of us passed and drained the bottle between us until the rain began to fall fast and hard. Hari unplugged her lips from the bottle's mouth and the three of us raced to Addo, our red and white prints plastered pink against our skin, our slippers losing traction in the rock-studded mud. In the rush to shelter, we left our Bibles on the farm.

At the house, buckets were already lined up on the veranda collecting the downpour as Addo House girls stood naked under the water falling from the sky. Brempomaa found us as we started peeling off our clothes, on our way to take advantage of the shower. "So you won't be drinking *fermɛ* again?" Hari scowled. Brempomaa turned to me and Ivy. "What about you?"

I frowned at Brempomaa for the guilt she was trying to make me feel for indulging in one of the few things that made me laugh and forget where I was, enduring a water crisis when I should be at home taking steamy showers for granted. I wasn't like her. I couldn't balance heavy buckets of water on my head. I couldn't fight. I needed some help being strong. So I would be drinking *fermɛ* again. I didn't see what it had to do with God or being a Christian.

Meanwhile, Ivy stood on the edge of our circle with a look of sadness on her face, weighed down by her newfound faith, I guessed.

Rain fell heavily for the next seven days, creating ravines and filling them to overflowing all over campus. During the day, our sandals dug into and slid against the slippery red mud. The stench of the new latrines Madam had built for us stunk to the heavens. The flies had a field day. At night, mosquitoes bred in the stagnant waters.

The following Sunday, SU was more packed than ever. Brempomaa, Ivy, and I joined the rows of girls wearing cloying perfume and powder at their necks. Hari had refused, grunting at Brempomaa's invitation.

Those seven days, we slept like rocks because we knew our buckets would still be full when we woke up. Then the rain stopped as abruptly as it had started. We tried SU again and prayed for it to rain, but a week passed with no answer. Desperation settled over campus once again. The water ran out and girls got their period and had to drink knicker-flavored water again.

19

I woke up to the familiar chorus of *Slap! Squawk! "Ah!"* It was my first Christmas in Ghana. I smiled as I walked past the burnt black nub of mosquito coil to the kitchen. I peered through the door's screen, watching Enyo run after the dingy white fowl, Bits nipping at her heels while Moko yawned, bored by it all. I poured myself a glass of crystal-clear ice water, letting the odorless liquid rush past my tongue. *Ahhhh!* I exhaled, happier than I'd ever been to drink a glass of water, and let out a loud belch.

It felt so good to be back at Auntie's, to hear the hum of the freezer, to sleep on a thick mattress, to eat food I didn't have to pick weevils out of, to drink water that didn't have color, taste, or scent. I left my drained glass next to Auntie's sewing machine and stepped out to sit on the red earth. Bits turned at the sound of the door and ran my way.

"*Afyehyiapa!*" I gave Enyo the traditional Christmas greeting as I scooped Bits onto my lap. "As for you, I won't wish you a happy Christmas," I shouted at mean little Moko. Like she cared. She yawned again and ducked deeper into her shed. Enyo ignored me too, focused on her moving target, the knife in her hand. When the deed was done, she looked up, seeming to notice me just then as she walked over with the decapitated chicken.

I stood, letting Bits go so I could hold the door open for her, and felt a twinge of guilt as she laid the chicken aside to pick up and wash the glass I'd left on the table before she started plucking.

"I'll pluck," I offered quickly.

Enyo turned to give me a condescending smirk as she pushed my hands away and started to pull at the hen's feathers. I wanted to help her, just as I had wanted to help when I'd come home and Auntie Irene honked the horn and yelled for her to come and help us bring my trunk and chop box inside. I'd forgotten what a luxury it was to have Enyo around and I marveled that my life at Dadaba was her life here.

I felt guilty for letting her push my hands away when I started to unpack my trunk but proud of her at the same time. Now that I knew what it was to fetch water in a heavy metal bucket, sweep a plot with a short broom, and wash my clothes in hard water that didn't easily form suds, I appreciated that she did it better than I did. She was a worker, and so she was entitled to the remaining tins of powdered milk and Milo chocolate drink she opened to see how much was left. I stayed awake that night trying to imagine what life would be like with her name, her parents, in her situation.

"Good morning." Auntie Irene's voice was scratchy from sleep when she walked into the kitchen.

"*Afyehyiapa,*" I said.

Auntie Irene shook her head and laughed at me. "*Afyenkobɛtuyɛn.*" She returned the customary reply through her nose, making fun of my accented pronunciation. "Lila, go and have your bath and get dressed. We have to go to the airport. Your mum sent you a suitcase. Then we have to go to church."

My head snapped up at the mention of Mum's name as disappointment came over me. Mum and I were now letters and sent suitcases. How much longer was this break going to continue? I'd spent my first weeks in Ghana replaying in my mind what Mum had thought she'd seen Ev and I doing on the living room floor that day. Then she had written, so casually, so callously, "Lila, it doesn't matter what did or didn't happen anymore . . ." I wanted to see her. To stand in front of her, wave my hands in front of her face, and make sure the Mum I knew still lived in her body—because none of it was making sense.

She'd always told me, "Everything happens for God's good reason," but the last three months in Ghana had been devoid of reason from what I could tell. I was just there—floating from Kumasi to Cape Coast, from Addo to the classroom, from the chapel to the farm, like a down jacket feather in the hazy red dust. Was this "good" to God?

Auntie Irene clapped her hands at me like the prefects at Dadaba, and I was grateful for the interruption. "Quickly, Lila. There's no time to boil water."

Thirty minutes later, we pulled away from Auntie Irene's bungalow. I scanned the University of Science and Technology's campus as it flew past my open window, the dry wind beating my face. The only hint of Christmas was the Christian music broadcast from the secular radio station, but that was normal, just like it was normal for everyone to go to church—whether it was a chapel, mosque, or shrine. In Ghana, the secular and the sacred are mixed nuts in the same bowl.

Last year this time, London had been cold and it had rained. Mum had made me wake up early in the morning to go to church, then help her cook four different dishes that spoiled weeks later because the two of us couldn't finish all that food. Then she'd made me sit by her as she *Afyehyiapa*-ed her way through her phone book, handing me the phone at intervals to say hello.

"What are you mixing in your mind, Lila?" Auntie Irene lowered the radio and gave me a quick sideways glance.

"Nothing—just thinking that Christmas in Ghana doesn't feel like Christmas."

Auntie Irene smiled, switching gears on the motorway that led to Kumasi Airport. "I think it's quite peaceful."

She jerked the car to a stop, shouting a greeting over me at Uncle Fifi. "Uncle Fifi, *afyehyiapa-oh, afyehyiapa.*" Auntie Irene chuckled, handing me a crinkled cedi note to give him.

Uncle Fifi's face lit up. "*Afyenkobɛtuyɛn.* Lila, how was your first term at Dadaba?" His hand closed over my mine.

"They bothered her a little bit," Auntie Irene answered for me, "but she's okay. Aren't you, Lila?"

Uncle Fifi smiled at me. "They worried you over there, eh? Well, that's to be expected. They test you, but you show them what you are about and they back down. You will be stronger for it all, eh?"

The front of the airport was lined with more people than I expected to be arriving and departing on Christmas Day. Auntie Irene and I took our place among the waiting as arriving passengers started to wheel their bags out into the heat.

"Rose!" Auntie Irene flagged down a small woman in a wilted pantsuit. Back in London Mum had always sent things to Ghana this way, preferring a human courier to the "black hole" she said the Ghanaian post office could be when it came to packages with Abrokye stamps.

We exchanged greetings, took the suitcase and envelope Mum had sent, and made our way back home.

"Okay, put the suitcase down and call Enyo into the car. Quickly! Else we'll be late for church."

Enyo was ready and waiting when I stumbled through the door with the suitcase. She had on a ruffled pink dress, white patent leather shoes, white gloves, and a white hat—the kind of outfit Mum used to dress me in for holidays till I revolted at eleven and told her I would not wear white patent anything ever again.

"*Ei!* Enyo, *wei* dear, you are looking sharp," I lied.

Enyo basked in the compliment, clutching her starched white handkerchief.

"Let's go. Auntie's waiting in the car."

Auntie Irene started the car and handed me the envelope Mum had sent. "You forgot to take this in."

I shrugged and opened it to find two £10 notes and a picture of me from when I was nine years old.

In the picture I was wearing the pink and white outfit Enyo now had on. I looked in the rearview mirror and noticed then that the dress was pinker at the seams, where it had been let out to fit Enyo's thirteen-year-old body. I turned the picture around. Mum's scribble read, "Easter 1987."

After church, I opened the suitcase Mum had sent to find old and new clothes, a rice cooker for Auntie Irene, and bars and bars of Cadbury Fruit & Nut. I gave Enyo three of the chocolate bars instead of the pair of jeans she told me she liked as she hovered while I unpacked. She gave me one-word answers the rest of the day and avoided my eyes across the dinner table that night, but I didn't care. I felt bad, but I didn't want to give her my clothes. They were all I had to remind me I had come from somewhere else.

"I've been trying your mum all day, but I can't get through. Everyone is calling Abrokye," Auntie Irene said with a frustrated sigh as she dished out our plates. "Tomorrow, we'll call your mum and thank her for all these nice things."

That night, the three of us ate the chicken Enyo had roasted with rice, and yam. We each drank a bottle of Coke in front of the evening movie, *A Christmas Story*. Right after the part when the boy gets his tongue stuck on an icy flagpole, the lights went off.

I groaned, watching the TV glow radiation-black in the sudden darkness.

"That would be my cue to go to bed," Auntie Irene said. I heard her bamboo chair creak with relief as she stood up and shuffled away.

"Let's wait. Maybe it will come back on again," Enyo suggested. We gave up after a few minutes and felt our way through the blackness to our room.

That night, I dreamed of a laterite-red Christmas. Instead of an evergreen towering over gift-wrapped presents, we had a hibiscus tree with buckets of water under it. A chicken with a halo around its head sat perched on the topmost branch.

20

The first study prep of second term, I received a letter from Mum. The mail girl shimmied her way through the arrangement of desks to stop at mine. "*Broni,* I have a letter for you." She waved the blue airmail so I could see the stamped image of Queen Elizabeth's face—and see that it wasn't a postcard this time.

I tried to snatch it from her hand, but she wanted a bribe.

The mail girl cocked her head at me. "I don't mind if you want to come to my room after prep and settle your bill."

"What bill? It's her letter, just give it to her!" Brempomaa hissed, color burning her cheeks and ears at the injustice. The prefect monitoring our classroom gave us a warning look.

"Fine. How much?" I whispered.

She smiled the way the woman in the market had when Auntie Irene had bought all that *chofi* from her. "Two hundred cedis."

I sucked my teeth and gave her the money before ripping open the folded blue paper, which was bumpy from the impressions of Mum's pen.

"She's coming!" I told Brempomaa breathlessly. I wanted to leap from my seat as I read on. Her cousin had died. *I'll be there for the funeral—and your birthday!* Mum was coming for me!

She hadn't been to Ghana since before I was born, and there had been funerals before. But she was coming now. I had to make sure I left Ghana with her.

That Sunday, I went to SU with Brempomaa. While the other girls raised their voices in prayer for a school water tank, I prayed to God that a mosquito would inject me with malaria. If Mum saw me on an infirmary sickbed, gentian violet staining my oozing mosquito bites, she would have to take me back to London with her.

I made myself sick in anticipation and vomited up my *kenkey* and fish dinner the night before she came. I went to the infirmary. Auntie Nurse examined the thermometer that had been in my mouth through her spectacles. Then she landed a combination slap-punch on my ear.

"There's nothing wrong with you."

I rubbed my ear at her painful diagnosis, pissed off as I walked the dark campus to prep. The picture I had been painting of Dadaba in my letters to Mum wouldn't look as miserable as I had hoped.

That night I couldn't sleep. My armpits were itching wildly and I was literally short of breath as I tried to construct my appeal to Mum. I needed to show her Ghana hadn't been good for me, that I was worse for it. When I finally drifted off, I dreamed Mum was ringing Pay-Shee's bell. It kept ringing and ringing and ringing until it was time to get up.

I felt unbelievably drained as I pulled myself out of bed. A deep red stain—it looked like a child's drawing of a butterfly—added a new pattern to the multicolored cloth I slept on. I checked the back of my nightie; the impression was deeper.

"Menstruation," Hari observed.

I nodded like I'd been expecting my period, but the truth was, I had just gotten my period for the first time. I did as I

had watched my roommates do and sprinkled a little medi-
cated powder onto a sheet of cotton wool, folded it over,
then wrapped T-roll around it to create a maxi pad. It almost
seemed too late that Mum was coming now, I thought as I
squatted to adjust my homemade pad. She had missed my first
period.

21

On the Friday Mum came, S'ter Penny came to call me out of Mr. Kiss-Say's pop quiz on the biology of urination. I ran the first few feet but slowed my pace as I got closer to the parked Rover. Mum and Auntie Irene were inside. I dropped my head and shoulders and filled my eyes with sadness so Mum would feel guilty, but when she saw me the biggest smile I'd ever seen on her face lit up her eyes. She jumped out of the jeep in her heels and slipped on the gravel. I couldn't help but laugh. As I helped my mother gain her footing, I noticed a small stone, the color of Brempomaa's eyes, sparkling on her finger.

"*Lila!*" Mum pulled me to her sweaty stomach. She snapped her fingers at Auntie Irene. "Irene, get me the camera." Mum whipped out a crumpled tissue and dabbed away the beads of sweat dripping from her hairline. "Goodness, it's hot."

The video camera Auntie Irene passed to Mum gleamed shiny and silver amid the red dust around us.

"See how much money I'm saving with you here?" Mum winked at me.

Just like that my laughter evaporated. The desperate anger, frustration, and betrayal I'd felt those first weeks in Ghana crashed in violent waves around me again. So my being in Ghana wasn't about Everton or a break? I knew then, with dejection so strong it paralyzed me for a second, I was going to be in Ghana for a long time if I was in Ghana so Mum could save money.

"Irene, I don't see the red light," Mum said, completely oblivious to the shadow that covered my face.

"I pushed it," Auntie Irene insisted.

"Well, it's not recording if I don't see the red light."

I studied Mum now. She looked different. She looked good. Happy. Fatter. *Better.*

"I pu—"

Mum ran on her tiptoes to the other side of the camera and pushed a button. A red dot of light now emanated from the camera.

Auntie Irene shouted in triumph. "*Now* I see you!"

"Lila, give us a tour." Mum stretched out her arms, performing for the camera.

"Mum, I don't want to . . ."

"*Ei!* Irene, you weren't kidding, oh. Listen to the accent on this one." Mum laughed at me, her accent no thinner than mine.

"Oh, Felicia, you've made the girl angry." Auntie Irene finally noticed.

"Have I?" Mum cupped my face in her palm, that ring resting cold against my burning skin.

I had dreamed about Mum coming for so long, but our reunion was turning out to be an opened faucet with no running water. I was in Ghana because she was trying to save money? For what? To buy a video camera? So she could wear that ring on her finger? Mum read the accusation in my eyes.

"I brought you some Fruit & Nut, and Bounty, and Lilt." My favorite chocolates and soft drink.

That night, when Mum left, I broke a square of Fruit & Nut

and bit into the little bit of London. The chocolate tasted different on my tongue now. It had been fine when I ate the ones she sent over Christmas break, but this time phlegm collected in my throat and coated my tonsils from the rich milk chocolate. The Lilt had a nagging chemical aftertaste. I realized then that if I were to get on the plane to Heathrow right now, the London I had left wouldn't be there—because I wasn't the Lila who had left.

Mum was right. I didn't sound like myself. My English accent had slowly humidified to the thick, slow, gelatinous Ghanaian way of speaking. I wanted to go home, to save myself before I changed into an altogether different person, but when Mum came back to visit me on my birthday the following week, she told me, "Lila, you're growing into a good woman." It surprised me to hear her say that.

"You think so?"

"I really do. Ghana has been good for you." I started to recite my carefully rehearsed monologue about how not "good" my experience in Ghana had been, but she turned her back and handed me a Pyrex bowl. "Go and call your friends to help you take the food to your room. I'd love to meet them."

I went to our classroom to call Brempomaa, Hari, and Ivy as Mr. Kiss-Say collected their quizzes. "Your mother is here, eh? I will come and meet her. I have a letter for my sister over there." He followed us out, leaving the classroom rudderless.

"Hello, Madam, I am Lila's biology teacher," he said, introducing himself, and chatted with Mum for a while before he gave her the envelope. Mum gave him some money.

"Look after my girl, okay?" she told him in Twi.

"Of course." Mr. Kiss-Say put his arm around me now. Mum took pictures of us and Mr. Kiss-Say overstayed, cheesing for the camera.

"Okay, Mr. Kiss-Say, I'll see you again, eh," Mum had to say before he left us.

When we were alone, I introduced Mum to my friends. She gave them all five-pound notes and told them also to take care of me before pressing a ten-pound note in my hand.

"Whoa, you are rich," Auntie Irene said patronizingly.

I tucked the money in my pocket and directed my girls to the Rover, which was loaded down with Pyrex bowls of different sizes filled with home-cooked food: meat pies; a Ghana salad of hard-boiled eggs tossed with baked beans, onions, tomatoes, and greens under a heavy drizzle of salad dressing; a teddy-bear-shaped cake; and more Cadbury chocolates.

"I'm leaving on Tuesday," Mum announced when I came back alone to say good-bye. "So you won't see me till—"

"Till when?"

Her voice had that same shake in it as when she told me I was going to Ghana, not Auntie Flora's. "Till you've finished your O's."

I almost fainted when she said that, but for once I had a definitive answer. I would be in Ghana for the next three years.

22

That night, I got drunk on the farm with Hari, then paid the ₵200 to get into the dining-hall-turned-nightclub for Jams. The dining hall benches were stacked against the back wall and the traces of powder that had collected at the folds of some girls' necks glowed in the black light. The room was thick with bodies and body odor masked by powder and perfume. Girls writhed against each other as LL Cool J filled the room. *I need an around the way girl!*

Hari and I danced together but alone, lost in our drunken thoughts. I closed my eyes, feeling each drum, snare, and riff jolt my leaden limbs into action.

"You can't dance!"

I opened my eyes and S'ter Ashiaki was in my face, laughing at me as she pulled me to her in the darkness. I looked around for Hari. She was off in a corner dancing close with our house prefect. S'ter Ashiaki and I danced together at arm's length at first. In her thick Ghanaian accent she started to sing the lyrics to the Sade song playing and now I was laughing.

S'ter Ashiaki pulled me closer. *"This is no ordinary love,"* she sang into my ears and I laughed some more, airlifting out of my body to look at the room full of sweaty girls gyrating against each other to Sade. I couldn't stop cracking up.

"What's so funny?"

I gestured for her to look around. "We're all girls in here."

"But there are no boys," she said. *She has a point,* I thought as I slow-danced with her until the bell rang, my eyes closed, pretending she was Ev. The lights came on and we walked back to the dorm hand in hand.

S'ter Ashiaki suggested I sleep on her bed, which was kitted out with a heavy Ghanaian cloth covering her mosquito net. I joined her under the opaque cotton cloth and melted onto her mattress. It was the same flimsy piece of market foam that mine was, except it was on a wooden board that didn't sag into a U shape when I lay down on it. I fell asleep against her hot-water-bottle-warm body, which moved up and down slowly with her breathing.

When I woke up, I wasn't sure if it was morning, noon, or night. Under the cloth-covered mosquito net was a world the ringing bell couldn't enter.

My tongue felt thick and hairy as I rubbed it against my lips. My throat was as dry as the Harmattan winds. I heard my roommates stirring around me and I was glad it was a Sunday so I didn't have to go anywhere or do anything until chapel that evening. I just lay in the blackness remembering Jams and all those girls pressed up against each other, nervous energy rushing blood to my armpits, making them itch, when I realized I was in S'ter Ashiaki's bed.

I jumped when S'ter Ashiaki stuck her hand under the cloth and net holding two smooth, mottle-skinned mangoes. She crawled in beside me, and I saw her nipple push through the thin cotton of her oversized Microsoft Windows nightshirt. She took my hand and started to bring it to her breast.

"I'm not, I don't . . ." I gently pushed her away.

"Then why were you fucking with me at Jams?" *Fawking,* she'd said.

I got off her bed, climbed back onto my saggy mattress, and started to laugh. Hard. S'ter Joe-See punched my mattress and let out an "Ah!" and a "Shit!" as her fist slammed into the chain links that kept me from dropping onto her head.

"Stop shaking the bed!" she complained. I couldn't stop giggling.

"Heh! Are you laughing at me?" S'ter Ashiaki poked her head out from under her cloth and net.

For once I didn't think about how I would never have been in this situation if I were in London. I let it go because I was here—in this situation. And you know what? It wasn't the end of the world. I pulled my pillow over my head and laughed tears down my face until I drifted back into sleep. When I woke up and hopped off my bed to urinate behind the laundry lines, S'ter Ashiaki looked through me. She never spoke to me again.

23

At morning devotion the next day, Madam took the stage with a small man who stood on his tiptoes. He was wearing acid-wash jeans, and a big black camera swung from his neck.

"Good Morning, Duchesses," she said. Brempomaa and I exchanged a *Give me a break* glance as we rose with the rest of Dadaba to return the greeting, all eyes on the strange man in our midst.

"As you all know, the inter-house games will begin this weekend and *National Geographic Magazine* in the U.S. has sent Mr. Agyekum here to Dadaba to do a photo essay on it." She beamed proudly. "I'll let him say a few words."

Mr. Agyekum came forward. "Duchesses, huh? Is that right? I like that." He looked to Madam for confirmation.

"Yes, they are duchesses." She nodded firmly. I wondered why she didn't do anything about her duchesses not having water.

"As your headmistress has said, I am here from the States. I take pictures for *National Geographic,* the *New York Times, Time* magazine . . . and for a long time I've wanted to photograph Ghana to show the Western world more than the bloated stomachs and fly-covered children they see from the news feeds on CNN and BBC News.

"I will be at Dadaba for the next two days. I'll be at your morning services and meals, in your classrooms and in your dormitories . . ." He turned to Madam before clarifying, "That is, I'll be there after the siesta bell till before you go to prep. So try to be decent, eh?

"And of course, I wouldn't miss your inter-house games. I understand I should be rooting for Ofori House."

The Ofori House girls around the chapel roared in affirmation as the rest of us screamed, "NO!"

The photographer turned to Madam and said, "Or should I place my bets on Danquah?" He elicited the appropriate squeals from Danquah's residents.

"Or?"

"*LAMPTEY WILL WIN!*" An overzealous girl in yellow print shot to her feet. The whole chapel shook with laughter, even Madam.

"*Addo!*" S'ter Joe-See shrieked.

"*Yoooo,*" he laughed. "I'll be there to photograph you all."

24

"Ah! Sit still!"

"Bε you are tickling me!" I giggled, my throat rolling under Hari's hand as she painted my neck with a powder puff.

"Okay, I'm done." She held up a mirror in front of me and I giggled some more. Between my overpowdered neck and the wreath of hibiscus blossoms Ivy had pinned in my hair, I looked like I was about to perform some fetish ceremony, and I wasn't the only one. Just about every girl in my room was covered in white powder and red hibiscus, sporting our house colors with pride.

"Y'all ready?"

Brempomaa was at our door in our blue and white PE uniform. She picked up one of the red flowers on Hari's bed. "I'm half-Addo, half-Ofori," she said with a wink as she hid the stem in her thick blond Afro.

Every Dadaba girl got into the inter-house games. We forgot there was no water as we generated sweat, running in the dry heat to the school field. We were sectioned off by houses, with each section brandishing or wearing some representation of their house colors. Danquah House girls waved milk bush branches. Lamptey House girls painted their faces with the yellow pollen of the flowers that grew from the milk bushes. Ofori House girls wore the blue PE uniform.

"*Addo dunna kpɛkpɛ! Lamptey dunna kpɛkpɛ! Danquah dunna kpɛkpɛ!* BUT"—the Ga chant was broken with English to make the following point—"*Ofori dunna bodo! Bodo! Bodo! Bodooooooo!*" (*Dunna* meant "bum," *kpɛkpɛ* meant "hard," and *bodo* meant "soft," Ivy translated for me.)

S'ter Joe-See led a taunting section of Addo House girls down the field. At the Lamptey House group, S'ter Joe-See led her followers in chanting, "*Jinsoh!*" Urine! At the Danquah House group they stopped to kick up dust with their sandals. "Grass! Under our feet!" They teased the Ofori House section: "Lie blue! Lie blue!" The houses in turn waved red Magic Marker and nail polish–soiled cotton wool pads as they roared, "*Wowo! Osmo!*" No teacher stopped to ask where the contraband nail polish had come from. It was our day.

Madam Afisiafi was the only damper on the fun as she stalked the stands calling unlucky girls at random and shearing off their punks. Meanwhile students crossed the field to buy snacks. The tuck shop had moved to the field and in addition to the regular fare of *boeufs* and sugar donuts, off-campus vendors had come to sell *chofi*, fried yam, and *kele wele*. The photographer from morning devotion was on the field too, spying Dadaba girls with his long-lens camera.

"Can I take you?" the photographer asked me. He pointed at Hari, Brempomaa, and Ivy. "All of you." We came together and smiled for his camera. "Now by yourselves."

Together we were natural, but alone, we each sat for him stiffly, self-consciously, a little suspiciously, treating the camera the way Ghanaians treat *bronis*. When he left we became ourselves again.

The next evening, S'ter Penny came to get me out of chapel. Auntie Irene was waiting at the roundabout. "You got your wish. Your mum has sent you a ticket."

25

If words could split a person in two, Auntie's words did to me. I wanted to rocket off the ground and scream my thanks to the Lord—and I wanted to cry. I had been waiting to hear Auntie Irene or Mum tell me I could go home since I'd stumbled onto the Ghana-bound flight in my sweater and jeans, but now I had friends and dogs. And it would be cold in London now.

"When am I leaving?"

"Tomorrow. We don't have time."

"Can we call Brempomaa? And Ivy and Hari?" I asked as S'ter Penny and I sat in the car. Brempomaa had looked so worried when S'ter Penny had come for me.

"I can't call them out of chapel unless it's an emergency, Lila. You know that."

I sighed, wondering if S'ter Penny would have done it if she still thought I couldn't understand Twi. "But I have to say good-bye to them." My voice rose above the engine, the car's headlights cutting through the night. Auntie shushed me with a look through the rearview mirror.

"We don't have time for all of that, Lila. I told you your flight leaves tomorrow and we have a lot to do before then. You can leave your friends a note and write to them when you get back to London." She stopped the car in front of Addo. "Now, hurry up!"

I jumped out of the car without another word. I should have been ecstatic, but something didn't feel right. What had made Mum change her mind *now*? I swallowed my apprehension and silenced the questions knocking around in my head as I watched S'ter Penny unlock the door to my room. *You got your wish,* Auntie had said, and I had. I was going back to London!

"Heh! Hari! What are you doing in here when you're supposed to be at chapel?" S'ter Penny stood by the light switch now.

I looked up, surprised. Sure enough, Hari was lying on her top cot, her face looking like the chicken Enyo had cornered. Hari had told Ivy and me to go on to chapel ahead of her when she still wasn't ready after the warning bell sounded.

"Oh, S'ter Penny. I have my period." She offered up her usual excuse, doubling over melodramatically. I had to laugh. No one was giving this girl an Oscar in this lifetime.

"Take off your pants. Let me see the blood," S'ter Penny dared her.

Hari gave it up and straightened before dropping to her feet with a smirk, a Mills and Boon novel falling to the floor with her. *Only Hari . . .*

I turned to S'ter Penny. "She can help me pack."

S'ter Penny pursed her lips. "Hari, I'll deal with you later. Help Lila pack her things. Quickly! Her auntie is waiting downstairs. Lila, I'll be back," S'ter Penny told me. She kept her face stern, but smiled at me with her eyes. "I'm going to call Brempomaa and Ivy." She left Hari and me alone before I could say thank you.

"Where are you going?" Hari asked me.

"Back home."

A shadow passed over her face when I said that, even though I hadn't stepped in the path of the dangling lightbulb.

"I knew you wouldn't last a full year here, *broni*," she told me, hopping back on her bunk, watching me dismantle my mosquito net.

I should have known Hari would be angry. She had never fully trusted me.

"I didn't know my mother would send for me. She told me when she came that I was going to be here till after O's," I tried to explain as I crumpled my net together with my bedsheet.

"Well, when you go there, don't go and exaggerate about this place."

"What do you mean by that?" I folded my mattress over the net and sheets.

"Go and tell them the truth about Africa."

"Of course," I said, surprised she would say that. "I mean, what am I going to say? That we drank homemade alcohol and menstrual water?" I teased her.

She didn't laugh. I sighed, impatience with Hari, excitement, and apprehension coming together to knot my stomach and tickle my armpits. I didn't have time for Hari right now. I hurriedly gathered my things as Hari sat back on her bed frowning at me.

"What's taking you girls so long?" I turned to see S'ter Penny with Brempomaa and Ivy and ran to hug my friends.

"I'm leaving!"

"Lila, your auntie is waiting to get on the road, so be quick," S'ter Penny warned me. The three of us ignored her and stayed huddled together for a few seconds, Ivy crying like someone had died while Brempomaa and I laughed at her, wiping her pouring tears.

"Ah! Ivy, stop that crying! You people, she has to go." Hari got down from her bed. "Ivy, come and help me with her chop box. *Bronis*, get the trunk and mattress."

We separated and got to work shoving the last of my loose bits into my trunk. I gave Ivy my bucket and pail and left my towel, pants, and sponge, still wet from my evening bath, swinging from my bed rail. Tears sprang to my eyes as I stopped at the doorway to look around the room. It was crowded with bunk beds and buckets, messy with hanging uniforms, sponges, and knickers. As if on cue, a mosquito settled on my arm. Hari slapped it harder than she needed to.

"We don't want you taking malaria over there," she said, cracking a sneaky smile.

I pulled her close for a hug. "I'll miss you the most," I whispered, thinking it was what she wanted to hear.

"Liar," she said, pulling away. "Let's go." We bent to pick up my boxes and walked them to Auntie's Rover. After we loaded the back of the truck, they waited to see me off. Auntie Irene opened her bag and handed me some bills to give them. I gave the cedis to Brempomaa. She would share them fairly.

"Go with God," she told me, her face puffing and glistening with tears.

"I have no choice, right?"

"Write to us. Every day," Ivy said, and made me promise to.

"Ah! You too! Will you even have the time to read a letter every day?" Hari sucked her teeth and shook her head before turning back to me. "Just don't forget us, okay?"

I nodded at her. "How can I?"

"Okay, girls, it's time to get back to chapel." S'ter Penny emerged from the house clapping at them. She stopped at the car and ducked into the window. "Lila, *ekyere.*" *We'll see you again later.*

I nodded, feeling for some reason that I would see them again, even though I hoped it wouldn't be at Dadaba. As we pulled away from them I said good riddance to Dadaba. If I never saw the place again, it would be a blessing. But I would miss Hari and Ivy and our nights on the farm drinking, dancing, and laughing under the moon and stars. I would miss Brempomaa, my sister *broni* from Brooklyn, who could carry a bucket of water on her head like a Ghana-born even though she didn't look or speak anything like one. I would never forget them.

26

I couldn't shake the chill that had seeped into my bones from
the moment Auntie Irene and Enyo had waved good-bye
to me at Kumasi Airport. It stayed with me till we landed in
Accra and I transferred to the second aircraft. It got colder as
the flight attendants marched through the narrow aisles spraying the plane with mosquito repellent, and colder still when the
plane taxied into Heathrow six hours later.

I should have listened to Enyo.

"Is that what you're wearing on the plane?" she had asked me
with wide eyes when I walked into the kitchen earlier that day,
dressed for my flight.

"Why, what's wrong with this?"

"You can't get on the plane in jeans. You have to wear a
dress."

I remembered the Ghanaians in line at Kumasi Airport my
first night, all dressed up in their suits, dresses, *kabas,* and *slits,*
swollen ankles spilling out of dusty shoes. "Why? I want to be
comfortable."

"You have to look posh when you travel so the people who
are greeting you in Abrokye will be happy to see you."

Auntie Irene rolled her eyes at Enyo. "Let's eat. Enyo made your favorite—chicken and fried plantains with *jollof*."

"Send for me when you are over there and I will come and cook for you."

Auntie Irene pinched Enyo's earlobe. "Silly girl! What house does this child have for you to come and cook for her in? Do you want to be a maid forever?"

Enyo's head dropped when Auntie Irene said that.

"You'll finish school soon and move on to better things," Auntie Irene continued, her tone softening. "Who knows whether someone will be cooking for you one day?"

I nodded, but Enyo looked into her plate as she ate. When l finished my food, I left Enyo to wash the dishes while I went outside to say good-bye to the dogs.

"Lila, we only have a few minutes before we have to get to the airport," Auntie Irene called after me just as Bits ran up and scratched my feet, then my cheeks and ears with his warm rough tongue. I walked over to Moko, still cradling Bits. She snarled when I came close.

"Oh please, Moko. You know you're gonna miss me." I picked her up for the first time and she bit me.

"*Heh!* Moko!" Auntie Irene thumped her over the head after I dropped her on the floor, but Moko looked untroubled as she opened her mouth, exposing her teeth in a big wide yawn.

"Well, she didn't break your skin, thank God." Auntie Irene rubbed my arm. "I'll go get some Robb." She returned with the small round tin and massaged the mentholated grease where Moko's teeth had chafed my inner elbow. "Okay, we're all set. Enyo, let's go."

Enyo had already packed the Rover with my suitcases so I took the passenger seat for the last time and watched the hibiscus trees and red earth move outside my window. I listened to the news radio playing, not really listening to the forced British accent of the newscasters. Six months had passed since Mum had made Ghana my reality for an indefinite amount of time, and just like that, just when I'd started to become used to it, I was going home.

You should be happy, I thought again as Auntie Irene slowed in front of the airport. But it felt as anticlimactic as Mum's visit to Dadaba had been.

I couldn't wait to take clear, clean water and long, hot showers for granted again. I wanted to escape the swarms of restless flies by day and stinging mosquitoes by night. I wanted to ride over tarred roads that didn't rattle you to your bones as you bumped over dirt and rocks, swerved around gaping craters, and barely missed falling into open gutters.

But I would miss Auntie Irene's harsh softness. I would miss Enyo's permanent smirk that proved she knew exactly what was going on even though she pretended not to. In London there would be no s'ters. Or fresh fried chicken. I would never forget the *Slap! Squawk! "Ah!"* of a chicken's last minutes. It would be strange not to hear a sentence with an "oh!" or "ah!" or "heh!" or "ei!" thrown in. Ghana would always be a part of me now.

"*Ei!* You just got here and you are leaving us?" Uncle Fifi clapped me on the back when we stopped at his gatehouse. "Don't forget us, oh," he said, echoing Hari's words to me.

"She can never forget this place." Auntie Irene laughed, caressing my cheek.

"What you are saying is true. She is a Ghanaian. Ghana will always be her home."

The last time Uncle Fifi had said that I'd bristled, but now it didn't feel so wrong. I still felt like London was home, but I was starting to think maybe home wasn't about where you were born, or where you lived even.

We left him at the gate and the beggar-looking porters bum-rushed us.

"S'ter, make I help you!"

"*Broni!* I go help you get your bags on the plane!"

"Ah! Relax!" Auntie Irene barked at them.

"Oh, madam, *sɛ wo nim, kakra yɛ be di nti*"—*You know we have to do what we can to eat*—one of them said as he threw his elbow at the man standing in his way, his other arm pulling my suitcases from Enyo's hands.

Auntie Irene handed me my passport and ticket at the check-in desk and when I was all set, we lingered at the threshold of the "No Passengers Beyond This Point" area.

I wrapped my arms around Enyo, then Auntie Irene, filling my nose and chest with her powder-fresh scent one last time.

"Ah! Lila, you are acting as if you won't see me again. If not there, then you'll see us right back here," she said with a wink at me.

I started to tell her I would do everything and anything to never have to come back to Ghana, but I knew better than to say never. Anything could happen. I gave Enyo, who was crying now, another squeeze.

"You can write to each other," Auntie Irene pointed out.

Enyo nodded as she mopped her face with her hankie. "*Zo nuede,*" she said in Ewe. "That means 'safe journey.' "

I turned to follow the other blue-passported passengers and disappeared from their sight down the corridor. I waited with the other passengers to board the small plane that would take me to Accra's Kotoka International Airport before I'd transfer to the plane that would bring me back to London.

27

"Welcome back," the man behind the customs desk at Heathrow said, smiling at me as he flipped through my passport. I smiled back. Hearing his accent and just being back home felt surreal. "Ghana, eh? Let's have a look in your bag then."

He unzipped my suitcase. "Now what's this?" He wrinkled his nose as he pulled out the snails Auntie Irene had wrapped in polyurethane bags for Mum. "And this?" He held up the bag of *chofi* with just the thumb and index finger of his rubber-gloved hands.

"Food," I said, summoning my crispest English, self-conscious about the Ghana in my voice.

"Taste good?" he asked, zipping up my suitcase.

I nodded as I put my suitcase back on the trolley and wheeled it into the arrivals hall.

The moment I walked out, I heard: *"Lila! Lila!"*

I followed Mum's voice till I saw her face. She was glowing like a streetlamp on a foggy day and waving like a hooligan at a Manchester United game. I smiled nervously, excitement, anger, and insecurity rushing through me at once. My heart was pumping in my armpits.

I walked stoically over to her, not sure how to act because

I wasn't sure why she had let me come back. I wanted to wrap myself around her and melt into the velvety soft wipe of her hand against my cheek, but I wanted to carve her face up too, with the stone in her ring. I wanted to let her know that whatever she thought she had seen me and Ev doing that day she would never see again. I would not so much as think about a boy in her presence. I wouldn't do anything that would give her an excuse to take a break from me again.

"Hi!" she wailed. As we got closer, I started running to her because I loved her—and in the end she had made things right. I was back home with her in London where I belonged.

She was running to me too, but she seemed slowed down. As I got closer, I saw that she was dragging something—someone—along. *A man.* He was very tall—like a basketball player—with skin the color of black olives and glossy black hair with an island wave to it. I stopped running.

"Lila, this is Ronan." Mum smiled even brighter when she said his name. "Ronan, this is Lila."

He nodded and stepped forward, taking my hand in his. The chill I'd felt now broke into a clammy sweat in my palms and under my arms when I saw the band on his finger. The stone in his ring was the same color as the stone in Mum's, the ring that had winked and stuck its tongue at me when Mum had come to visit me at Dadaba. I hadn't guessed the obvious that day, that a man had given her the ring.

"Hello, Lila." This Ronan had a husky Caribbean accent.

I flung his hand from mine and turned to Mum for an answer. "You're married?!"

Mum's eyes darted over to Ronan.

"I love your mother," Ronan answered for Mum, "and yes, my intention is to marry her."

I almost laughed at the irony of it all. Mum had sent me

to Ghana for being a girl, for liking a boy—so she could get her groove on with this coolie wearing a yellow-stoned ring? All bets were off. I wasn't going to play perfect so Mum wouldn't send me away again. The worst had happened already. She'd sent me away and I'd come back just fine.

"Oh, I thought your intention was to *spoil* her," I said. Mum's eyes met mine quickly before she looked away, embarrassed. "Don't ever think you are special to them, Mum. Right?"

Mum ignored the words—her own words—as I followed her and Ronan out into the cold drizzle to the car park and a shiny silver sedan. "Did you give up the Opel while I was in Ghana saving you money?" I continued.

The Mum I knew would have slapped me by now, but her eyes checked in with Ronan again. "This is Ronan's car, Lila."

Ronan sighed, producing keys. "I keep telling your mother this is *our* car. Has she always been a *me, mine* person?"

Mum's cheekbones were about to pop through her face from all the smiling as Ronan pressed a button on the key ring that silenced the alarm and unlocked our doors. He put my suitcase in the boot before taking his seat behind the wheel.

"So, Lila, your Mum has told me so much about you," Ronan began as he turned the key.

I wish I could say the same, I thought. It wasn't enough that Mum had yanked me from London to Ghana without warning, but now she had just as abruptly interrupted my life in Ghana to foist this new boyfriend on me.

"She tells me you don't like those silk flowers she loves to set up all over the house either. Let me warn you, Lila. They're *everywhere . . .*"

"Oh, Ronan!" Mum giggled, swatting him playfully.

". . . the fake flowers, the plug-in air fresheners . . ."

I turned to look out the window, wishing they would just

shut up, as I swallowed my thickening anger. *At least I'm back in London. She could've left me in Ghana while she got married and started a new family with Ronan,* I told myself.

I focused on the passing scenery, marveling at the fact that I'd been in Ghana that morning. Change just happened without explanation and there was no use wishing things could be as they were. So I tuned Ronan and Mum out and let London reintroduce herself to me.

Where everything in Ghana had some red in it—from the soups we ate to the dirt roads we bumped along—everything in London was black, ash, or brown. There were colored accents: doors painted cobalt blue; spring-green parks; red, white, and yellow off-license shop signs; and nail-polish-red buses. Some windows had pale blue, butter-yellow, and lavender decorations up for Easter, which was a week away. But the city's base colors were muddy brick-brown buildings, cloudy gray skies, and rain-slick black tar roads that stretched out in narrow lanes and wrapped circles around white and fluorescent-green reflectors at the roundabouts.

Compared to Ghana's dirt roads, it felt like we were riding on air as Ronan drove on and made a sharp turn just after the Lewisham Shopping Centre. He parked in front of a semi-detached duplex and bent to lift the lever that opened the boot.

"We're here." Mum turned to watch my reaction.

"What?"

"I bought this while you were in Ghana!" She skipped out of the car as Ronan opened the door. "You think I've been sitting down while you were in Ghana?" Mum asked me, pride mixed with excuse in her voice as I walked into the new house.

I didn't answer her. I just looked around the semidetached duplex Mum had moved into while I was gone, scratching my underarms as Ronan set my suitcase down. Ronan wasn't lying.

Mum's bogus bouquets were everywhere, as were the air fresh-eners that filled the house with the cloying fragrance of fraudu-lent fresh.

"Your mother's done well, hasn't she?" Ronan said. Mum beamed that annoying grin again. "Don't worry, not everything has changed on you. I don't live here. I'm just up the road with my daughter, Chardonnay. She's about your age."

I sighed with relief. Thank God he didn't live with us.

"You have your own room," Mum said.

"Where is it then?"

Mum caressed my cheek with the back of her hand the way she used to, the way I'd wanted her to at the airport. "You want to see your room, eh?"

I rolled my eyes, moving away from her hand. I was angry and exhausted.

"Mum, just show me my room so I can go to bed."

28

"*Lila!*" Mum shrieked me out of my concentration.

"Yes, Mum!" I turned the volume down on my Walkman and took my pen off the airmail I'd been writing to Brempomaa.

"*Lila!* Auntie Irene's on the phone."

I caught my reflection in the mirror on the wall as I galloped down the stairs. I touched my hair, thinking of Ev for a minute. I had bumped into him at Safeway with his mum.

"You look different," he had said.

"You do too," I said, studying the soon-to-be dreadlocked knots that now sprang from his scalp and the fuzz on his upper lip; he looked much like the gang of boys at the bus stop.

"I heard you went to Ghana," he said.

I nodded.

"Your mum still crazy?"

I nodded again with a smile.

"I'll give you a call, yeah."

I nodded, hoping he would. In just those six months I'd been away all of my friends had moved on. I called but they didn't call me back. Everton never called either. It was just as well. We lived in a new neighborhood. It made me sad to think how fickle those friendships had been. I wondered if my friendships with Brempomaa, Hari, and Ivy would survive.

"Lila! Where are you? My minutes are going! And stop stomping down these steps. She's stomping around like she bought this house," I heard Mum complain to Auntie Irene.

"I did. Everything in here we went fifty-fifty on," I told her, reaching for the phone.

Mum sucked her teeth into the phone. "Don't mind her! Your auntie is hearing everything you're saying, Lila." She pulled me close, moving the back of her hand slowly, softly from my temple to my cheeks, stopping to pick at a pimple. "You're getting your period," she announced.

I started to move away from her, annoyed that she would mention my period when she hadn't been there the first time I'd gotten it. She forced me onto her lap. I wrestled around to the side of the sofa.

"Hi, Auntie."

"*Hi, Auntay.*" Auntie Irene made fun of how quickly my English accent had returned.

"Mum keeps saying I sound Ghanaian." I evil-eyed Mum.

"My card's about to finish," Mum said as the calling card beeped its last-minute warning on cue.

"Don't mind her. Your Mum tells me her boyfriend is coming over for Easter tomorrow."

"Hmmph!" I grunted.

"You like him that much?" Auntie Irene started laughing. "Oh, why? I hear he has a daughter too, your age, that goes to your school."

I grunted again.

"Lila, be nice."

"I'll try, Auntie."

"That's my *sweet* girl." She chuckled.

"Where's Enyo?"

"She's here breathing heavy, eager to chat with you."

"Hello?" I smiled when I heard Enyo's soft voice. "How is it over there?"

"It's . . . the same, Enyo." I couldn't get into how so not the same it was with me sitting on Mum's lap.

"*How is it?*" she asked me again.

I sighed. I knew she wanted to hear about streets paved with gold and all the soft drinks you could drink. "Well, it's cold and rainy. We live in a new area and I'm in a new school. It was really lonely at first because I didn't know anyone . . ."

"You knew Chardonnay," Mum interrupted.

I ignored Mum. I didn't know Chardonnay. We were in the same class, but Ronan's daughter did not speak to me and she did her own thing at lunch. I had tried to be her friend, but she didn't seem interested.

"But I got a job!" I continued, smiling into the phone. I worked at the Safeway near the shopping center. "It's great. I get on so well with everyone there. We're all a big clique of friends." I didn't add the fact that I had a boyfriend too. I smiled at just the thought of Gamal. I couldn't wait to see him.

"Auntie wants to speak with you," Enyo said, bored.

"Lila," Auntie Irene said, "be good to your mother, you hear?"

Mum fingered my cheeks again to squeeze the pimple.

"Mum!" My hands flew to cover my oozing pore.

She handed me a tissue from the peach-colored tissue box cover on the sofa-side table.

"Let me say bye-bye to your mother."

I handed Mum the phone and got up to leave. "Lila, we're still on to get your hair done, right? We need to do something with that hair. Let it flow." Then she said to Auntie Irene, "I don't understand why *o'n ma ni ti* flow . . ." Mum didn't like my short cut and wanted me to get a weave.

"I have to go to work," I muttered as I galloped back up the stairs.

Ronan had helped me get the job at Safeway two weeks after my return to London. Mum had been against it, but Ronan had said, "You let the girl go all the way to Ghana by herself, but you won't let her work and make some money for herself?" That certainly earned him points. Safeway was my escape from Mum and where I got to be with Gamal.

I turned the radio on, pulled off my shorts and T-shirt, and examined myself in the washroom mirror. I jiggled to the music, pumping my pelvis as if Gamal was my reflection. I pulled on my shower cap and stepped under the hot spray. Before I could finish lathering, Mum was in the washroom. She lowered the music and turned on the vent.

"Lila, how many times do I have to tell you to turn on the vent while you're taking a shower? The wallpaper will peel."

"*Okay,* Mum."

"You know we're going to *Auntie Flora's* tonight, right?"

She dropped Auntie Flora's name like it was normal, like she hadn't prevented me from seeing my father's sister for years, then used her as the ruse to trick me into packing for Ghana. I refused to give her the satisfaction of asking why, after all this time, she was letting Auntie Flora see me. "Mum, I can't tonight, I'm working late."

"No, you're not. You don't get overtime to be working late for those people."

I rolled my eyes. "Mum, I'm about to be fifteen."

"Not for a few months. Lila, your shift ends at five thirty; I want you home by six thirty latest."

"No, Mum."

The curtain rings scraped loudly across the metal rod as Mum tore the shower curtain to the side.

"Mum, water's getting all over the mats."

Mum looked down and pulled the shower curtain half-closed. "What do you mean 'no'? Lila, you've been saying a lot of things and I've been letting it go because I want us to be at peace, but you are here because I paid for you to come back. Six hundred pounds, Lila, for you to sit on that plane, and let me tell you, I have the six hundred pounds to send you back."

"Then send me back, Mum." I pulled the curtain back, my shower time spoiled by Mum's bleating.

"I could have left you there, but I was the fool."

I rolled my eyes at the shower curtain. "No, Mum, I was the fool. You left me in Ghana to—"

"Oh yeah, I abandoned you. You never opened a letter to find any twenty-pound notes in it?"

I started laughing.

"You didn't have any food in your chop box," she continued. "You never got any visitors. You were all alone."

"Mum, you sent me ten pounds, like, three times."

"Five times, and one pound is six thousand cedis. You know what the average Ghanaian man could do with six thousand cedis?"

I sighed, just wanting her to leave me alone so I could be alone with my thoughts of Gamal. "Mum, can I have some privacy?"

"Privacy? You're sleeping with him, aren't you? That Paki boy at Safeway."

I sighed, stepping out of the bathtub and out of the washroom, leaving Mum to wonder as I went to get dressed in my room. *No, Mum, I'm not sleeping with him*—but it was enough to make me want to, I thought to myself. That way if she sent me back to Ghana there'd be a real reason to blame it on. I pulled on my T-shirt, jeans, and boots and clip-clopped out of my room, past Mum's bedroom and down the stairs, a surge of excitement rushing through me in anticipation. In less than an hour I would be seeing Gamal Abdeel Azziz.

29

G amal was in aisle four unpacking a shipment of McVitie's Milk Chocolate Caramels. I tousled my spikes for his benefit, momentarily abandoning my mission to replace the carton of tampons a customer had left at the till because she hadn't read the "one discount per household" clause on her coupon. I surprised him with a kiss from the back.

Gamal had been my first kiss. Those first few days at Safeway he and I got close as he trained me. Between showing me where the mop was stored, how to price items, and how to spray the produce so water didn't get all over the floor, we had a laugh at our manager, Tom, and ate the odd packet of crisps when no one was looking. He would disappear for pockets of time and come back with hooded, bloodshot eyes. The first time I asked him, "What happened to you?"

He giggled like I'd just said the most hilarious thing he'd ever heard in his life. Then he kissed me. His lips firmly pressed mine. Then his tongue pushed my lips apart. It felt weird—I could taste the crisps on his tongue—and amazing! My stomach and my *pipi* seemed to stir uncontrollably into one as my armpits started to itch. I hoped I was doing it right. When we separated, he asked for my phone number.

Now he pinned me against the shelves for a longer kiss. I

thought I was going to melt the chocolate off the biscuits until I heard the squeaky shuffle of Tom's rubber soles.

"Azziz?"

Gamal and I sprang apart as Tom approached, straightening the MANAGER pin at his lapel.

"What're you doin' here?" Tom asked me, the permanent red stains on his milk-white cheeks growing in circumference as he fumed. "I sent you to drop off those sanit'ry napkins ages ago." His voice squeaked like his shoes. "Go on, get out of here."

"They're tampons, Tom, not napkins." I corrected him just to see his cheeks get even redder.

Tom sputtered, sending out a dribble of spit. "Just go, Lila."

I backed out of the aisle with a wink and smile at Gamal and skipped to Toiletries.

At Safeway, I might have had to listen to Tom's shit, but I didn't have to take it. Within Safeway's fluorescent-lit walls, I wasn't Mum's child, subject to whatever she thought was good for me. I wasn't a *broni tuntum*. I was Lila, responsible for doing price checks and cleaning up spills, and in between I could go ahead and kiss a boy if I wanted to. Everything I did and didn't do started and ended with me—even if I was starting to wonder who "me" was.

Since I'd come back to London, everything felt like an out-of-body experience. I listened to myself speak, and I heard myself forcing my English accent back. I watched myself bump to a song, not sure if I really liked it or was just saying I liked it because everyone else thought it was wicked. These were things I couldn't communicate in letters to Enyo, Brempomaa, Hari, and Ivy because I just didn't know how to articulate my disillusionment, excitement, and overwhelming insecurity at the newness of it all.

I wanted to fit in so badly. To be the English girl from Peckham I'd been before Mum's need for a break/Ronan's dick had made me the Girl from Ghana. I wished I had Brempomaa's strength to be okay with being different, which essentially meant being okay with being alone. Ronan's daughter, Chardonnay, was like that.

In a lot of ways, she reminded me of Brempomaa. Tall, thick, and chalk white (her mum was English), Chardonnay wore an armful of silver bangles that jangled when she walked and a thick smudge of makeup around her eyes. She painted her nails with Wite-Out.

Chardonnay didn't seem to mind being friendless. I watched her in class, in the yard, and in the cafeteria, holding court over invisible subjects. I went to sit by her in the yard my first day at the Peter and Paul School. She looked my way as she fished in her bag.

"Have you got a light?"

I shook my head, thinking how ironic it was that Mum thought I was a bad girl when this girl, her precious Ronan's daughter, smoked!

"Do you smoke?"

I nodded. I had smoked my first cigarette with Gamal in the Safeway car park the day after we kissed.

She arched her eyebrows at me. "Felicia doesn't know that, does she?"

"Course not."

She stood in her boots. "Let's go then."

I followed her to the hole in the fence that separated the school from a row of welfare flats and around to the small alleyway near the flats' rubbish Dumpster. A few other kids were hanging out in the alley puffing away.

Chardonnay started rummaging through her bag again and pulled out a ziplock Baggie holding three of her own cigarettes.

I wanted to ask why her cigarettes were skinny at the ends and thick in the middle, but I didn't want her to think I didn't know what was up.

Chardonnay put one cigarette in her mouth and walked up to the closest boy in the alley. He kissed Chardonnay's cigarette with the burning end of his. Smoke curled between and above them, and Chardonnay gave him a Wite-Out-painted thumbs-up as she curled her thumb and forefinger around her cigarette and took a deep breath. I wondered why she was being so precious with the cigarette, holding it so delicately. She passed it to me.

I took it and sucked in the way I'd just seen Chardonnay do it. Fire caught in my chest.

"This is not a cigarette!" I handed it back to her as a coat of phlegm instantly salved my burning throat.

"You don't smoke weed," Chardonnay fumed. "Why'd you say you did?"

"I thought you meant cigarettes," I said, feeling stupid as I now recognized the scent that clung to Gamal when he came in from the car park with his red eyes.

"Don't fucking tell my dad." She put out the joint, dropped it into her Baggie, and walked off, leaving me in the alley with the other smokers.

"You joining us afterward?"

I looked up at Gamal, who was now holding a price gun. "Where you going?" I heard myself adopt the choppy cadence of his East End dialect.

"Fred's for a few pints and a tenner."

"Course." I wiggled my thumb at him. Now I knew what a "tenner" was.

"The blitzkrieg is on then." The gold cap on Gamal's incisor glinted as he pushed the gun into my face. "Now get the prices right."

I watched his back, a wallet chain dangling from the pocket of his jeans and swinging with each switch of his hips. "Azziz, my arse is bigger than yours!" I called after him. He stuck it out, his boots clack-clunking across the glazed tiles.

It was 5:51 when Tom pulled down the gate and released us to go our way. Drizzle began to dance on the puddles.

"*Shite!* It's raining!" Gamal pulled his hood over his head and took my hand. We were running through the black car park behind our coworkers Annie and Fred when I heard my name.

"LI . . ."—I cringed, letting the cigarette between my fingers fall into a puddle as the second syllable of my name dropped—". . . LA!"

I doubled my pace, tightening my grip around Gamal's hand, but the shrill call came again, louder, as headlights burned our backs. *Pim! Pim! Pim!* Mum pelted me with her car horn.

"LILA!"

Mum was alongside us now, window rolled down a crack. I dropped Gamal's hand.

"Mum." I turned to her like I hadn't heard the horn, my heart pounding, my armpits itching.

"Hello, Ms. Adjei." Gamal stuck his hand through the crack of open window. Mum ignored his hand.

"Hello," Mum said icily.

"*Ei,* Lila, look at you. Your mother's photocopy," Auntie Amerley said. I peered into Mum's open window. Auntie Amerley sat on the passenger side, grinning so wide I noticed the gap in her teeth had gotten bigger in the time I'd been away in Ghana.

"When I told Auntie Amerley you were back, she made me

come and pick you up so we could all go to Auntie Flora's to-gether."

I rolled my eyes before turning to Gamal and the group.

"Later then?" he asked me.

I squeezed Gamal's arm. Mum's eyes followed his hand to the waist of my jeans, which he squeezed gently in response. Waves of giddiness shivered through me as I got in the car and watched the lot of them run through the increasing downpour as we drove past.

"How old is that boy?" Mum looked at me through the rearview mirror.

I ignored Mum and sank lower into my seat. Gamal was nineteen but I wasn't telling her that.

"Did you see his gold teeth? And he was smoking cig'rette." Auntie Amerley pronounced it *see-gret*. "Ah, ah, ah, these kids," she clucked. "Anyway, Lila, how was Ghana?"

"Awful."

"Don't mind her," Mum advised. I turned to look out my window and count the streetlamps as Mum and Auntie Amerley ignored me, gossiping about Auntie Flora the rest of the ride.

30

"*Ei!* Is the place for her alone?" Auntie Amerley covered her mouth with her fist when Mum turned into Auntie Flora's driveway and parked next to a midnight-blue BMW. "And she has a Beemer. *Ei!*"

"This isn't where Auntie Flora used to live," I said, remembering her old flat near Camden Market, which had been quite posh as well. This house was the real deal—a detached English brick house guarded by a pair of pruned shrubs.

"She moved," Mum said as she gave Auntie Amerley a look, then checked the rearview mirror to see if I was listening before she told Auntie Amerley something in Ga. I didn't understand Ga, so all I could piece together from Mum's answer were the random English words—"man," "married"—and "*shika*," which sounded like the Twi and Fanti word for "money."

Auntie Flora answered her door in a silk swirl of color, swathed in an emerald-green *buubuu*, jeweled ruby slippers, and gold bangles stacked along the length of her slender arms. Her long hair floated around her shoulders, parted at the middle, just like I remembered her.

"Is that Lila?" She looked past Auntie Amerley and Mum and folded me into a skinny hug. "How long has it been?" She held me at arm's length to have a look at me, then took my hand and stepped aside for Mum and Auntie Amerley to enter.

"Five years."

"Let's not ever let that much time pass between us again," she said to Mum's back.

"Yes," I agreed, curiosity now getting the better of me as I stood in Auntie Flora's home. What had happened that Mum was talking to Auntie Flora again? I wondered how my father figured into their reconciliation, if at all.

"Felicia, you didn't tell me how beautiful Lila had become," Auntie Flora said, cupping my face. Her hand smelled like roses. "She's a woman."

"Not yet," Mum said, walking past the foyer to settle on one of the stuffed, cream-colored couches in Auntie Flora's living room.

Auntie Flora flashed me a wink and a smile. "Come. Come. Let me give you the grand tour."

She walked me through the living room. Everything was cream and cranberry, from the walls to the pillars of candles that stood around the room frozen in mid-drip, to the fat throw pillows scattered in cozy little corners, to the rugs that swallowed the heels of my boots. I could practically see my reflection in the black wood floors at the edges of the rugs.

She pulled me through an archway to a black and white washroom. A massive photo of Auntie Flora naked was printed onto the shower curtain. "Yes, it's me," she answered my wide eyes. "They can put a picture on anything these days."

There were other black and white photographs of Auntie Flora when she was younger and Auntie Flora with friends dotting the walls. There were pictures of me too. I picked up one from ages ago of me, Auntie Flora, and her then boyfriend Uncle Roger at Thorpe Park.

"Remember that day?" she asked me. I nodded as she led me to her bedroom. "Please." She shook her head and looked down at my boots. I backed out and off her white carpet and looked around from the door. Her bed was an oversized cushion hidden behind a mosquito net that converged into a point just below her very high ceiling.

I thought back to my bunk at Dadaba. I never imagined a mosquito net could be so glamorous. "Your house is beautiful, Auntie Flora."

"Thank you, dear," she said, though it sounded like "Of course it is."

She disappeared behind a mirrored door. "I have something for you," she called to me. I took in the room more comfortably as I waited for her to reemerge. There was a mirror above the mosquito net that looked down on her bed!

I had forgotten how enchanting Auntie Flora was. I remembered her swooping into the tiny living room in our house on Benjamin Road before we had stopped seeing each other, wearing a peacock-printed poncho or a feather necklace or some other wildly beautiful "piece" she had "picked up" from her travels or her magazine job. She would take me to watch boring dance shows or eat dinner at restaurants where I was the only child in the room.

The only kid-appropriate activity I recall us doing was going to Thorpe Park. We went with her boyfriend Uncle Roger, and I remember him complaining about her choice of shoe as she slowed us down, catwalking through the park in wedge heels and short-shorts.

Auntie Flora appeared from behind her mirrored door holding a fold of gold fabric. She shook it out into a blouse. "Try it on."

"Now? Mum's waiting."

"I've been waiting five years. She can wait a few minutes."

I took the soft shiny piece from her, not sure what I'd wear with a gold top. I pulled it on and Auntie Flora straightened it over my hips so the fabric stretched smooth and tight over my body just under my bum. "This dress was made for you," she declared.

"It's a dress?" I wrinkled my nose at Auntie Flora. "I thought it was a top."

"That's the great thing about fashion, Lila. You can wear it any way you want. But I think it suits you as a dress." She turned me around to face the full-length mirror leaning against the wall behind me. "Ugh." Auntie Flora dropped her head into the curve of my shoulder. "Look at that body. To be fourteen again . . . It's yours. Happy Easter."

I studied my reflection. I looked like something out of a fashion magazine in the glossy gold design. I followed Auntie Flora out of her bedroom and through the hallway, stopping at the small alcove lined with shelves of *Harpers & Queen* magazines.

"You have so many magazines, Auntie Flora."

Auntie Flora switched on the overhead light and I walked into the small niche in the wall.

"This is every magazine *Harpers* has put out since I started working for them," Auntie Flora said proudly. "Each one immortalizes a little blip in time—a true, important, granular record of our culture." She paused. "Do you know what 'granular' means?"

I shook my head.

"Then you should've said so. Don't be afraid to ask questions."

I thought about Auntie Irene's impatience with all my questions and how my time in Ghana had trained me to learn by watching, not asking. I wasn't sure which way was better now.

" 'Granular' means you're so intimately close to something,"

Auntie Flora continued. "You're down to the grains that make it up."

I ran my fingers across the magazines' spines, looking for the September 1990 issue—the month I'd been sent to Ghana. I imagined how a magazine of my life would have immortalized the months I'd spent in Ghana.

The cover of my first month in Ghana would have me with a shoulder-length frizz ball of hair, tears in my eyes. In the second my skin would be darker and the soles of my London shoes worn from Ghana's dirt roads. The third would show me with my punk haircut, fuller in the cheeks from all the *jollof, chofi,* and fried plantains I'd been eating. The fourth would show me sitting on an overturned bucket, at the end of a long line of girls waiting to fill their buckets under the slow-dripping tap. The fifth would show me swilling *fermɛ* under the stars. The next would show my powdered neck stretched like a peacock's, the Addo House cheering section behind me.

I wondered what ever happened to that photographer's pictures, the one from *National Geographic*. "Auntie Flora, do you have *National Geographic*?"

"*National Geographic*? The only animals I'm into are the ones on my plate and the ones my shoes, bags, and coats are made out of."

"Flora! *Lila!* Where are you?" Mum called from the living room.

"Come on." Auntie Flora took my hand. "Introducing your daughter," she announced as Mum and Auntie Amerley absorbed me in the gold dress over my jeans and boots. "Doesn't she look beautiful?"

Mum's mouth soured down. "It's too tight."

"She's fourteen, she's supposed to wear tight clothes."

"She's supposed to be hitting the books," Mum countered.

Auntie Flora clasped her long hair back into a ponytail, then released it to fall to her shoulders again. "Oh, Felicia . . ." She started to say more to Mum but ended there. "Lila, come help me serve your mum and Amerley some drinks. What'll you have to drink?"

"Coke," Mum and Auntie Amerley said in unison.

I followed Auntie Flora into her kitchen. It was official. There was nothing in Auntie Flora's house that didn't look like the inside of a magazine. Everything in her kitchen was shining silver, glittering glass, or wood polished to a mirror finish. Heavy-looking iron pots dangled from an overhead rack over the work island in the middle of the kitchen. Auntie Flora set glasses and a sparkling silver serving tray on the island.

"Lila, take out the ice and Coke, and the cranberry juice for me."

As I finished pouring the Coke into Mum and Auntie Amerley's glasses, Auntie Flora pulled a long-necked crystal bottle out of a cupboard and poured a few sips of the clear liquor into her glass.

"Now you can throw the cranberry on top." She winked at me. "Put some in your mum's drink too."

Mum liked her tot of sherry every night before she went to bed, so I knew she would appreciate the drink. She would also appreciate Auntie Amerley not knowing about it, since Auntie Amerley didn't drink. I took the bottle and poured the amount I'd seen Auntie Flora put in her glass. "*Ei!* Lila, it's too much. You have to count out your pour." She splashed the Coke and liquor into her gleaming silver sink, then dropped three new ice cubes into the glass and demonstrated. "One, two, three, four," she counted as she poured into the glass, then covered it with Coke. "Let's go." She handed me the tray.

The rest of the night, Auntie Flora, Auntie Amerley, and

Mum spoke loud Ga around me until Mum gently poked me awake.

"Lila, we're leaving." Auntie Flora handed me a canvas bag with *Harpers & Queen* emblazoned across it.

"Your T-shirt," she explained. I looked down at the gold dress I was still wearing.

"Auntie Flora, thank you."

"No problem, Lady Lila." Auntie Flora put her hands together like she was praying and gently bowed her head. "I like your hair," she concluded after staring at it a long time.

"You like this hair? She looks like a boy," Mum said. I rolled my eyes.

"Your mum doesn't know style," she whispered to me. "You remind me of my youth," she continued.

Mum looked at me weirdly. "It's getting late," she said.

Mum and Auntie Amerley hugged Auntie Flora. When it was my turn, Auntie Flora wrapped her thin, rose-scented arms around me.

"I want you to come and spend next weekend with me, Lila. We can go shopping, get you something other than these baggy clothes to wear," she said when we parted, still holding my hands.

I turned to Mum.

Mum started to shake her head, but Auntie Flora spoke first. "I'll pick you up on Saturday morning."

When we were in the car, Auntie Amerley and Mum gossiped in Ga from the minute we backed out of Auntie Flora's driveway till Mum dropped Auntie Amerley off.

When we got home I ran up to my room, took off everything except the gold dress, and put TLC into my player. Mum opened my door holding a photo album.

"Still in that dress?"

The phone rang. I ran past Mum to the silk-flower table at the bottom of the stairs where the phone was based.

"Come to Fred's."

"Gamal," I whispered, running up the stairs. I closed my door, then my eyes as I flopped backward on my bed, hitting the album. "Ouch! I wish I could."

"What?"

"Nothing." I pulled the album from under my back.

"Come to Fred's," he repeated.

I heard people in the background. "Who's there?"

"Annie and Fred, and they're saying, 'Come to Fred's. Come to Fred's.' *Come.*"

"I can't." I opened the album. Mum was pressed against my father in a tight metallic minidress not unlike the one I was wearing. I sat up to get a better look. She was looking at him, clutching him tightly. He was looking at whoever had taken the picture, his face open in laughter. I remembered his booming voice that day we'd spoken on the phone; he was so happy to be alive, happy that his twins were alive. He had mentioned the twins' names, I think, but I couldn't remember them now.

I turned a page. Mum was smiling again, glowing like she had at Dadaba, Ronan's ring twinkling on her finger. On the opposite page, my father was hugging Mum and Auntie Flora.

"You coming to Fred's?" Gamal's voice brought me back to the phone.

"Gamal, how'm I going to get past my mother?"

"Haven't you ever snuck out? It's not like the house keys are swinging from your mum's hips like she's a jailer. Listen, if you're not here in an hour, I'm coming to your house and shouting 'Free Lila!' outside your mum's bedroom window."

I shivered at the horrific thought, the vision of Mum chasing Ev still only a six-month-old memory. "G'bye."

I walked to Mum's room with the album. "Mum?" I called to her, hoping she had fallen asleep so I could creep away to be with Gamal, but she was awake, sipping a glass of sherry and watching television in the dark.

"Come." She threw back the covers.

I crawled in next to her. "I had fun at Auntie Flora's tonight. Thank you for making me go."

"And you didn't want to go."

"I just said . . . Never mind." I opened the album again even though I couldn't see the pictures in the dark. Mum stretched her arm to turn on her bedside lamp. The album was open to a picture of my father and Mum swaddled in wool coats. Mum was holding me.

"That was our first winter in Abrokye." She frowned at the memory.

In the picture beneath it, Mum was decked out in a sequined top that reflected disco lights on her skin and mine. "*Ei*, that day, your father and I were ready to go to the nightclub, but you kept wailing and wailing when I put you down." Mum smiled, shaking her head. "The poor babysitter said you cried nonstop till we came back." She closed the album abruptly. "So you were on the phone with that Paki boy, eh?"

Mum hadn't unleashed the Tirade since I'd been back, but I knew it would not go away quietly. I braced myself.

"His name is Gamal, Mum."

"I didn't like that he was smoking, Lila. Lila, these boys out here—"

Before Ghana I would've just listened to her rant about boys and *pen-usses* and their collective desire to spoil me, but not now. Not after packing for Auntie Flora's only to be shipped to Ghana. *No.* I got up to leave. She pulled me back to the bed.

"You don't ever walk away from me when I am talking to you. Do you hear me?"

I looked past her, through her. Bored.

"I know you think I sent you to Ghana for Ronan, but it isn't true, Lila."

I looked at her now. "When'd you meet him, Mum?"

"After you left, actually." I almost wished she had met him before and that he had plotted to get me out of the country so they could see to their relationship. Now it went back to making no sense.

"Then why did you send me away? You made it seem like it was because of Everton being here—but nothing happened between us. He started walking me home because some stupid boy was harassing me after school. He came in so we could do our homework together. When you came home that day, we were playing video games. That's it."

Mum exhaled deeply. "Lila, Ronan is the first man that's been in my life since your father and I split. In all the years we've been here together, have I ever introduced you to a man that was not a relation or someone from work or someone from church? Have I?"

"No."

"Well, the *loneliness*"—she grimaced at the word "loneliness" like it was spoiled milk she had accidentally tasted—"Lila, it *gets* to you. I pray you never know what it feels to be as lonely as I was."

"How do you think I felt in Ghana, Mum?"

Mum snorted. "I don't think you know the kind of loneliness I'm talking about, Lila." She looked away now. "Lila, everything I've ever done is for your good. Forgive me this one time that I wanted to do something good for myself."

So she admitted it. Ghana had not been about what was good

for me. It was a selfish lapse in her judgment as my mother and a betrayal of our relationship—our friendship.

"I still believe, Lila, that everything—good and bad—happens for a good reason. I've stopped pretending to understand the logic in that reason though. There is no human logic that can understand it. But there is faith."

I boiled inside when she said that. There *was* logic. She was acting like Ghana had happened by accident, like she hadn't lied to me about going to Auntie Flora's only to send me to Ghana. She had *chosen* to trade logic—and me—not for faith, but for a man. She had just said so herself.

"Bring me the phone," she said.

I nodded and collected it for her. She would talk to Ronan all night, as usual, and wouldn't hear a thing when I walked out the door.

31

" **S** top. I'm sorry."

I clapped Gamal's back and he rolled off of me. "I don't know why it hurts so much, but it does." I was trembling as I spoke to his back, his jeans coming up over his skinny bum. "You pissed off at me?"

Gamal laughed. "It's your first time. It's supposed to hurt. Come on then, get ready. I'll call you a cab before Ms. Adjei starts driving around looking for you."

"I'm sorry," I kept saying between long moments of silence as we waited in the cold for the taxi to pull up.

"Come here." Gamal opened the jacket over his hoodie and pulled me to his chest. "Stop saying sorry," he said.

I stayed pressed against the soft heat of his hooded sweat-shirt until the taxi pulled up. "Did you lot call a cab?"

Gamal kissed me and waited till I climbed into the car before handing the driver some money. I melted into the vinyl folds of the seat, the lingering bouquet of cigarette and weed smoke dragging my drooping lids down. The cabby's sharp speeding turns might as well have been a hand rocking me to sleep.

"Hello?!"

My lips were saliva-sealed to a vinyl button in the seat when

I looked up groggily. For a minute I thought we were in the wrong place.

"This isn't Benjamin Road. This isn't Peckham," I said angrily.

"You said Lewisham!" The cabbie started smacking his forehead. "You said Lewisham!"

"Oh, yeah. Sorry, we just moved here—it's here," I mumbled, scurrying out of the car. The cabbie muttered a curse at me before screeching off, leaving me to the jingle of my keys. I fumbled with the locks, my fingers losing patience with my brain's insistence on repeatedly fitting the wrong key into the door. In the distance I heard a car door slam. My armpits started itching from the irrational fear that Mum would hear it. I could hear my blood pumping through my body, gurgling with each pump of my jumping heart. *Pump. Gurgle. Pump. Pump.*

When I finally opened and gingerly closed the door behind me before tiptoeing upstairs to my room, I heard, "Lila?"

Pumppumppumppumppumppumppump! Gurgle! Mum was outside my door. I slid under my bedspread. Thank God she didn't open the door.

I woke up with Auntie Flora's face over mine.

"Up, up! We have a date!"

She stepped back and opened my closet. Her arms stretched out, making her a kaleidoscopic T shape. Turquoise, pink, red, and purple flew at my eyes from the floor-length knit kimono that draped her angular frame. A proper camera, like the one that photographer had used to snap us at Dadaba, swayed like a handbag at her hips. She turned to look at me over her outstretched arm.

"Jeans, jeans, jeans—and everything else is black or brown. You need color."

Mum barged into my room. "Don't go and spend too much money."

Auntie Flora closed the closet door. "Too much money wouldn't be enough for my niece."

"And nothing too short or tight, Flora."

"You wore the dress to bed?" Auntie Flora asked me, ignoring Mum as I sat up. "I'm glad you like it so much, but it's Azzedine Alaïa, Lila. You have to give the craftsmanship of that dress its proper respect."

I pulled the dress over my head and gingerly laid it on the bed for Auntie Flora's benefit. "I'll take a quick shower and get ready."

"Ugh, that body . . . ," I heard Auntie Flora say as I disappeared into the washroom in my bra and knickers.

"Don't forget to turn on the vent," Mum called after me.

32

"You can order whatever you want," Auntie Flora announced.

After shopping all morning, we were at a Thai restaurant near Hyde Park. I scanned the menu and shrugged. The endless list of curry dishes was unfamiliar. Green curry. Ginger curry. Massaman curry . . . "Do they have fries?"

"Bush girl." Auntie Flora laughed at me.

I looked down at the menu again and rolled my eyes. I knew she would have something to say. At every shop we went to she ridiculed the clothes I picked out until I gave in and just let her buy what she had picked for me.

The waiter stopped at our table. "Are you ready to order?"

Auntie Flora pointed at me to go first. I showed the waiter my choice, hoping he wouldn't announce it so Auntie Flora would scoff at it, but of course he did.

"Pad Prik Thai," he repeated with a nod, and scratched at the palm-sized pad he held.

Auntie Flora checked the menu. "Noodles? You can have noodles anytime."

"That's what I want."

She frowned.

"The Pad Prik Thai is delicious," the waiter offered.

"I want you to try one of the curry dishes. The green curry here is so good."

I gave the waiter a dirty look as I took the menu from him. "Okay, let me look at the menu again."

"Try the kaeng khiao wan kai," Auntie Flora suggested, trying too hard to pronounce the name of the dish properly. I suppressed a giggle. She handed the waiter our menus. "And I'll have the same."

I bent to slurp my water.

"That's not for drinking, Lila, it's for stirring." Auntie Flora pulled the stiff black straw that had come with the glass from my lips and folded her cloth napkin over it. "So, what's your favorite thing that you got today?" she asked excitedly. She bent to pull the bags from between my legs and took out the lime-green tank with spaghetti straps. "I know you weren't too keen on this color, but it really suits you," she gushed. "We dark girls shouldn't be afraid of color." She held up the sheer bra and knickers set next. "You don't have to show these to your mum," she said. She met my eyes. "Lila, have you had sex?"

I thought about the searing pain I'd felt as Gamal's *pipi* pushed against mine. "No."

"Your mum tells me you like a Paki boy at Safeway. You can do better."

I sighed. I loved the way everyone thought they knew what was good or better for me. "Auntie Flora, what does that mean?"

"It means, is he in school? What does he want to do with his life?"

I shrugged.

"Always aim for the best, Lila. You hear me? I know you're young, but you have to think about your future. Always. Secure yourself. Look out for men who will add, not take away. And you need to be surer of yourself, Lila. You're always shrugging. As a woman—a *black* woman—you can't afford to come off like you're unsure about anything." She took a long swallow of her wine. "So tell me what you're going to wear first."

When we got back to Auntie Flora's house, she walked through each room with a barbecue lighter, her coat of colors splashing behind her as she lit the candle pillars in her path. I followed her from the living room to the hallway to the toilet but wandered back into the living room when she went upstairs. The heady scent of roses wafted from the candles filling the first floor of her house. She returned to the living room in a silk black and white kimono, ruby slippers twinkling on her feet. She held a yellow and brown kimono for me.

"You can put this on."

After a long day of Auntie Flora pushing her opinions and life lessons on me, I was a little over her, but as she made her glamorous entrance I couldn't help but crack a smile, in awe again. It was nice the way she made everything feel like something out of a magazine or film—like an event. I took the kimono from her and ran up to her room to change.

Candles on both sides of her bed flickered. The mosquito net was folded up into a loose knot over her bed. I took off my clothes and ran down the stairs on my tiptoes the way Auntie Flora did so the kimono skirt could fan out behind me. Then I ran upstairs and did it again.

"Lila, you okay?" Auntie Flora called to me.

I found Auntie Flora in the living room sipping a glass of wine.

"It's so good to have you back, Lila," she said, cradling me. "I was against your mother sending you to Ghana, you know. Your father was too." She paused to finish her wine. "I don't like to talk bad about your mother. I've made a vow not to get involved in what goes on between her and my brother anymore, but your mother . . ." Auntie Flora shook her head. "She's a hard woman, Lila. She's a hard person to live with, harder to love."

"Well, I wouldn't know how my father is to live with or love," I told her, pulling away slightly.

"That's not your father's fault, Lila," Auntie Flora pressed. She paused for a second, set her lips in a fine line before announcing, "She sent you to Ghana without telling your father. Did you know that?"

I don't know how she expected me to react to that bit of information, but I felt nothing but impatience. What was the point of her telling me all this? Was I supposed to hate Mum and love my father?

Whatever had happened between them, she let him call me. He didn't have to call just on the holidays. And the same planes that flew out of London and Ghana flew out of New York as well. Why hadn't he ever gotten on one to visit me? Or sent for me?

He had never written. Never sent a card. It was one thing to see pictures of him and speak to him on the phone a couple times a year, but the fact was I didn't know the man. That was no one's fault but his own.

"Auntie Flora, if my father really wanted to have a relationship with me, nothing could stop him," I told her.

"Lila, he only just got his papers. He couldn't travel before."

I sighed. "He couldn't call more? Write? Have me come visit him?"

Auntie Flora nodded. "Maybe he could have . . . ," she answered finally. "Anyway, forget it. I'm just glad you're back home in London where you belong."

That night I lay next to Auntie Flora flat on my back trying to see if I could make myself out in the mirror above, in spite of the dark. I raised my arm and thought I saw the yellow of my kimono sleeve fall in a soft crush around my armpit, but it was just too dark to be sure what I was seeing.

I wondered what Brempomaa, Hari, and Ivy were doing right then. Was Brempomaa fetching water? Had Ivy gone back to sneaking to the farm and drinking *fermɛ*? Who was S'ter Joe-See terrorizing now that *broni koko* and *broni tuntum* weren't in pitching distance?

That night I dreamed that Brempomaa, Hari, and Ivy flanked my father wearing tight gold minidresses. He was puffing on a cigarette and blowing smoke into their faces, so they moved out of his way. Auntie Flora appeared from a corner to take the cigarette from his mouth and put it under a cloth napkin. Then she put him on her lap. Then the napkin burst into flames. An invisible hand knocked a glass of water with lemon over the fire. To Auntie Flora's fury, it spilled on the gold minidresses too.

A grinding sound woke me up.

"Fresh juice?" Auntie Flora asked me when I walked into her kitchen the following morning. She switched a lever on the machine in front of her and the grinding sound roared from it. I noticed the cutting board and the massive bowl of chopped-up fruit next to it. "It's peach-plum-orange juice with a kick of ginger," she said as she fed the thing more fruit. "Come help."

I went to stand by her. She stopped to cup my face with a sticky hand before she held her other hand out. I passed her a handful of mixed fruit.

"So, more shopping today? We can go get breakfast after our juice and then head out to the shops."

I was exhausted just thinking about another day with Auntie Flora. Making an event out of everything was nice and all, but sometimes it was fun to be still, calm, and quiet too. Suddenly I yearned for the languid lull of a joint. "No, thank you, Auntie Flora."

Auntie Flora switched the juicer off. "You didn't have fun yesterday?"

"Auntie Flora, thank you for everything you got me. Can I go home now? I forgot that I have some schoolwork to—"

She whirled around to face me. The skirt of her kimono spun like a windmill around her feet. "Why?"

I shrugged.

Auntie Flora gritted her teeth. "What did I tell you about shrugging? Say what you need to say."

"I just want to go home."

"*Why?* Did I say or do something, Lila?" Auntie Flora turned around and switched on the juicer again, which I thought was odd as she wouldn't be able to hear my answer. "What's your reason?" she shouted above the din. "If you can't tell me, I won't take you home till this evening, like we originally agreed."

I looked at the digital clock on Auntie Flora's stove. If I left Auntie Flora's by eleven, I could catch Gamal smoking a tenner on his lunch break in the Safeway car park.

"I have to go to the toilet."

As Auntie Flora juiced on I ran up the stairs and shed my kimono for my boots and jeans and the neon green tank top Auntie had bought me. I fuzzed my spikes with a hand and walked out through the front door. I could still hear the juicer going.

"Gamal!" He was in the car park smoking a joint by himself as I expected.

"Lila!" He took in a long toke, pulled me close to him, and exhaled it into my mouth. I held the smoke in and exhaled it back into his mouth. He turned his head to the side and spewed out a cloud of smoke.

"I got off the clock early. Come to Fred's with me. He and Annie are already there."

33

Fred and Annie weren't there. The sun was low, the lights were off, and our eyelids were leaden from the marijuana we'd just shared. At some point Gamal had put music on and leaned in to kiss me. He moved a breath's distance from my face. I closed my eyes and his tongue was in my mouth, then it was in my ear, then it was on my breasts. I felt like satin, like nothing and no one—not even Mum—could hold me in hand because I would slip out of their grasp.

He stood me up to pull my top off all the way. My jeans were already an inside-out crumple around my boots. His saliva dried cold on my goose bumps as he slipped his head through the opening my bound legs created and moved his mouth toward my *pipi.*

"Gamal, I want to stop."

He moved back. "Okay."

I quickly pulled my jeans up to my waist.

Gamal got up and put his arm around me. We sat in the darkening room, quiet until the music faded.

"You okay?" he asked finally.

I nodded.

"What are you thinking?"

"That my mum would kill me if she knew where I was."

Gamal pulled me close to his chest. "I think your mother would understand better than anyone."

I pulled away from him. I had told him about the loneliness talk Mum and I had and didn't think he needed to be bringing it up to try to convince me to have sex with him.

"Gamal, I'm leav—" A heavy knock rattled the door of Fred's small flat.

"Is Lila in there?!"

Auntie Flora?! I could see her peering through the window on the landing outside Fred's door. I dropped to my knees. "My aunt!"

"What?"

"Lila! Is Lila in there?"

Gamal turned to the door. Auntie Flora could see him now.

"Hello! Hello!" Her voice was muffled by the windowpane. "Lila! Lila! Is Lila in there?"

We crouched low and quiet until Auntie Flora left. "Oh my God. I have to go now."

"I'll walk you out."

How had Auntie Flora found Fred's place? Gamal and I walked quickly through the open corridor outside Fred's flat that looked out onto a busy street of blurry white headlights and red taillights flying past each other. Auntie Flora stood at the foot of the stairs.

"I'll call you later," I told Gamal.

"I knew you'd be with the Paki so I went to Safeway and made your friend tell me where you'd be."

"Who?"

"Her name was Annie," Auntie Flora said, turning to face me. "Listen, I won't tell your mum where I found you if you don't tell her you had a miserable time with me. Okay? I honestly thought you were having fun. I took you shopping. I got you stuff girls your age don't even know about . . ."

I rolled my eyes.

"You're not going to tell your mum you hated being with me, are you?"

"I didn't hate being with you, Auntie Flora."

Auntie Flora's back melted into the curve of her bucket seat with relief. She started the car. "Where do you want to go for dinner? Anywhere you want to go."

"Kentucky's," I said, suddenly realizing I hadn't eaten anything but the slice of peach I'd popped into my mouth at Auntie Flora's that morning.

Auntie Flora made a face. "What kind of auntie would I be if I took you to eat that junk? It's poison, that fast food."

I sighed. "You said anything *I* want."

"Uh-uh." She shook her head. "Anything that's *good* for you. How about Nando's? That's a compromise."

I rolled my eyes and turned to look out the window. Auntie Flora was still talking. "Trust me, you'll love it. Want to hear some music?"

Auntie Flora pushed the CD sticking out of its player into her dashboard and sighed when the lilting chords vibrated through the car, turning up the volume. "This is a classic you're listening to, Lila—'The Girl from Ipanema.' You may not appreciate it now, but you'll see. When these white people are talking about 'The Girl from Ipanema,' you can say 'Yeah, I've heard it.' When they ask you if you've ever eaten Thai food, you can say, 'Course I have.'" She adjusted her voice to the deep-throated nasal accent of English aristocracy. *Course I have.* "These things are important. Trust me. It's all about creating the impression you want people to have of you."

I remembered how Auntie Irene switched accents at the airport and at the market. I did it too, overdoing my English accent when I first came back from Ghana, lest anyone hear a trace of the Kumasi and Cape Coast that had crept in. I remembered how at Dadaba I did subtle things to remind people I was a *broni*. And it wasn't just about accents or intonation. At Dadaba it had been about powder as well. Once we had powdered down no one knew who had had a bath because her parents had sent her a barrel of water and who hadn't bathed in days.

"You know, I've been thinking about what we talked about yesterday," Auntie Flora said, slowing the car down as she looked for parking. "About your father, and your mother sending you to Ghana, and you know what? I'm convinced it was a good thing. It gave you an experience that separates you from everyone else. You just have to learn how to use it to your advantage."

34

When Auntie Flora dropped me at home, Ronan and Chardonnay were over.

"What happened? Everything okay?" Mum asked before I closed the door.

"Did you have fun?" Ronan chimed in.

Mum frowned at the Nando's takeaway in my hand. "Oh, I made dinner. We were waiting for you to eat."

"Well, you can still sit with us while we eat. I'm starving." Ronan rose to his full gangly height and clapped Chardonnay on the shoulder. "Char, you didn't see Lila?"

Chardonnay smiled prettily. "Hello, Lila," she said in the most dulcet of tones.

"Lovely to see you." I gave her the fake right back and ran up the stairs.

"Lila, come right back after you wash your hands. I'm putting the food on the table now," Mum called after me.

When I got back downstairs, Mum had finished laying out a spread. There was Ghana salad, rice and beans, red stew, and corn on the cob.

"Felicia, this is delicious," Ronan said, heaping food onto his plate. Mum giggled and glowed, as she did whenever Ronan was within eyesight or earshot. He turned to me and Chardonnay.

"So, you two have some classes together at school, right? Tell me, Lila, does Char have any friends?"

Chardonnay sighed loudly.

"I never hear her talking about anyone . . . ," Ronan added.

"Nothing and no one to talk about really. That school is crap," I answered.

Chardonnay looked my way. I could see she was deciding maybe I could be cool.

"As for Lila, everything is crap," Mum said. "I should go and bring the letters this girl used to write me when she was in Ghana."

"Mum, I don't know what school was like when you were in Ghana, but Dadaba was a nightmare." I started to tell them about how all 1,400 of us girls lived by the rusty old bell that Pay-Shee shook around campus—waking up, bathing, cleaning up, praying, learning, singing, eating, and drinking at each gong. How we used to drink water that had dirty knickers in it because running water was hard to come by and it was the only way to prevent your water from being stolen. How the dining hall flies wouldn't let you eat in peace. How the girls danced together at Jams. How that photographer had come to capture it all.

"Sounds like Jamaica!" Ronan chuckled. Mum giggled. Chardonnay looked amazed.

The next day in the schoolyard, I saw Chardonnay bending to disappear through the hole in the fence that led to the smokers' alley.

Chardonnay sold weed, I now knew. I felt the pounds in my pocket from my Safeway check and followed her, a smile curving my lips at the thought of how happy I would make Gamal if I surprised him with a bag of weed.

"How much?" I asked as the clock chimed that our lunch break was over.

"How much is what?" Chardonnay tried to play dumb.

I raised my eyebrows at her.

"I've got tenners," she said finally.

I exchanged a £10 note for an earring-size bag and started to walk away.

"You going to smoke that all by yourself?"

I shrugged. "You want to smoke some with me?"

Chardonnay motioned for me to give her my weed. She sprinkled the small dried leaves onto a rolling paper and spun it into a joint. She lit it, puffed, and passed it to me. I took a sip of the smoke and exhaled a cloud. She looked impressed. "I see someone's become a smoker."

I said nothing as I took another pull.

"So that was some story you were telling about Ghana," she said.

"That wasn't even the half."

I told her about how we used to mix *kenkey* and sugar water in old Coke bottles, bury it on the farm, then get drunk off the exhumed *fermɛ* days later—the music blasting from Jams at the dining hall our inadvertent sound track. I told her about how I'd stumbled into Jams drunk one night and S'ter Ashiaki had tried to make out with me. And how we used to shit in plastic bags or on paper torn from our notebooks, then hurl it into the bushes behind the house mistress's house because the toilets didn't flush. How girls had started praying for, fighting over, and stealing water—just to be clean. Then, finally, about that day the rains came in the dry season and we all showered under the smoke-colored sky.

When I was done Chardonnay handed me my £10 back. "You need to get paid for that story."

~

"Look what I got." I waved the bag of weed Chardonnay had dashed me like a prize. Gamal took it and put it to his nose. "Not bad." He led me out of the toiletries aisle.

"I have to price these," I protested.

"We have to smoke this," he answered with mock urgency, marching me through the aisle and round the corner, past Fred, who was spraying the vegetables in the peninsula where the produce, frozen foods, and pharmacy sections met.

"You lot going to smoke?" he whispered after us, dropping his hose to follow.

"No," Gamal answered over his shoulder, marching toward the automatic doors.

"Sharing is caring, Gamal, didn't your muvva eva teach you dat?" Fred was at our heels. "Ann." Fred motioned Annie over.

"Oh brother," I muttered. Ever since Annie had given Auntie Flora Fred's address to find me, I did not want her knowing my business.

"Where're you lot going?" Annie asked loudly. She stopped mopping to catch up with us.

"Let's just invite Tom then." Gamal rolled his eyes.

I snuggled into Gamal's plaid shoulder as we followed the automatic doors swinging outward into the car park. Gamal loosened his fingers around mine to pack a pinch of the herb into the pipe he kept in his pocket. "Light me up." He turned to me and I was ready with a flame.

Annie's loud laughter tickled the rain clouds beginning to darken the bright sky. "You look like Popeye with that pipe in your mouth."

"Uh guh guh guh guh." Gamal aped the Popeye laugh and took another sip of the smoke before passing the pipe to me.

"Who do we have to thank for this teatime treat?" Annie asked after she'd had her pull and passed the pipe to Fred.

"Private Dancer over here." Gamal wrapped me up from behind.

"Private Dancer?" I twisted to look at him.

Gamal let me go and dipped to the ground to demonstrate. "Her auntie is standing outside your door, peeping in, yeah. *'Is Lila in there? Lila?'* " He put on Auntie Flora's voice, making us all crack up. "And this one hit the floor like a dancer," he told them.

Annie sighed. "Sorry about that, Lila. It was like your aunt put me under a spell. You can't lie to a woman wearing a turquoise jumpsuit."

"We should go back before Tom comes looking for us." I squeezed Gamal's hand before I led the group back into Safeway and returned to my work. Tom was there holding the price gun I'd left on the shelf.

"Where were you?"

"Toilet."

"Right." Tom shoved the price gun in my hand.

35

"*L*ila!"

"Yes, Mum!" I chased my voice to Mum's bedroom, where she was sitting up in her bed sipping a glass of sherry.

"What are you doing?" she asked, shifting under her duvet to make room for me.

"Nothing."

"Come and sit with me for a bit." Her voice was low and soft.

"Mum, I have loads of schoolwork." I started to leave the doorway of her room.

"I haven't seen you all day," she said.

"Mum . . ." I wanted to lock myself in my room and talk to Gamal into the night.

"Okay, go, go." Mum's voice was hard again. She took another sip of her drink. I sighed and got into her bed.

"Before you get in." She drained her glass to the ice cubes and handed it to me.

I sucked my teeth and left her room to refill her glass.

"I'm waiting for the day when I will send you and you won't suck your teeth." Her voice followed me downstairs. I rolled my eyes on the way to the kitchen. When I returned with her fresh glass of sherry, Mum pushed the covers back for me.

"Thank you, dear." She hugged me tightly, leaving a moist lip print on my temple. "So when are you going to do something with this hair?"

"Mum . . ." I squirmed out of her embrace.

"You were crying when you had to cut your hair for Dadaba and now that you can wear it long, you keep it short." Mum sighed and looked up at the sky before pulling me to her heart again. I could hear it knocking softly against my head. "Lila, I'm glad you're here. I missed you when you were in Ghana."

"You did?"

"Of course I did. You're all I have."

I looked at Mum again. Her eyes glistened in the flickering light of the television set. She was spinning the amber stone around her finger with her thumb. Something had happened with Ronan.

"What's going on, Mum? Is it something with Ronan?"

"There is. Nothing. With Ronan." She took another swig of her drink. "Anyway, you can go. I'm fine."

"No, I'll stay." I wanted her to be clear that I was there for her, so Loneliness wouldn't feel the need to send me away again.

"No, no, it's fine. Go and do your schoolwork, okay? Oh, and you got a letter from Ghana."

I left her and ran to the table at the bottom of the stairs where Mum kept the mail, keys, and other miscellaneous papers. My letter was under the fake-flower pot, rubber-stamped with the Cape Coast post office seal. I peeled apart the envelope's gummy flap, the glue stretching like okra as I ran back up to my room to read it.

"Lila, stop running all over the place. It's late." I heard Mum's voice before I closed my door.

Two pictures were wrapped in the letter. I laid them on my

pillow, pushed them together, held them up, and shuffled them before finally reading the letter.

These are the pictures that photographer took of us! Brempo-maa wrote. *He came back and brought the magazines with him—we each got one. I asked him for the ones he took of us and he sent me four copies of these!*

In other news, there were rumors that S'ter Joe-See had gotten pregnant!

Madam came to devotion and told us she was disappointed in us. "Duchesses don't gossip," were her exact words. She told us Sister Josie was just sick with a severe case of malaria and would be back to write her O'levels. I'm sure. She's probably in the village now, having an abortion as I write—I just want to know who the father is?!

Meanwhile, there is still no water, but the tanker comes more regularly now. Madam has sent a letter to all the parents telling them that if they send water to just their daughters, they should be warned that it will be common property. She's started enforcing it too, but so far, only the teachers and prefects are getting that water. My parents came to visit me and now Dadaba is their new project. They're raising money for a school tank.

Hari is still Hari—raising hell. Ivy and I are praying she'll submit to God once and for all.

What about you? Are you reading your Bible? Praying without ceasing? I pray for you daily—and MISS you! It's almost like you weren't here . . .

Those six months I'd spent in Ghana felt like a dream now. Only the stories, memories, this letter, these pictures were proof it had all been real.

36

"Lila."

I was high. I had just walked in the door from work and my plan was to scuttle upstairs to wash my face, brush my teeth, then listen to music in my room till I fell asleep, but Mum was awake, watching television.

I crossed the threshold of her room halfway. "Mum?"

"Lila, come."

"What is it, Mum?" Marijuana-induced paranoia—*marinoia,* Gamal called it—gripped my fast-beating heart.

"Your father wants you to spend the summer with him in New York," she announced.

My buzz was instantly killed, leaving a dull headache. "Here we go again . . ." I was just beginning to feel settled into London life again. I had a boyfriend. And I didn't even know my father. I hadn't heard the man's voice since the Christmas before I went to Ghana. "Mum, no. I told Safeway to put me on the full-time schedule for summer."

Like she hadn't just heard me, Mum said, "He told Auntie Flora he wants you to go to him once school closes for long vac. They're going to Disney and they want you to come."

"Mum, you prevented me from seeing Auntie Flora because

she put me on the phone with my father. And now I'm meant to spend a whole summer with him?"

I stepped into Mum's room all the way and looked for her glass of sherry to explain this crazy change of heart, but her bedside table was empty. The flickering images on the television were over- and underexposing her face. My armpits started itching as I remembered the look on her face the day she drove past Auntie Flora's to Heathrow and left me to board the plane for Ghana. The same guilty yet unapologetic expression tightened her jaw. She avoided my eyes.

"I'm going, aren't I?"

"I think it will be good for you to go, Lila. I've been holding you back from your father and it's time you got to know him."

I stomped out of her room, wondering how and why I had gotten back here again. This time she was being up-front about the fact that she was sending me away, but I was still at the mercy of Mum's—and now my father's—random will.

The next day, I left for Safeway without a word to Mum. I was down the street when I heard my name.

"*Lila!*"

I turned to see her at our door in her nightclothes, the wind whipping her with the belt of her morning gown.

"What?" I shouted.

Mum narrowed her eyes at me. "Excuse me?"

I rolled my eyes and performed the right answer in the right tone of voice: "Yes, Mum."

"You couldn't even tell me you were leaving?"

I rolled my eyes again. "Mum, I'm going to work."

"Have a good day. I love you," she said with a smile that begged me not to be mad with her.

I shook my head, bitter laughter scratching my throat in spite of my hurt, anger, and frustration. She was disrupting my life, but she didn't want me to be pissed off? I ran to catch the bus and once I was on it, I sprinted to the top level so I could watch London crawl below.

When I got to work, Gamal followed me into the lockers as I put on my apron. I crumpled into his arms.

"What's wrong?"

"My mum's forcing me to go to America for the summer."

Gamal waited for me to say more, not sure why I was upset. I pulled away from him. "I *don't want* to go!"

"Why not? America's meant to be brilliant."

"She can't just keep sending me to different continents because she's feeling lonely!" He looked at me like I was just being dramatic. I started to walk away. "Forget it."

"Wait!" His arm snaked out to catch me around the waist. "Where in America you going then?"

"Disney," I whimpered.

"Which one?"

"What?"

"Disney World or Disneyland? There's two in America, innit?"

"I don't know which one."

"You should find out. There's meant to be a big difference between the two."

I rolled my eyes at him. "This isn't a joke, Azziz. What about us?"

"Haven't you ever heard of the phone? The post? I'll write you love letters."

I sighed. That was all sweet, but I knew things wouldn't be the same when I got back, just like things hadn't been the same when I'd come back to London. So much could happen in three months.

Anyway, what did I expect Gamal to do about it? There was

nothing he could do. "Let's go before Tom sends the blood-hounds looking for us."

We nearly smacked into Tom as we pushed the locker room's swinging doors outward.

"For chrissakes, would you make sure there's no incoming before you exit!" His cheeks were a fuming shade of fuchsia. "This where you two been the whole morning?"

"We been in here five minutes, man. We're entitled to a break." Gamal sucked his teeth and started to swagger away.

"Not *before* you start working!" Anger shot from Tom's neck to his face, deepening the rose color of his cheeks. He blocked us from leaving for a minute, stretching his sleeve out to lean against the doorpost, but then shook his head and stomped off into the fluorescent horizon of aisles, pushing the mop and bucket he had come to get.

"What's your problem?" Chardonnay asked me as I frowned at the joint she passed me.

"My mum's sending me to my father's for the summer."

"Why's that a bad thing?"

"I don't want to go. I just feel like . . . urgh!" I pounded my fist in the air, dropping the joint.

"Careful!" Chardonnay leaped to catch it, her big white hands closing around it before she screamed from the burning pain.

I couldn't help but laugh at the surprising grace of Chardonnay's acrobatic leap as she went after her precious joint.

"What are you laughing about?"

"Nothing. You all right?"

She put the joint to her lips and sucked in. "Yeah, I'm fine." She choked the words out with smoke before licking the burn on her palm.

"Come on then."

"Where we going?" she asked, huffing and puffing from too many years of pot smoking and the energy she'd just exerted to save her joint.

I took her to Safeway and as I expected, Gamal was where he always was at two in the afternoon.

37

I was high as a prepubescent boy's voice, taking another toke of smoke, when Mum's jeweled hand came out of the sky and landed with a crash across the hill and valley of my forehead and eye. Gamal's mood ring pipe fell from my hand and glittered to the ground. I heard the tinkle of shattering glass on a two-second delay, another two seconds after my brain registered the pain of Mum's surprise strike. At just the same time, Tom shuffled out of the store, his pinched English face pointed in our direction.

"Is this where you been the whole time, Azziz?" He stopped to take in the scene. Mum's hand was repeating her crash landing across my face in rapid succession. Chardonnay was giggling.

"What are *you* doing out here, mate?" Gamal wanted to know. "Aren't you meant to be doin' your job?"

"That's what I'd like to know!" Mum turned her rage on Tom when she saw the MANAGER label on his Safeway apron. To all of our surprise, she started clocking Tom. "You let [*bang!*] these kids [*smack!*] smoke drugs when they are supposed to be working for you!" *Thwap!*

"Hold on now. Hold on. *Hold on!*" Tom screamed, his face

and neck on fire as he started throwing his clenched fists about in wildly awkward karate chops. His tantrum stopped Mum's strikes. "Azziz, you're fired. Lila, you're fired. The rest of you lot, GET YOUR ARSES OFF THIS CAR PARK NOW OR I'LL HAVE YOU ARRESTED!" He turned to Mum, his voice dipping to a whisper. "And *you*. If I EVER see you at this Safeway again . . . YOU'RE GOIN' IN FOR ASSAULT AND BATT'RY, DARLIN'!"

"This is bollocks," Gamal stated, and stomped off.

Chardonnay's sinsemilla-laced snickers graduated to raucous laughter, fat tears streaking her eyeliner down her cheeks. "Chardonnay, come on—*now!*" Mum pushed her as she dragged me by the ear to the car. I noticed then that in her other arm she was holding a bag of groceries.

"You people didn't even offer to carry the groceries," she said as she slammed her door and started the car. "No phone. No telly. No music. No job. No friends. No—"

"No life," I mumbled at my window as Mum started listing the terms of my punishment. Her hand came down on me again, hard. Chardonnay was doubled over and shaking with hysterical laughter.

"Close your mouth now, Chardonnay!" Mum ordered. She drove us home and we sat stiffly in the living room while Mum left a message for Ronan. Ronan came by to pick up Chardonnay after work.

"Uncle Ronan, hi." I smiled, genuinely happy to see him.

"That's what you're doing now, Lila? Getting high?" He turned to his daughter. "Wait in the car."

"Lila, go to your room," Mum told me.

I went upstairs and heard Mum and Ronan whispering to each other for several minutes before the door slammed.

"Lila can't talk on the phone because she was caught smoking drugs," she explained to someone who called for me later that night. It was probably Gamal. In spite of all the shit I was in, I had to I laugh. *Drawgs,* Mum had pronounced it in her Ghanaian accent.

Now I couldn't wait to go to America.

38

I ignored the in-flight film moving on the screen above my head, the actors' voices whispering from the earphones around my neck as I studied my father and his family in the photo Auntie Flora had given me. My father was dark black, like me, and shiny bald with a full mustache and beard. His wife was the color of red clay, like Ghana soil. She had a half smile on her face, but her eyes squinted warmly. Their children sat on their laps—the girl with too many ribbons in her hair on my father's, the big-headed boy on hers.

The whole flight, I'd been fidgeting with this photograph. Tucking it in my envelope of travel documents, then plucking it out. Curling the Kodak paper in my fist, then, before it creased, letting it spring back into flatness. Huffing warm circles of breath onto the glossy veneer, then wiping my fingerprints off with my sleeve. I was nervous.

On one hand I was unimpressed by the supposed significance of meeting my father. I wasn't nine years old anymore, needing to pin a personality to the booming voice on the other end of the line. Ever since that day we'd spoken on the phone in Auntie Flora's flat, the day he'd told me he'd just had twins, my father had become to me like something I had left on the bus.

He was just gone. There was no way to get him back. Someone else was enjoying him now.

I'd settled into being okay with this, holding tight to Mum and whatever else was in front of me. Now change—instigated by Mum—with its perfectly imperfect timing, was shaking the sediment up to the top.

On the other hand, I was titillated. I had grown up feeling guilty about wanting to know my father. Mum had made me feel like any desire to connect with him would be a betrayal. *She* was there with me. *She* had sacrificed. *Everything I do is for your good.* But he was still my father, the man with the big phone voice and photogenic smile. I'd always been curious. And now I was going to meet him.

My stomach curdled as I scratched my underarm, thinking of what the summer ahead had in store for me. The idea that we were going to Disney World was just so random. Was Mickey Mouse going to wave his magic wand and create a relationship for us?

Once again I would have the Stranger's job of deciphering a new dynamic and figuring out wherein I fit. I'd have to be sensitive to this family's moods, get used to their quirks, learn their inside language.

I'd be at the mercy of a stepmother who probably didn't want a reminder that her husband had been married before. I'd be a big sister to two when I was used to being the only one. And I'd have to be sweet about it all because I was the Stranger invading their turf. And just when I finished the work of getting to know them, I'd be leaving.

I resented Mum for putting me in this situation again and for not being strong enough to handle her full responsibility to me. She wasn't allowed breaks from me, just like I wasn't allowed breaks from her. She was my mother and I was her daughter. I was born to be her responsibility.

I was hurt and wished, as I had when she went off on her "boys and pen-usses" tirades, I could reach her in that bitter, broken place and let her know how much I loved her.

I sighed, willing my thoughts to stop running laps in my head, and turned to the panorama of scattered cloud puffs outside my window. Some looked like the thin smoke rings Gamal sometimes impressed me with in the car park, some like the thick and fluffy cotton wool I'd used for pads at Dadaba. Each cloud was trapped, suspended in this midair moment, just like I was in this moment, with a plane full of strangers. Mum had said she'd stopped looking for the logic in God's good reason, but I hadn't.

I needed understanding, and not the "Only Jesus"–"In Him We Live Provisions"–"Thy Will Be Done Hair Salon"–"God's Way Chop Bar" kind of understanding. I wanted a why-couldn't-Mum-and-my-father-just-have-stayed-married understanding. Why-couldn't-Mum-just-handle-her-loneliness-like-every-other-single-mother-and-keep-me-with-her understanding. Why-wasn't-there-just-running-water-at-Dadaba-for-chrissakes understanding. I was after a why-did-Mum-have-me-come-back-to-London-only-to-send-me-to-my-father's-just-months-later understanding.

Worn out by the questions, I leaned my head on the window. When I woke up, the air hostess's face was within an inch of mine. She had that pissed-off grin air hostesses get by the end of a flight after having to repeat the same thing row after row.

"Headphones, please. And I'm gonna need you to put your seat in the upright position." She said "gonna" like Brempomaa. America, here I come.

I sat up and handed her my earphones. She added it to the ones lining her arm from wrist to bicep, like so many bracelets, and went on to tell the passenger two rows behind me to adjust his seat as well.

My nap had been calming, sort of. All the anxiety I felt now lay in a thin film of sweat on my skin. I was sticky and clammy and hot and cold at the same time. I shifted in my seat. That's when I felt the first syrupy drops of my period moisten my pants. I looked out the window as I added *Why now?* to my understanding list.

"Thank you. 'Bye now," the air hostess repeated again and again, scraping my nerves as I moved closer to the door.

I wondered how many times she had said those words in the last five minutes, how many times she would say them in the next week, how many new personalities she would have to deal with. Her job was to be the perfect stranger.

I moved through the tunnel connecting the aircraft to the airport terminal. In the first toilet I found, there was a sanitary napkin dispenser hanging on the tiled wall, but I needed a twenty-five-cent coin to buy one. Since all I had were pounds, I stuffed my crotch with a wad of T-roll and waddled out of the toilet to the immigration line.

"You come all the way from London by yourself?" the red-nosed immigration officer asked me in an accent I'd always thought actors exaggerated for the *New Yawkiz* they played on film. He took my landing card and thumbed through my passport. "How long you visiting New York for?"

"Just the summer."

"You visiting family?"

"A family. Yes."

"*A* family or *your* family?"

I nodded, not clarifying what I'd meant. I was visiting my father and *his* family. The immigration officer stamped my passport and I moved on to baggage claim.

I wrestled my cases, tagged HEAVY, off the moving belt and dragged them through the customs stop, avoiding eye contact with the uniformed agents. Mum had told me not to mention the *chofi, colby,* logs of yam, palm oil, and *shito* she had sent me with, and now I knew why as I passed the sign prohibiting bringing in meat products, vegetables, and fresh fruits.

I wheeled past the customs agent seated at the inspection desk without trouble. The automatic doors parted to reveal New York.

39

I pulled my suitcases behind me, swiveling from left to right, scanning the markered names greeting DR. LAKSHMI, ELIZABETH FEINBERG, attendees of the SLOAN KETTERING MEMORIAL ONCOLOGY CONFERENCE. A group of young men holding letters formed a chain to spell out H-E-W-A-N-T-S-T-O-M-A-R-R-Y-Y-O-U. But I didn't recognize my father or his family in the waiting crowd.

I moved out of the passenger-pickup traffic and found a seat, using the opportunity to take in New York. JFK was a massive port of passing people bathed in Safeway-esque fluorescent lighting. Asians and Hispanics, blacks and whites, and uniformed airport staff crisscrossed each other to sell and sweep, meet and greet, roll and drag bags.

Beyond the airport's revolving and sliding-glass doors, just in front of the shadows cast by the surrounding airport buildings, I could see the late June sun baking a line of people waiting for taxis. So far, New York didn't look that much different from London, except it seemed bigger and sunnier.

"Lila," a voice boomed above my head.

I looked up to see my father, his bottom and top rows of teeth meeting perfectly in the middle of a dazzling smile. He opened his arms to hug me, pulling me into the hard muscles of his stomach. My armpits flared on contact as cheers erupted behind us. We turned to see the girl "he" wanted to marry crying and hugging her new fiancé.

"Hello," my father greeted me.

He was tall, four heads taller than me, and his long, muscular legs seemed longer in the shorts he wore. I followed my eyes down to my own legs, lean and long like his, though I was short like Mum.

"Hello," I returned as his other daughter took my father's hand. The girl's eyes were as big as 20p coins.

"Daddy! Let's go-uh!"

"Nana Yaa, lower your voice," her mother said, nudging the girl's head to face me, simultaneously revealing the little boy behind them, who was also wearing shorts. The boy and I had our father's legs.

Nana Yaa narrowed her eyes at me. I could see her deciding whether she was going to be nice. "Your hair looks funny-uh," she said finally. My hands flew to my head self-consciously.

"*Nana Yaa.*" My father's tone warned her to behave and she instantly wiped the look of mischief from her face and threw her arms around me in a dramatic squeeze, like she'd been coached to do so.

"*That's* my girl." Our father beamed at her. Jealousy pinched me as he scooped her up to his hip and nuzzled her stomach, sending a shiver of giggles through her body.

We don't know you, bitch, her eyes glared at me. *Fuck you,* my eyes glowered back. "Hmmph!" she grunted through her nose, resting her head on my father's shoulder.

"Yaw, get out from behind your mother and greet your elder sister," my father demanded.

Yaw reached to shake my hand as his mother's eyes smiled warmly at me—the same way they had in the photograph. "Yaw, do you greet your big sister with a handshake?" He clung to his mother instead of embracing me. She shook her head and stepped forward.

"Don't mind him. I'm Julie." *Joo-Li,* she pronounced it in her Ghanaian accent, pushing past my personal space border to crush my breasts in a squishy hug. I tried to ignore the nagging itch under my arms as I stood trapped in her awkward cuddle, until I saw my father scratch the nerves out of his own pits. So this was where I'd gotten my armpit tick from.

"Shall we go?"

"Yes!" Nana Yaa squirmed in her father's arms until he let her down and ran ahead of us with her brother in tow, chanting, "M-I-C-K-E-Y! M-O-U-S-E!"

"Nana Yaa! Are you the only one here that we all have to hear your voice?" my father hissed.

Joo-Li ran to corral the children, leaving my father and me alone. I kept my eyes fixed ahead, my insides leaking into the wad of toilet paper. My father rubbed his underarm again.

We walked out of the airport into the early afternoon, past the island of passengers waiting for taxis and across the street to a vast car park. The sky was brighter and bluer than the airport windows had let on, and the air was a hot and muggy soup.

My father led us to a tightly packed minivan. The rear window was opaque with travel bags. A sticker plastered across it read NO JESUS, NO PEACE. KNOW JESUS, KNOW PEACE.

"Did you just come back from somewhere?" I asked as a rush of blood spurted into the T-roll.

"We're going straight to Disney." My father beamed at me.

Joo-Li sighed and shook her head as Nana Yaa opened her mouth to chant again, "M-I-C-K-E-Y! M-O-U-S-E!"

"Won't we be going . . . home . . . first?" I swallowed my spit, feeling weird calling their place "home." "Mum sent fish and yam. I should probably unpack." I was too shy to add that I would not make it out of the car park, let alone to Disney, without bleeding onto their van's vinyl seats.

"No, no, no." He twisted his head firmly. "We are on a tight schedule."

Joo-Li shook her head and smiled at me from her side-view mirror. "Your father likes his schedules," she informed me, "and his lists." She pushed a tape into the player and started singing loudly and badly along with the suddenly blaring music.

> Good! Working together!
> Working together for your good!
> Beeeee-cause you love the Lord!

The volume dipped at a twist of my father's hand, but Joo-Li continued to sing at the same level, her off-key notes crashing against the windows in the car. A few of her guttural notes flew past the gate of my eardrums, ricocheting like bullets around my skull. Nana Yaa closed her eyes, clapped her hands over her ears, and shouted above Joo-Li's singing. "M-I-C-K-E-Y! M-O-U-S-E!"

"*Nana Yaa. Now,*" was all my father had to say to shut Nana Yaa off. "Joo-Li," he continued, "we were supposed to ease Lila into our family. With that voice, you'll scare her away."

Yaw giggled, and Nana Yaa stretched out her neck to cackle louder as our father raised the music to a compromise volume. Joo-Li turned to me, waving her arms in time with the music like she was at a Scripture Union meeting. "Ah! Lila, are you scared?" I played my position as the Stranger and shook my head, smiling politely, trying to ignore the rapidly soiling T-roll in my knickers.

For better or worse, Joo-Li's voice and music were the sound track to my first hours in America, and though I wished my ears could follow my eyes out the window, I soon tuned her out and absorbed the view. I'd been expecting to see a close-up of New York's famous skyline—more of the toy land I'd seen when the plane nosed down or the postcard-sized Twin Towers and Empire State Building I'd seen at the card shops in London—but all I saw were the four- then five- then six-lane highways my father sped down, lined with dense green forest.

"Can you imagine? At one time this was all bush," my father remarked, meeting my eyes in the rearview mirror.

I looked at the road signs. Green and white reflector signs let us know we had entered this parkway, that expressway, this interstate. Under the signs and all around us, families, couples, old people, and dogs passed us in their sedans, jeeps, minivans, and station wagons, small overturned boats or bikes strapped to many of their roofs. Some of them overtook us. Some tailgated. Several stopped short when a police car or suspected police car was in sight, causing my father to curse and Joo-Li to repeat, "Jude, *boko.*" *Relax.*

I craned my neck to see the drivers of the oversized trucks that rumbled next to us, some of them with sharp-looking steel rods packed onto their backs. I tried to erase from my mind the potential freak show of one of those rods flying off the truck and straight through our windshield. Many of the trucks had a sign at their back asking, HOW AM I DRIVING? I wondered what would happen if I called the provided 1-800 number to answer.

"You're quiet, Lila," my father said, breaking the spell of my drive-by hypnotism. The car was humming with the rhythm of everyone else's light snores and measured breathing. I wasn't ready to talk to him alone. I dropped my eyelids, pretending to sleep until I did.

40

According to the digital clock on the dashboard, I'd been pressed between Nana Yaa and the car door for fourteen hours.

"It stinks in here-uh!" Nana Yaa bleated.

Joo-Li sucked her teeth. "Roll down your window."

"Daadeee! *Someone* in the car smells-uh!" She threw an accusatory glance my way and pinched her nose. I wondered if Nana Yaa really could smell the blood that had soaked through my T-roll pad, knickers, and jeans. I reshifted my balance to the bones of my bum, afraid to get comfortable even though I knew I had already soiled big time. *Why* did I have to get my period right before meeting my father and his family?

"Then go to sleep. Look at Yaw. He's sleeping nicely."

"I can't sleep, Mommy! It stinks-uh!"

Joo-Li turned to my father's profile, which now bobbed along to the playing tape. *Good! Working together! Working together for your good!* Now I knew the words as well. The tape had looped over and over again from New York to Pennsylvania, Delaware to Atlanta.

"Jude, help," she laughed, exasperated.

"Who wants McDonald's?"

"Me!" Nana Yaa bucked in her seat at the offer.

My father veered the car onto a right-hand exit and followed the red sign that announced a McDonald's, Bob's Big Boy, and Shoney's Restaurant all up ahead. He parked between an oversized truck and a dark plain of evergreen trees. The soft shine of the restaurants' lights glowed warm and gold in the dark distance. My father stretched out of the car and let out a coyote howl of a yawn.

"Now who's scaring who?" Joo-Li asked him.

I smiled to myself at Joo-Li's dig. Nana Yaa snickered as well as she bounced out of the car with him. "Oh, Daddy! That was a loud yawn!"

"Lila, what will you have?" he asked me. In my mind I could see Auntie Flora frowning as I ordered a double cheeseburger, large fries, and a Sprite.

Joo-Li lowered the music when Nana Yaa and my father were gone. "I told your father we should leave tomorrow so you could unpack, but he wouldn't hear of it. He wanted your first memories of America to be about fun and family—Disney World." Her eyes met mine. "Your father really lobbied for you to be here."

I wasn't sure how to respond. Was I supposed to pat my father on his bald head when he got back to the car or pin a gold star over the embroidered horse on Joo-Li's polo shirt?

Joo-Li changed the subject. "So Flora says your mother bought an apartment?"

"Yes, she has." I did not want this woman thinking she could pump me for information about Mum.

"She has done well." She gulped, noting the change in my tone. "Anyway, we're happy you're here." She raised the music's volume again. She didn't sing this time. I kept silent until my father and Nana Yaa opened their doors, immediately filling the car with the smell of grease and meat.

"Yaw! We have McDonald's!"

Yaw twitched in his sleep at his sister's shriek and suddenly I felt wet heat seep under my jeans.

Pap! Nana Yaa slapped her twin. "Yawwwwwww-uh! You made pee-pee!" The boy blinked confusion back at his sister, his big, pretty eyes glistening in the dark.

"Ah! Big boy like you peeing on yourself?" My father sucked his teeth as his arm jerked round and round at his side, opening his window. Joo-Li pulled Yaw out of the car and speed-walked with him to the nearest toilet.

"I have to pee too," I lied. By now, my knickers were a bloody puddle.

I ran past Joo-Li and Yaw toward the McDonald's hoping to beat them to the toilet, praying they couldn't make out the stain on the seat of my jeans in the dark. I tried the washroom door when I got into the restaurant. It was locked. ASK THE MANAGER FOR THE KEY, a handwritten sign way above eye level instructed.

"Excuse me, are you the manager?" I asked the uniformed woman behind the counter, my hands behind my back, though they couldn't possibly cover the massive soil. "I need to use the loo." I wiggled and hopped and squeezed my face to make sure she wouldn't point me to the RESTROOMS FOR CUSTOMERS ONLY sign hanging behind her.

The woman stared at me blankly for a second. "Ohhh, you mean the bathroom," she said, handing me a key on a heavy metal ring. I nodded just as Joo-Li and Yaw walked in.

"Oh! You've soiled yourself!" Joo-Li announced.

I sighed as she followed me into the open bathroom.

"You p-p-p-peed blood?" Yaw asked me with a stammer, kind of titillated by the idea.

Joo-Li handed Yaw his change of jeans and knickers. "Yaw,

concentrate on what you need to do." She turned to me as I self-consciously shed my own knickers and jeans. My knickers were slick with blood. I dripped onto the small, square tiles as I started to wash my pants with the syrupy pink soap I squeezed from the dispenser.

Joo-Li laid a wad of tissue under me. "You're not washing well, Lila." She took my jeans and scrubbed the denim seat against itself until it was spotless. Then she washed my knickers. As I held my jeans and knickers up to the hand dryer I remembered Ivy and that day we had washed the pile of S'ter Penny's and my prints. The same feeling of gratitude washed over me. Joo-Li slipped a few quarters into the tampon machine on the wall and passed me a handful. "Next time, just tell me what you need."

41

The woman behind the check-in desk at the Orlando Hilton handed my father the card-keys to our room. Wilted from the twenty-hour ride, we followed behind him like zombies and all but fell to the floor from exhaustion when he opened the door. Even Nana Yaa, who had "M-I-C-K-E-Y"ed her way down America's east coast, was practically asleep standing up.

Joo-Li tumbled into the full-size bed nearest the window and the twins joined me on the other one—only to be awakened by gunshots. I opened my eyes in panic. It was my father slapping his palms together to make explosive, hollow sounds.

"Upupupupupupupupup!" he chanted. The rhythm of his voice mercifully lulled me back to instant, blissful sleep—until he clapped me on the back. "We have four days to cover three parks and I'm not losing a morning to sleep."

"Jude . . . ," Joo-Li protested groggily.

"You can sleep in the car." Reluctantly, we all filed out of the room.

The twins were able to sleep once we got on the road, but I closed my eyes in vain. My *pipi* throbbed, raw from all the blood gushing from it and the coarse irritation of my slightly damp jeans. The air conditioner blasted in my face. I opened my eyes to close the vent but still felt the chill.

"How is your mother?" My father broke the silence, his eyes darting to the rearview mirror, noticing I was awake. This time I answered him.

"She's fine. The same." I felt eyes on me and looked in the direction of their heat. "Do you know my mum?" I asked Joo-Li.

She shook her head.

My father changed the subject, turning to his second wife. The two of them launched into conversation, leaving me alone to look out the window again.

"Okay!" my father said, jerking the hand brake up. Nana Yaa and Yaw breathed raggedly in deep sleep, their limbs entangled in a sweaty knot.

"Nana Yaa! Yaw! Wake up!" Joo-Li leaned over the backseat to poke them awake. I pried them apart.

"Nana Yaa, Disney!" My father baited her. He got out of the car and poked his head through the open window of the backseat. The girl groaned and with her eyes still closed, she held up her arms through the open window frame. Our father scooped her up right through it.

"Jude, you'll be carrying her around all day," Joo-Li warned him as she took Yaw's hand.

My father shrugged. We stopped behind him at the long queue to buy entry tickets. He jutted his hip out for Joo-Li to dig his wallet out of his pocket when we got to the front of the line.

The man in the shaded booth straightened to begin his speech. "Welcome to the Magic King—"

"I want the three-day package," my father said, silencing him.

"Sir, we have several different p—"

"No. No. No. We want the three-day package." My father splayed the bills out neatly and Joo-Li and I had to laugh at the man's surprised face. I'd only been with my father for a little more than twenty hours, but I already knew the man behind the booming voice was a bully.

My father collected the tickets and we walked in. I turned every which way to take in our surroundings. Red brick streets crisscrossed through a fantasy of perfect little houses on perfectly manicured lawns, decorated with hedges clipped to look like different Disney characters.

"AAAAGH!" Nana Yaa's sudden shriek sent itches crawling under my arms. "M-I-C-K—Mickeeey!!" She shimmied down and out of our father's arms and ran to the man in the mouse costume.

"Mickey" must have been dying a slow death under the heat-trapping head of his costume, but he bobbed his permasmiling plastic face and waved his white-gloved hands. Children seemed to materialize from every corner of the park to rush and circle Disney World's biggest star. Camera bulbs began to flash excitedly as a crowd of parents directed them. "Get closer to him, Nigel!" "Laura, look this way!" *"Melissa!"* one woman hissed at her daughter through clenched teeth. Yaw hung back, frozen by the flurry of activity.

"We're lucky to see him so early in the day." Melissa's mother, a woman with salmon-pink skin, white-blond hair, and an Australian accent turned to tell Joo-Li, satisfied that her trip's mission had already been accomplished. "We were told we might have to roam the Magic Kingdom all day before we caught sight of him." She pulled Melissa to her side and turned to steer her down the red brick road.

"Yaw! Mickey wants to take a picture with you." Nana Yaa beckoned her brother.

"He *d-d-d-does*?" Yaw's head snapped up and his eyes nearly jumped off his face. He walked timidly toward the larger-than-life figure and took the oversized, gloved hand Mickey extended. The biggest smile stretched across Yaw's face as my father immortalized the moment with his camera. I caught the spirit of Disney World from Yaw at that moment and let myself fall into the experience. I was in America, in sunny Florida with this new family—my family for the summer.

When Mickey bobbed his head good-bye, I went for my little brother and took his hand. "Let's try that ride!" We ran to the back of the long queue for a ride called Space Mountain. Not one to be left out of anything, Nana Yaa ran to catch up with us and took my other hand.

"No. No. Wait." My father pulled a neatly folded map from his back pocket and shook it open. "Okay. Let's see. Where are we? The Magic Kingdom? That's right . . ." Joo-Li rolled her eyes.

"Lila, come," he said, summoning me.

I moved off the line and walked with my siblings to our father's side.

"If we want to see everything, we need to strategize. We are here." He traced his finger down the page and stopped to cover what he wanted me to see. "If we start here, we'll have to go to this ride next." He moved his finger to another dot on the map.

"Um, okay," I said, wondering why we needed to plot fun.

"Oh, look. It says children under fifty-one inches cannot go on this ride." Joo-Li started to take Yaw's hand as his fingers tightened around mine.

"Daadeeee!" Nana Yaa stamped her feet, threatening to throw a tantrum on the red brick.

The woman in front of us nodded at Joo-Li in empathy, then pointed with her head at the three boys at her hips.

"We can go on another ride," I offered, thinking to myself this trip was going to be bollocks, as Gamal would say, if we couldn't go on any adult rides.

"No, I'll stay with the kids. You and your fath—"

"No. We are all getting on the ride," my father intoned.

"Let's just go." I started to walk away, but my father took Yaw and Nana Yaa's hands from mine and stayed on the fast-moving line. When we got to the front, the attendant shook his head at the twins and pointed at the sign. "I can't let them on this ride." His tone was almost as firm as my father's.

Nana Yaa began to whimper.

"Excuse me, but these kids are eight years old," he lied.

The man shook his head at my father, apparently experienced at dealing with spoiled kids and their lying parents. Nana Yaa began to cry.

"Jude, I'll stay with them," Joo-Li said, relieved the attendant wouldn't be bullied.

"No, we are getting on the ride." He turned to the man and changed his tack, scratching his armpit before he began. "Sir, we drove all the way from New York to bring my kids to this very ride. My daughter here just came from England, straight from JFK—didn't even unpack her things. This is the first time I am seeing her since she was three years old. Her mother and I divorced a long time ago and it's been very difficult for all parties involved."

I avoided the attendant's eyes, completely mortified. Apparently, in addition to being a bully, my father was a big mouth!

"Jude." Joo-Li put her hand on his arm to shut him up.

"Can we go on? All of us?" he asked.

The attendant stepped aside to let us through. "Have a good time."

My father walked past him with the biggest grin on his face.

"Was that necessary?" Joo-Li asked her husband.

"Yes," Nana Yaa answered for my father. He swept her off the red brick and tickled giggles out of her.

"I don't even like roller coasters," Joo-Li complained to me, looping her arm through mine. "Someone just died at Great Adventure on one of these rides."

"Ah, it will be fun," my father said, dismissing her fears, as we stepped into our seats.

Joo-Li flinched when the security bar started to lower over our laps. "Lila, I'm scared." She gripped my arm tighter and buried her head into the nook of my neck and shoulders. Then we were hurtled into starry, air-conditioned blackness.

I closed my eyes and swallowed my heart as we rocketed to the heights and plummeted to the depths of Space Mountain, twice. Surround sound passenger screams joined my own, ringing in my ears. My underarms itched with excitement. I loved it!

I opened my eyes to check on Joo-Li. Her eyelids were wrinkled shut, fear twisting her face as hologram planets flew at us. Nana Yaa was also completely spooked. Yaw was tittering uncontrollably. When we crashed to the ground for the finale, my heart was pumping faster than it had the day Mum had caught us smoking in the Safeway car park. The cars of the ride drooled out of the black tunnel into the blinding sunlight.

"That was wicked!" a boy roared behind us in a hoarse voice as he stumbled like a drunk out of his car. We wobbled as well as we waited for our heart rates to calm and our eyes to adjust.

"That was amazing!" I squeezed Yaw, who started giggling again.

"Daddy, that was scary-uh!" Nana Yaa sniffed, tears slipping from her eyes as she clung to him.

"You were the one that wanted to go!" Joo-Li said roughly,

pissed off. Now that we were in the sun again, I could see that Joo-Li's skin was starting to turn a strange shade of olive. "I'm feeling sick," she announced just before she splattered the chunky pink and yellow mess of her half-digested McDonald's dinner onto the red brick. A park attendant instantly appeared out of nowhere to clean it up.

"This heat is murder. You need to get her home." A sweating woman stopped to fan Joo-Li with the visor of her Mickey Mouse cap.

My father nodded politely at the woman, but we stayed when she left us alone. Joo-Li had not been kidding about my father and his schedule. There was no way he was wasting a minute of the three-day package.

My father was a bully, but he was a fun bully. He conspired with the twins to get them on the rides they were too short to go on—"Stand on your toes," he told them—and alternately badgered and sob-storied the attendants until they relented and let the twins on their ride.

We made it to It's a Small World, a ride they were tall enough to get on, as the sky was starting to turn an inky blue.

"This ride is not for the faint of heart," the attendant said, flirting with me. "You sure you want shotgun?"

"What?" I asked him.

"Shotgun. Front seat. Let me guess, you're from . . . ?"

"London." I nodded, enjoying the attention.

"They make 'em strong in London, eh?"

"She's a tough cookie," my father confirmed, clapping my back almost as hard as he had to wake me up. An overwhelming wave of pride crashed over me even though I knew he was just saying that. He had no personal proof of my strength.

~

The ride back to New York was much like the ride to Florida. Joo-Li's Christian music filled the car and she sang along loudly with backup help from Nana Yaa. I tried to mute them as I stared out the window counting the road signs, craving a joint with Gamal.

My father exited at a rest stop just after we crossed the Georgia border and parked in the Shoney's Restaurant lot. None of us had said we were hungry, but we ordered and wolfed down the greasy food when it came, comfortable enough in our separate introspections to skip any forced small-talk.

It hadn't been a bad idea after all to go to Disney World straightaway, I decided. Four days stuck together in a car and hotel room had fast-forwarded us past the awkward preliminaries and exposed everyone's personalities. Now, no matter what happened the rest of the summer between my father, brother, sister, and stepmother, we would always have Disney.

42

"I want you to stay here with us. Past the summer. Finish high school. Here." My father's pronouncement came out in fragments, or maybe that's just how my still-jetlagged mind processed what he was saying the evening we got back from Florida.

We had reached their white-shingled, red brick, four-bedroom house in Valley Stream, Long Island, not more than half an hour ago and I was still unpacking my suitcase in the room they had set up for me with hideous vine-printed wallpaper borders running along the tops of the plum-colored walls. I noticed a Bible verse woven into the curve of the vine. ALL THINGS WORK TOGETHER FOR THE GOOD OF THEM THAT LOVE THE LORD, it read, the same message Joo-Li's music had preached on the long ride to and from Florida.

"You think about it and we'll discuss it with your mother in the morning."

He walked out before I could say *What? Wait! No!* I had to kill this quick. If I didn't stop this idea from growing, I knew Mum would go for it.

"Dinner's ready!" Nana Yaa smacked into our father on her way into my room. "Ouch, Daddy!" She giggled, collecting herself from the thick blue carpet.

"Okay, I'm coming." I stalled, trying to organize my thoughts as I felt my way around my suitcase for slippers. Where had I put them? I unzipped a pocket and found several folded-up sheets of paper. These were the papers Helen the air hostess had given me on the flight to Ghana. *Write everything you're feeling right now, then read it again a week from now. You'll be surprised how different you feel then,* she told me. I fell onto the edge of my bed and unfolded the pages.

I've just lost everything and I don't know why . . . I had written that day. I didn't feel different. I had lost so much in the shuttling between London and Ghana, and now what I had started to get back in London was about to be lost if my father succeeded in convincing Mum to make me stay in New York. I tore the pages up and walked out of the room barefoot.

When I entered the small dining room, the family was all seated, an empty chair between Nana Yaa and Yaw waiting for me.

Joo-Li smiled at me. "We have to tell your mother thank you for all the food she sent."

I nodded, noticing then the yam Mum had sent me with, boiled and sliced on my plate with stew. I noticed too the words painted on the plate and glass in front of me: A MAN CAN DO NOTHING BETTER THAN TO EAT AND DRINK AND FIND SATISFACTION IN HIS WORK.—ECCLESIASTES 5:18. The same Bible quote was embossed on the paper napkins corseted by thick wooden napkin rings.

"Nana Yaa, you can dim the light now for prayers," Joo-Li said.

Nana Yaa jumped up to fade the lights, twisting the knob until the glasses created prisms on our skin.

"Before we pray," my father began, pausing to scratch his armpit, "I want to let you all know I have asked Lila to stay with us for as long as she likes."

In the soft light I saw Joo-Li's smile evaporate. Her head snapped up. Yaw grabbed my arm and beamed up at me. "I'm hungry-uh," Nana Yaa said, rolling her eyes at me.

"We'll call your mother tomorrow to make all the necessary arrangements."

"Wait a minute." I started scratching both my armpits. "I have to stay at my school. It will be hard for me to catch up," I continued lamely.

"From what I understand you haven't been too focused on school these days, doing drugs and chasing boys when you're supposed to be working," my father said.

I gasped in unison with Joo-Li, which made Yaw giggle. Mum wouldn't have told my father about the Safeway incident, so it had to be Auntie Flora.

"Jude, *ekyere*." *Not now,* Joo-Li said. She nodded in the direction of her kids. "Now, let us pray." Her voice was soft as cotton as she asked the Lord to bless our meal. When she was done, Nana Yaa and Yaw passed their plates so she could dish out their food. My father started eating as if he hadn't suggested a complete life change for everyone at the table. His bald head gleamed in the gentle light as he bent to receive a slice of yam from his fork.

I could see from the uncomfortable look on Joo-Li's face that she didn't want me to stay any more than I did. Maybe together we could dissuade my father from this mission. I liked my father and his family fine, but it was presumptuous of him to think that he could uproot me after so many years of staying away. I had a life back in London and it wasn't his or Mum's right to disrupt it. *No.*

After dinner, I followed Joo-Li into the kitchen.

"I don't want to stay," I told her at the sink, standing under the IF YOU WANT TO BE GREAT IN GOD'S KINGDOM, LEARN TO BE

A SERVANT OF ALL plaque that hung on the cupboard above the sink. "I know you don't want me to stay either."

Joo-Li whipped her head around to face me when I said that, but she didn't deny it.

"If he asks my mother, there'll be no turning back."

She wiped her hands with her THE TRUTH SHALL SET YOU FREE dishrag even though her hands weren't wet. "It's already been decided, Lila. Your mother spoke with your father before you came here. We had planned to talk to you about it later, together, but your father was so excited."

I felt myself losing balance and breath. Once again Mum had lied and jerked my life out from under me and there was nothing I could do about it.

"It will be good for you, and for all of us. Your father wants to know you. I want Nana Yaa and Yaw to know their big sister. And I think you're a lovely girl, Lila. I do want you here."

I stopped listening at "good for you." Once again, the adults in my life thought they knew what was "good" for me. "I want to call my mother," I said through my closing throat.

"It will be past midnight there, Lila. We will call her tomorrow." She turned on the faucet and started to wash the dishes. Before I could walk away, she handed me a dishrag. "Stay. Dry."

43

"Let me come home, Mum," I begged Mum early the next morning.

My father and his family watched me from the table between mouthfuls of their *banku* and okra soup breakfast. Nana Yaa raised her hands high to see how far the okra would stretch before it broke, the strands clinging to her skin.

"Nana Yaa, *stop it.*"

"Mum, do you hear me? I want to come home now."

Silence.

"MUM!"

Nana Yaa started laughing.

"Lila, you can have this conversation another time," my father warned me in that voice that got Nana Yaa to stop playing with her food.

"Lila . . . ," Mum began.

"Mum, I don't want to hear anything else except 'You can come home.' "

Mum sighed again. "By all means, come home then, Lila. Why don't you come now?" She started laughing dryly.

"Send me my return ticket!" I gulped for air, my chest getting tighter and tighter as my mother had a chuckle at my misery.

With all that was in me I hated her. "I'll hate you forever for this." I ran to my room and slammed the door.

I heard footsteps banging after me. My door launched open and my father filled the doorway. "Come out of this room now and finish your food."

"No. I'm not hung—"

"I didn't ask if you were hungry."

I looked at my father, his dark handsome face set in the same determined angles that got Nana Yaa and Yaw on those rides at Disney World. Wasn't he supposed to feel awkward and nervous and guilty around me? Yes, he was my father, but we were not on those terms. I looked at him again. He looked really pissed off.

"Up. *Now.*"

I walked to the kitchen with my father at my heels. Joo-Li was clearing the table, but he stopped her.

"She'll do it after she eats." He sat opposite me as I trembled with the spoon in my hand. "I'm not your mother," he said. "I don't run away—or send people away—I deal with the issue at hand. No matter how hard it is."

It was an odd thing to hear from a father I hadn't seen since I was a toddler. "Then why weren't you around to deal with me?"

"Jude, you have to go to work today," Joo-Li said, trying to give him an out.

I looked over at Joo-Li, who was quietly hovering the way Enyo did. I knew now why Mum was in London and Joo-Li was here. Mum didn't hover on the sidelines. She couldn't. When she lost control, she walked or pushed away, just like my father had said.

My father rubbed his armpit, scratched his neck and then his chin, then he rubbed the shine off his head. "I wanted to be," he said finally, "but I didn't have my papers, so I couldn't travel. Your mother knew that when she left New York."

"We lived in New York?" Mum had always presented it as if he had left us. I remembered the pictures in that album Mum had thrown on my bed. Had those pictures been taken in New York?

"We left London and moved here together. Then your mum left." He still seemed pissed off about it. Now I was pissed off too. Why hadn't Mum or Auntie Flora ever told me? Was that another thing that had been withheld for my "good"?

"Jude, go to work." My father looked at my bowl, which was emptier than it had been when he'd sat down, and walked away. Joo-Li came to sit next to me.

"It won't be bad living with us, Lila," she assured me. "Your mother, she has her reasons for wanting you here, we have our reasons for wanting you here, but God has His reasons too. Always remember, He works everything in our lives for our good."

I sighed. There it was again—this reference to what was "good" for me. I thought maybe Mum, God, and everyone else should start doing what was bad for me.

44

"Upupupupupupupupupup!"

I opened my eyes at the sound of my father's explosive applause. "We're going to church."

I looked over at the dawn-gray window. It was barely morning. My father was still standing in the doorway, his hands ready to start clapping again. I sleepwalked to the washroom.

When I was dressed, we filed out of the house and piled into the van. Once again, I kept my eyes out the window watching the neat rows of white, buttercup-yellow, and eggshell-blue homes on our block recede as we got on another thicket-lined highway. When we got off at the exit for church, the neighborhood was very different.

I counted three filling stations, two McDonald's, a cab stand, and a liquor store on the same long block. Bus shelters serviced rows of apartment buildings; huge signboards advertising trainers looked down from the tops of the tallest ones.

When my father turned off the main road, up a hill, and into the car park of the church, I thought to myself how strange it was that just a twenty-minute drive away people lived completely different existences. A plane ride away, five hours ahead, Annie and Fred were taking the piss out of Tom or in the car park sharing a tenner. Another plane ride away, Enyo was killing a chicken for supper while Brempomaa and the rest were plotting the night's fight for water. Why were things like this?

"I'm not coming back, Gamal," I told him over the phone as I took off my church dress.

"You serious?" he asked in his laid-back way.

"Serious as Tom." I referenced our red-faced boss, trying to make light of what was happening. We were breaking up. "Mum's shipped me off again. She and my dad had it planned from the beginning."

The doorknob turned, followed by a bang on the door. "Lila, I have to pee-uh!" It was Nana Yaa.

"I gotta go. My little sister has to use the toilet."

"You okay over there? Loving New York?"

"It's all right. I miss you," I told him.

"I'll call you."

"With what money? Write me," I said, knowing we would be good about keeping in touch at first until the need to document our lives so the other person would feel close would just stop making sense.

"I'll talk to you later, yeah?"

"Good-bye," I croaked, tears swelling my throat.

"Lila-uh!" Nana Yaa banged on the door again.

45

"We have to find you a school," Joo-Li said.

I sighed, feeling déjà vu as I remembered Auntie Irene sitting behind her sewing machine in Kumasi while Enyo washed the dog food pan. "Why can't I just go to the school you teach at?"

"Lila, I don't even want to go to my school." Joo-Li snickered. She reached for her Bible, which was fat with loose pieces of paper, and pulled out a crinkled, glossy brochure. "This is the school I want Nana Yaa to go to." She handed it to me.

"The School for Girls," I read. "Great name."

"They don't charge tuition. The board of trustees pays for everyone," she explained. "If you get into the School, you are set. The top colleges will be begging for you."

I flipped through the pamphlet. An old woman with feral eyes and wiggy pin curls burned a hole through me. *Matilda Villard*, the caption read, *founder/advocate for girls*. On the page after her bio, there was a picture of a group of girls smiling wide as horses in a room full of computers. On the next page another clique of girls wore overalls and Wellies on a farm, a dreadlocked woman smiling in front of them. Lumpy tubers pushed through red earth around them and—it was the farm at Dadaba. *Our* farm.

I checked the caption to make sure I was seeing right. *The School for Girls Rotary Club planting yams on the farm at Dadaba Girls' Secondary School in Ghana, 1989.* The school had been at Dadaba the year before I'd gone there! I stretched out the folded paper like an accordion.

"Nice, eh?" Joo-Li asked me.

"This is my school!" I showed her the picture.

"Ah, yes. You went to Dadaba. You see how God works? You're already connected to the school. We'll find out when the test is."

I didn't know how God worked. All I knew was that according to Mum and Joo-Li's Christian music, he was working everything out for my good.

"Do me a favor and wake your brother and sister up for their baths," Joo-Li told me.

I walked into Yaw's room and shook him up. I noticed his children's Bible on the floor and picked it up. I had never really read more than the Bible verses quoted at Scripture Union and church or on the lorries in Ghana.

I leafed through the pages of pictures and text, many torn and colored over, and flipped back to the first page. "In the beginning God created the heavens and the earth . . . And God saw everything he made and behold, it was very good." "Good." There was that word again. *Hmmph.*

Brempomaa had said I had to be born again to experience God's good will and I had prayed for God to make me so, but I never did understand what it truly meant. For Brempomaa it meant defending people and herself. Fighting. To Ivy it meant she couldn't drink *fermɛ* anymore.

I had prayed for God to get me out of Ghana, and to be fair, He had, but in His own sweet time. At Dadaba, we had prayed for water and those rains had come to tease us before drying up again.

Mum had told me there is no human logic that can understand why anything happens, but there is faith. But when I thought about faith, I was in Ghana, with poverty, filth, flies, mosquitoes, wannabe English accents floating amid a swirl of red dust. I wasn't sure I had the faith to say "God's will be done" through all of that.

I shook Nana Yaa awake now. "Nana Yaa, get up. It's time for your bath."

I bathed them both and after dinner I went to my room to read. I wanted to read the Bible for myself and put everyone else's theories about what was good out of my head.

My father walked in. "You don't want to watch TV with us?" he asked me.

"No. I'm reading."

He smirked at the Bible. "Your mother has gotten to you."

I wished he wouldn't refer to Joo-Li as my mother, but I smiled so he would leave me alone to read.

I read past Joo-Li poking her head in to say good night, past Joo-Li checking on me in the middle of the night on her way to the kitchen for a glass of water. When I finally fell asleep, the stories continued in my dreams.

I saw a talking snake convincing a woman to eat a piece of fruit and a jealous brother murder his little brother because God liked his sacrifice better. There were fallen angels and the women who fell in love with them giving birth to giant babies. There were angels visiting a man and his wife and there were men demanding to have sex with these visiting angels.

This same man's wife turned into a pillar of salt for disobeying the angels and looking back at the city God sent the angels to destroy, a city she had called home. This same man's daughters got him drunk so they could have sex with him and have children.

I dreamed on about God telling a man to kill his son, only to send an angel to stop him from doing it. In my dreams, a man tricked his father into believing he was his favorite older son so he could get a better blessing, then this same man was tricked into marrying the sister of the woman he loved. Brothers sold their father's favorite into slavery and this favorite son became the head of the nation he entered as a slave.

A man who should've been killed as a baby grew up to free his people from slavery by leading them to cross a sea God parted so they could escape the army of slaveholders trying to trap them. The same sea engulfed their pursuers, killing them all.

I had read passages in the Bible before at Sunday school, but for the first time they seemed to connect. Each event set off another chain of events that made sense of the things that had happened before. I started to think more and more that the School for Girls–Dadaba connection was no coincidence.

46

The School for Girls didn't admit students based on test scores, we found out. They interviewed all applicants first, and, if accepted, then you took the test so they could see what your "learning style" was. As we drove to Manhattan for the interview, I felt a tickle in my stomach, in addition to the expected tingle under my arms. It was nerves but something else as well: purpose.

For the first time since Mum had driven me past Auntie Flora's house to the airport, I felt sure I knew where I was going. After seeing that picture of the girls on Dadaba's farm, things didn't seem so random anymore.

I looked outside the car window and for the first time saw up close New York's mirrored glass buildings scraping the sky, hot dog vendors on the streets, people coming from the shops loaded down with bags.

"Is that the World Trade Center?" I pointed at one building we passed.

"No, we're in midtown," my father answered. "The Twin Towers are downtown. Maybe after the interview we'll drive through Manhattan so you can see more."

"Good idea, Jude," Joo-Li said.

"This is Central Park," my father said, pointing with his head out the window as we cut through it. I couldn't see anything under the tunnel and by the time we came out, we were there.

THE SCHOOL FOR GIRLS—EST. 1901 was imprinted on a bronze plaque on the side of a town house building. THERE IS POWER IN THE PURPOSEFUL HEART read the inscription under the name. My heart leaped at the inscription. It was literally a sign that my attendance at the School for Girls was meant to be.

We passed the building. "Parking in Manhattan is impossible," my father complained. He sighed and stopped the car in front of the building. "You get out and we'll look for parking."

Joo-Li and I left Nana Yaa, Yaw, and my father in the car and walked up to the shining brass doorknob of the heavy doors. It was locked.

"Pull harder, Lila."

I tugged at the knob, but the doors wouldn't budge.

"Wait, I see a bell."

Joo-Li pressed the small white button in the stone wall and a buzzer emanated from the doors. I pulled again and we entered the School. A scary painting of Matilda Villard greeted us as it hung over an open door that read COMMON ROOM. The dead woman's penetrating eyes followed us into the room, where a receptionist was seated behind a huge wooden desk.

"Hi, you must be Lila," she said, smiling brightly, and shook my hand before turning to Joo-Li. "Miss Nikki will be right with you. Would you like some tea? Coffee? Water?"

"Tea, please," Joo-Li said. I nodded as I sank with Joo-Li onto the tan sofa.

"This is nice," Joo-Li whispered, tilting her head to look around. Massive paintings and photographs dressed the glossy cream-and-exposed-brick walls. The sun streaming in from the tall windows radiated from the gleaming wood floors.

The receptionist returned with a tray and set the two steaming cups and sugar packets before us. There was already milk in the tea; I smiled as I watched the beige swirl around my cup. Dadaba should have been like this.

"Miss Nikki is ready to see you."

"You have it already," Joo-Li whispered to me as I rose. "In Jesus's name."

I walked into the office the receptionist pointed me to. One wall was lined with books from floor to ceiling; the other walls were dominated by even more massive photographs. The woman from the picture in the brochure stood up to greet me, her golden dreadlocks almost the same color as the blond wood floors.

"Hello, Lila. I'm Nikki," she said to introduce herself, her pale brown hand wrapped firmly around mine. "So tell me about you," she instructed me as she took her seat.

"Well, I'm from Ghana," I announced with a broad smile, stressing my connection to Ghana because I thought it would be a shortcut to getting in good with her. Besides, where I was from seemed relative now. In Ghana, I had been the *broni* from Abrokye, and when I'd returned to London, I was the girl who had just come back from Ghana. Now that I was in New York, I felt like I was from both Ghana and London.

"Yes"—she nodded—"I knew that from your name."

I'd expected more of a reaction, but I continued. "I went to Dadaba Girls'."

"Really? Then you know we were at Dadaba in '89. But I hear an accent that doesn't sound Ghanaian . . . ?" She pronounced it *Guh-nay-an.* "How did you end up in Ghana?"

I shifted uncomfortably in my seat. I didn't want to get into all of that. Mum's aching loneliness. Her tricking me into going to Ghana. No. I ignored her question and launched right into my rehearsed Ghana story. The same story I'd told Chardonnay and Ronan, Annie, Fred, and Gamal—except Miss Nikki gave me no feedback. She maintained her polite mask as I fumbled and finally just stopped.

"Lila, your six months in Ghana were obviously life-changing, but I don't know *how*. One of the reasons we don't test girls first at the School," she continued, "is because character is most important to us. We want to know *who* we are admitting into our community. You seem like a wonderful girl, but based on this interview I can't invite you to test for the School."

I walked back out to the waiting room just as my father walked in with the twins. I started to cry so I wouldn't have to answer Joo-Li and my father's expectant faces.

"What happened in there, Lila?" my father asked me as we walked down the block, the School at our backs.

"I told her about Ghana, but she didn't want to hear about that."

"Ghana?"

I knew I wasn't making any sense, but that was because none of it was making any sense to me.

"You know, we should walk around a bit," Joo-Li suggested. "We drove all this way and it's a beautiful day. We'll get something to eat and show Lila some sights."

"McDonald's!" Nana Yaa, who had been quiet all morning, burst into her usual restless energy, and we walked away.

47

More than anything in the world, I wanted a joint, but I settled for a long hot shower. I stood under the hot spray feeling jumbled together, cursing Joo-Li for handing me that blasted pamphlet with the picture of the Dadaba farm in it.

When I got out of the shower, Nana Yaa and Yaw were jumping on Nana Yaa's bed. I could hear them squealing and carrying on from my room even after I closed the door and switched off the light. I buried myself under the covers.

The next day, Joo-Li took me to register for the ninth grade at John Bowne High School in Queens, where she taught English. After seeing the School's grand building, I thought Bowne must be the equivalent of Enyo's Sito school.

"It's not that bad here," Joo-Li assured me. "The American public school system is actually very good. It's the kids—the bad ones—that spoil it for everyone. But if you stay focused, you will get what you need out of it."

I nodded at her. "I guess the School wasn't where God wanted me to be."

"Maybe, maybe not." Joo-Li shrugged. "But life is half what God means for you and half what you mean for you."

What did *that* mean? Which was it? If everything happened for God's good reason, did my actions even matter? I sucked my teeth and looked out the window as Joo-Li's Christian music played on.

My first day at Bowne wasn't bad. I made a friend, Angela, who was cool. Her locker was next to mine and when I met her she was taping up a collage of Bobby Brown photos.

"Wush your name?" she demanded to know.

"Lila," I said.

She frowned. "Where you from?"

"London and Ghana," I explained, hoping I sounded worldly and not confused.

She frowned again and looked me up and down. "I'm Angela." She pointed to her collage. "You know my husband, right?"

"I'm sorry?"

She slammed her locker door. "That's right, I am not a 'baby mother' or any other stereotype applicable to the black teenage female," she declared. "I'm a married woman. Mrs. Robert 'Bobby' Barisford Brown."

I started laughing. I liked Angela immediately. We discovered we had the same lunch period on Mondays, Wednesdays, and Fridays, so we walked to McDonald's together and passed a cigarette between us as she went on and on about her boyfriend Denaun, who was in his first year at St. John's University and okay with being the other man in her life.

"Oh, shit!" Angela ducked behind a bush midsentence and yanked me to the ground with her.

"What?"

"I think she saw us smoking."

For a minute I thought she meant Joo-Li. "*Who* saw us?"

"Angela, get out from behind that bush."

I looked up to see, of all people, the dreadlocked woman

from the School who had interviewed me. My armpits started itching.

Angela straightened, brushing leaves from her jean skirt. "Miss Nikki, we were just—"

"Smoking, Angela. I saw you."

Angela sighed. "Please don't tell my mother."

Miss Nikki held out her hand and Angela laid her pack of cigarettes and lighter on it. "You know I'm going to, Angela." Angela's face fell as Miss Nikki looked my way.

"I know you."

I kept my face blank, the way she had at the interview.

"Lila Adjei, right? You were up at the School. What are you doing out here smoking, girl? You know they don't play that in Ghana. Get back to school. Both of you." She stood watching us until she was satisfied we were headed in the right direction.

"How do you know Miss Nikki?" I asked when she was out of earshot.

"That's my mom's best friend. I'm about to get in so much trouble. My mother is gonna kick my ass . . ."

Angela kept talking, but I couldn't think about anything except why we had run into Miss Nikki of all people. The next day, we took a different way to McDonald's so we could smoke in peace. Angela passed me the cigarette, and I took a deep breath of the noxious smoke.

"Miss Nikki hasn't said anything to my mother yet, but I'ma see her this Saturday. I know she's gonna say something before then . . ."

"Mmm." I shrugged, smiling at the fact that she had said "I'ma" instead of "I'm going to." I thought of Brempomaa and her "gonna"s and "wanna"s, Ghanaians' "Ei!"s and "Ah!"s, and the way we said "innit" and "yeah" in London. Language was so amazing.

". . . so my mother can be pissed at me while we looking at those pictures at the embassy."

"At the embassy?"

"Miss Nikki's husband is a photographer and he's gonna be showing some pictures he took while he was in Ghana at the Ghanaian embassy. You from Ghana, right? You should come."

48

I felt like we had walked forever before we reached the black and gold gilded gate in front of the Ghanaian embassy. Once again we couldn't find parking nearby so we had to park several blocks away. The warm but violent Indian summer wind was putting tears in our eyes and slapping our skirts around our legs as we marched against it. Nana Yaa refused to walk, so Daddy bent to carry her before Joo-Li yanked her down and made her walk.

"This is it," Joo-Li announced, looking up at the black star at the center of the red, gold, and green flag flapping above the gate.

We pushed the gate open and followed the sound of drumming past the red-carpeted reception area to a dark wood-paneled room. The sour smell of wine breath mingled with cigarette smoke and rose to the water-spotted ceiling. A small group circled a troupe of performing drummers.

Nana Yaa made a face. "It stinks-uh! And it's loud-uh!"

Joo-Li gave Nana Yaa's arm a sharp tug, making my little sister cry. Nana Yaa's crocodile tears solicited impatient looks from some of the guests.

"*Nana Yaa*," my father whispered sharply.

"Lila!" Angela rushed over to me swathed in bright blue Ghanaian cloth and a matching head wrap. "Hi, Miss Adjei," she said, smiling at Joo-Li.

Joo-Li smiled at Angela. "Hello, Angela. This is my husband and these are my children," she said. "Angela is in my fourth-period English class."

Angela politely shook each hand, then pulled me away. "You have to see these pictures, Lila!" When we were away from Joo-Li and my father, Angela sighed. "She hasn't said anything to my mother. I don't know why, but thank the Lord!" She giggled giddily, her arm still looped through mine as we stopped at the picture closest to us.

The photograph was called *City Girl,* a portrait of a girl in jeans and a Mitsubishi Motors T-shirt, braids flying around her face, a swirl of Ghana's red dust at her sandals as the tail end of a lorry zipped off. Next to it, a group of young girls balanced shining silver tubs filled with fresh pineapples, oranges, and *kenkey* on their heads.

"Is this what Ghana is like?" I nodded as we moved on to the next one. A large group of women were on the beach, some with babies strapped to their backs, buying fresh silver fish from a woman bent over a flopping catch. In the distance, wild gray pigs rutted around in the garbage-littered rocks beyond them. Beside this photo, a man squatted amid the pigs to shit. That was Ghana all right.

The photograph next to it showed a young white woman kneeling to photograph a group of raggedy-looking beach boys with the Cape Coast slave castle behind them. Another shot showed one of the beach boys surfing on a plank of wood that looked like a piece of one of the fishing boats parked nearby on the beach.

On the next wall, a watchman was caught sleeping at his

post, the lens spying him through the opening of a tall black gate. When I saw the chewing stick just about to fall from the watchman's lips, my heart stopped for a second. *Dadaba Girls' Secondary School, Cape Coast, Ghana,* the placard read.

"That's my watchman. That's my school. I went there."

"Really?"

I turned to scan the crowd for the photographer.

"Where's Miss Nikki's husband, Angela?"

"Uncle Ernie?"

"This is my school!" I shouted across the room. Miss Nikki looked my way as Joo-Li and my father walked over with the twins.

"That's right, you went to Dadaba." Miss Nikki took me in again, her light brown eyes starting from my growing hair to my stacked-heel loafers. "Ernie, come here."

The photographer, a coal-skinned man with a nappy widow's peak wearing a tweed blazer and pointy-tipped black shoes, strode over. I remembered him and that day he had stood onstage next to Madam in his acid-washed jeans.

"Ernie, this girl went to Dadaba."

"Really? This whole wall is from a spread I did at Dadaba," he told me.

"I remember the day you came to Dadaba and the headmistress introduced you at chapel."

I pointed to the next picture along the wall. It was Pay-Shee, shaking the bell.

"That's Pay-Shee, the bell girl. We lived by the bell at Dadaba. There was a rising bell. A work bell. A—"

"A *work* bell?" The white woman who had been looking at the photograph turned to look at me.

"Yes, we all had work assignments. Some girls had to wash the bathhouse. Other girls had to sweep the dorms. I was on compound duty. I had to sweep a plot the size of someone's yard every day." I moved on to the next shot. It was S'ter Penny. She was standing over kneeling girls just outside the chapel.

"We had morning devotion every morning, and if you weren't there when the bell rang the prefect on duty made you kneel down."

There weren't that many people in the room, but all twenty of them had now formed a loose circle around me as I explained the picture of the tuck shop, the hands waving money in Auntie Araba's face to buy the freshly fried snacks. And then there was a picture of us.

There was a blown-up version of one of the photos Brempomaa had sent with her letter. The four of us were completely unaware of the camera as we sat on the field, hibiscus in our hair, Brempomaa on the side in her blue and white PE uniform as we cheered and danced for the off-camera race. "That's me! That's us at the inter-ho—the inter-houses games, a sports competition between the houses."

My father looked from the photograph to my face. "Yes, that is you."

I moved to the last one. It was a close-up photograph of some girls with necks powdered from chin to cleavage. *Powder Necklaces,* the placard next to the picture read. I had never thought of the powder as a necklace, as some sort of adornment.

"A powdered neck meant you had bathed—that your mother or father had sent a barrel or jerrican of water so you had water to bathe with and drink. The girls that didn't have water started powdering their necks anyway," I explained.

"Ah, yes. When I went there was a terrible water crisis," Ernie confirmed.

"So powder was an indicator of class," Miss Nikki said, nodding. "Africans have a thing with their necks," she continued.

"All the photographs I've seen of the Kenyan women, or women in South Africa where they're wearing jewelry, it's these elaborate pieces that dress up the neck. I've always thought it was a symbol of pride. Like no matter what happens to us, who comes to try to destroy us, we always have something to stretch our necks about."

A chorus of "hmmmph"s rose around the room as the people who had congregated around me disbursed to study the photos for themselves or refill their plastic cups with wine. Miss Nikki and her husband lingered.

"You have an extraordinary story to tell, Lila," Miss Nikki said.

I shrugged. She had heard it that day at the interview and been unimpressed.

"Have you ever thought about writing a book based on your experience? Ernie's working with an agent right now who's trying to sell these photographs in a coffee-table book. Your story would give it more life." Miss Nikki scanned the room. "Carly!" She called over a chunky brown woman with short, springy dreadlocks. Introductions and business cards were passed over my head to Joo-Li and my father.

49

Carly, the agent, met with Joo-Li and my father, then they, plus Miss Nikki and Ernie, called Mum. It all happened so fast.

"You see it was good that I sent you there, Lila? You're about to be an author," Mum said when I took the phone off speaker.

"Yeah, I think New York has been good for me, Mum," I confirmed, but not because of this photography book I was about to help write. For whatever reason, New York was where it was all beginning to make sense to me. Sort of.

Mum had sent my return ticket to London just after I'd posed for Ernie's pictures. I went on that interview at the School so I could meet Miss Nikki. I didn't get into the School so I could go to Bowne and have my locker right next to Angela's. Angela and I got caught smoking so she could invite me to Ernie's photo exhibition so I could see the photographs and tell them my story so they could ask me to help write their book. Why I was even offered the opportunity, I don't know, but they were paying me $2,500 to write a few anecdotes about my time at Dadaba. That sounded good to me!

"Lila, I have something to tell you." Mum changed the subject with that nervous crack in her voice.

I looked at the phone in my hand, suspicious of what was

coming next. I'd heard that shake in her voice before, when she'd sprung Ghana on me minutes from Heathrow and when she lied about my summer in New York.

"What is it, Mum?"

"I'll wait to tell you in person."

"You're coming?"

"No, you're coming. Just for the Christmas holiday. I've spoken with your father about it."

So once again she was pulling me out of my life. There would be no book. I rolled my eyes. I didn't want to get into it with her with Miss Nikki and Ernie and Carly now in the living room. "Okay, I'll talk to you later, Mum."

When I hung up I went to the living room. Carly handed me a pen and a few stapled pieces of paper. I was to write a paragraph each for the seventy photographs Ernie had chosen to put in his book from those two days he had been at Dadaba. In exchange, I would be paid $2,500. I signed where she had X-ed.

"Why aren't you smiling, child?" Carly asked me.

I obliged her, but Mum's announcement that I was going to London for Christmas had me certain this good thing wouldn't happen for me.

I wrote like I was telling the story to Chardonnay or Angela. Miss Nikki said it was okay to embellish, so I did, welding memories together to create the most drama. "It's called *narrative nonfiction*," she told me.

Joo-Li agreed. "No story is ever really 'true.' It's all filtered through perspective."

I wrote during math and science period. On the days Angela and I didn't have the same lunch period I scribbled in a corner of the schoolyard or lunch room. When I was done, I gave my paragraphs to Joo-Li to read over.

I wanted her to read my stories right away, but weeks dragged on before she returned them to me with so many notes and red ink slashes on the papers they could've been framed and hung in a museum. I made all the corrections she suggested and submitted my finished paragraphs to Miss Nikki the day before Thanksgiving. We didn't have Thanksgiving in England, but I remembered seeing the newscasts on BBC about how Americans celebrated the day eating turkey and cranberry sauce.

On Thanksgiving Day, I woke up to Nana Yaa poking me.

"Nana Yaa? What-uh?" I had started dragging out the last syllable of my words the way she did.

"It's snowing-uh!" She squealed and clapped as I groaned, rolling my head to look out the window. The flakes fell in slow motion outside. Indeed, it looked like we were inside a giant snow globe that had been shaken. But more important, I smelled bacon.

I swung my feet over the edge of the bed and followed the fragrance of frying pork. Joo-Li was hanging up the phone with one hand and pushing the bacon around the pan with her other. "You just missed your mother. She wanted to give you the details of your flight. She said she'll call again." Joo-Li squeezed my shoulder and handed me the spatula. "Make sure it gets nice and cripsy, so we can add it to the stuffing." I smiled. She'd said "cripsy" instead of "crispy."

I pushed the bubbling strips of pork around until they shriveled. Joo-Li had done the turkey, peanut butter soup, and *jollof* the night before, so all we had to do was fry the plantains and make the rice balls.

I sliced the plantains and fried while Joo-Li waited for the rice to overcook so she could make sticky balls out of them. I thought of Enyo as I helped. She would be so surprised to see me cooking.

We cooked until the snow stopped and there was nothing but whiteness outside our windows. Nana Yaa helped us move the serving plates to the dining room and then Nana Yaa called my father out of his room. We sat around the dining table and just after my father prayed and we were about to eat, the phone rang.

"Lila, hi, it's Carly," she said when I answered. When Carly spoke I imagined block letters. "We LOVE your anecdotes. We couldn't stop laughing at the story about you shitting into plastic bags. INSANE. And you showered in the rain? You CAN'T make that stuff up. Anyway, we want you to write eight hundred words for the OPENING of the book. You know: WHY you went to Ghana in the first place. What it MEANT to you when Ernie came there. What it MEANT to see those photographs at the embassy that day. Ernie's gonna write an intro about the assignment *National Geographic* sent him on, what he saw, and the SERENDIPITOUS moment he met you. TAKE YOUR TIME with it. Get it to me in the NEW YEAR."

50

"Your ticket has come." Joo-Li walked into my room with a British Airways envelope.

I tore the envelope open. In two days I would be on a plane to Heathrow—arriving in London on Christmas Eve.

"Are you excited to be going home?" Joo-Li asked me.

For a second I thought about all the places I'd called home in the past year. The flat in Peckham. Auntie Irene's bungalow in Kumasi. Addo House at Dadaba. The duplex in Lewisham. Here in Valley Stream with Joo-Li and my father, Nana Yaa, and Yaw.

"I'm a little nervous," I admitted. I was anxious about whatever it was Mum had to tell me. I hoped she would let me come back. I was uneasy about seeing Gamal again as well. I wasn't even sure I would tell him I was there. What was the point?

"It's a shame you won't be here on Christmas Day," Joo-Li was saying when my father came into the room, adjusting his cap with one hand as he held his gloves in the other.

"We'll just have to have a *M'early* Christmas tomorrow then." He laughed to himself. "Joo-Li, you and Lila can prepare dinner tonight and we'll eat tomorrow."

"Oh we can, eh?" Joo-Li rolled her eyes, a smile crawling from one cheek to the other at the thought.

I smiled at my father. "That's a good idea."

"Good, then it's done."

"Well, let's go shopping then," Joo-Li said.

I got Nana Yaa and Yaw bundled up and soon we were stuck in traffic on the way to Waldbaum's.

Yaw put his head on my lap. Joo-Li shook him awake.

"Yaw, I am not carrying you in that supermarket; wake up." She turned to me for help. "Lila, bring a song."

"Excuse me?"

"A Christmas carol."

Yaw yawned.

"Else you'll have to carry him in the store."

"Hark, the herald angels sing!" I began.

Joo-Li and Nana Yaa joined me as Joo-Li shook Yaw till he sat up straight and started singing. We sang for about forty-five minutes, the car inching along Hempstead Turnpike till we reached Waldbaum's and circled the car park for another ten minutes looking for an empty space. When we walked inside, it was bumper-to-bumper shopping carts. It seemed everyone else had decided to have a "M'early" Christmas as well.

Joo-Li pulled a cart loose from the train of carts and Nana Yaa raced to her mother's side holding her arms up to be picked up and put in the child seat at the front. Yaw started to cry.

"I want to sit in the shopping cart!"

Joo-Li rolled her eyes.

"I'll get another cart," I said.

"No." Joo-Li held her arm up to stop me. "Nana Yaa, Yaw is going to get in the cart because he's sleepy, and you will walk."

Nana Yaa collapsed on the floor and started crying. Joo-Li dropped Yaw into the seat, pulled his legs through the square slots, and pushed on. "Lila, let's go."

I turned to see Nana Yaa look up in shock that Joo-Li was

actually leaving. She pulled herself up and ran to us, taking my hand when she caught up.

We must have been in the grocery store another two hours, crawling behind slow-moving carts to fill ours with boxes of powdered mashed potatoes, rice and farina, plastic-sealed trays of beef, chicken, okra, tomatoes, onions, and those little round orange and green peppers that did the work of a laxative if you accidentally ate one in your stew. We waited nearly an hour in line. Each till—even the express checkout—had at least ten shoppers waiting to pay.

I picked up one of the magazines at the counter to read. A dark black woman was on the cover. She looked like a Dadaba girl in a way, with that look of survival in her eyes and body language. Even though there was no powder at her neck, she was wearing a powder necklace, I thought.

After Waldbaum's we stopped at the Ghana market for *kenkey*. Joo-Li picked up some dried, salted *colby* fish, *shito*, and *gari*.

When we finally got home, Joo-Li and I got cooking. While Nana Yaa and Yaw sat in the dining room coloring, we chopped the onions, sliced the tomatoes, shaved the ginger, and poured them into the blender with rock salt and the laxative peppers. When I raised the lid off the blender after pureeing them together, the pepper essence was so strong I started coughing and had to spit up the phlegm in my throat.

Joo-Li put the balls of *kenkey* in a large pot of water to boil next to the pot of rice. Then she tore the plastic covering off the two large trays of beef chunks and dropped them into a large bowl.

"Lila, we need more onions," she told me as she started pulling spices from the cabinet overhead and sprinkling the bright red, orange, and brown powders over the dark red meat. "And ginger," she added.

I reached for the two gnarled fingers of ginger on the counter and started scraping their skin away. I chopped and watched into the night as we prepared tomato stew, groundnut soup, and palm nut soup between dishing out the fresh blended pepper, *kenkey,* and fried fish for the kids and my father.

"We'll make the rice balls tomorrow," she announced with a yawn.

The next morning, I woke up to an insistent push.

"M'early Christmas!" Yaw and Nana Yaa chorused.

I sat up and looked at the clock. It was seven thirty in the morning. My father was in the doorway slapping his hands to-gether. "Upupupupupupup!" As usual, he was unbearably bois-terous in the morning.

I dragged myself out of bed and followed my siblings and father into the kitchen, where Joo-Li was using a saucer to scoop sticky hunks of steaming rice into a small bowl, then slapping them around the bowl until they conformed to the shape of a ball.

"Lila, good morning!" She looked up to beam at me before turning to the kids. "Nana Yaa, set the table with the Christmas dishes, please. Yaw, turn on the music."

Nana Yaa and Yaw separated to complete their assignments.

"What can I do?"

"Start dishing out the food into serving plates and bowls." Joo-Li nodded at the gleaming cream-colored servers she had stacked on the kitchen counter, each of them painted with or-namented Christmas trees and gift-wrapped presents for the happy blond family around the trees.

I started ladling out the soups, then the rice and stew, and handed them to Nana Yaa and Yaw as Christian music filled the house. Joo-Li started singing at the top of her lungs.

"I thought my Christmas gift was peace from your singing," my father boomed out of nowhere, causing Joo-Li to almost drop a bowl.

"Jude! You've been sneaking around all morning!"

My father came up behind Joo-Li and buried his head in the curve of her neck. Her hand went up to pat his shining head as she continued with one hand to shape a rice ball into a perfect oval. "Go sit so the kids don't start getting restless," she told us.

Daddy and I obeyed and when she was done she joined us. "Nana Yaa, hit the lights."

Nana Yaa jumped up to do her favorite part, slowly turning the dimmer until the room was gray with the morning's natural light.

"Jude, we forgot the candles."

Daddy got up and opened a drawer in the dining room wall unit to produce a matchbook and two fat red candles with heads even fatter from where the wax had bubbled over the last time they'd been burned. He lit the candles and immediately, the heavy scent of sweetness filled the room.

"Shall we pray?" Joo-Li asked rhetorically as we all lowered our heads. I opened my eyes when she began because tears had started to slip from them. I would miss them. When I went to sleep that night, I realized I hadn't gotten any gifts or had my bath.

51

"Now boarding rows twenty-six through fifty-one," the uniformed attendant at the British Airways gate announced.

I slung one strap of my schoolbag across my shoulder and pulled my passport out as I joined the queue. The attendant matched my passport picture to my face before handing the small blue booklet back to me. "Enjoy the journey," she said.

I walked through the narrow corridor, smiled at the air hostesses who greeted me at the door of the plane, found my window seat assignment, and tucked my bag under the seat in front of me. The plane was freezing, so I wrapped myself in the staticky blanket that had been folded on my seat and waited for the rest of the plane to fill up.

As I rested my head against the window watching men load the belly of the aircraft with our luggage and the food we would be served, the words of the attendant at the gate struck me. *Enjoy the journey.* Why hadn't she just said "Have a safe journey" or "Have a safe flight"? But even as I thought about the fact that it was very possible the flight could be unsafe, I was calm.

I was more apprehensive about this big thing Mum had to

tell me in person, but whatever she had to say, I was prepared, I decided. I sighed and let myself doze off after the air hostess showed us how to get off the plane in case of a crash landing.

I woke up to the smell of food and the repeated query "Chicken or fish." I sat up, pulling down the table in the seat back facing me. I attacked my foil-covered tray of chicken and potatoes and fell asleep again. Before I knew it, we were landing.

52

I heard my name when I walked into the arrivals hall.

"*Lila!*"

Mum was with Ronan and Chardonnay.

"Hello, Lila, how was the flight?" Ronan asked, as if it wasn't weird that he was there. So this was what Mum needed me to know in person? That she and Ronan were back together?

"It was fine," I said. "I'm used to them by now."

"Oh, Lila's a world traveler now," Mum said.

Chardonnay rolled her eyes with me.

"It's good for a young person to travel a lot," Ronan said, "when they don't know yet to be afraid of the world. I told your mother you'd appreciate it one day."

When we got to the house, Ronan walked my suitcase into my room. Mum followed us into my room and stayed when he walked out, closing the door behind him.

She pulled me down with her as she sank onto the edge of my bed.

"Mum, what is it?"

"Lila, I'm pregnant," she blurted out, that smile she'd smiled at the airport spreading across her face again.

I looked down at her stomach and noticed that Mum did look a little thicker around the middle.

"Lila, I'm so happy," she gushed, throwing her arms around me. "Are you happy for me?"

I sighed. She was my mother and she was happy. "I'm happy if you're happy, Mum." I wondered what this meant for me.

"I am," she said, beaming. "We should get some sleep. Tomorrow is Christmas."

"Okay, Mum. Good night."

As I started to peel off my clothes, Chardonnay walked in and started to take off her clothes.

I looked at Mum. "They live here now," she said. It was only then that I noticed Chardonnay's boots lining the wall next to the closet.

Chardonnay snorted. "What? She didn't tell you?"

I sighed. *It's* all *good,* I told myself as I pushed Chardonnay's big arse closer to the wall so I could have room on my bed. *It's* all *good.*

53

My time in London was quick. Ronan, Mum, Chardonnay, and I ate the big Christmas supper Mum had prepared, then we went to see a movie. I spent one night at Auntie Flora's. She made me dinner and let me have a glass of wine in celebration of the book. I didn't see Gamal, but I spoke with him. He told me Annie was his girlfriend now.

"You mad?" he asked me.

"Course not," I said. I wasn't really lying. It hurt more than I could comprehend just thinking about Annie resting her head on Gamal's shoulder, having a laugh with him, swallowing his marijuana kisses, so I just put it out of my mind. The reality was, I lived in New York now.

Chardonnay and I smoked a joint once behind the house, giggling at the memory of Mum slapping Tom in the Safeway car park that day. At night, I worked on the intro to Uncle Ernie's book into the dawn.

We spent New Year's Day shopping for baby stuff. Ronan waited patiently in the car as Mum dragged Chardonnay and me to every shop in Lewisham Shopping Centre.

The day of my morning flight back to New York, Chardonnay gripped my arm. "She's *your* mother. Why do you get to leave?"

I laughed uneasily, shaking her off of me as Ronan beeped the horn for us to come. Anything could happen and Mum could make me stay.

Ronan waited in the car while Mum, Chardonnay, and I darted in and out of the shops buying biscuits, chocolates, and last-minute foodstuffs from the Ghana market on the street Mum and I used to live on in Peckham. When we got back home, Ronan made Mum sit while he made sure the zippers closed around my bursting suitcases. Mum just beamed, watching him.

Just when we were ready to leave for the airport the phone rang. I got a sinking feeling in my stomach. Here it was. Mum didn't want to get it, but Ronan picked up. He handed me the phone. It was Carly.

"I just got you a BOOK DEAL. Ernie's publishers LOVED YOUR PART and they want you and Ernie to go BACK TO GHANA, to your school, to shoot some more pictures and for you to write more. And they want you to write a book of your OWN! About YOUR experience! They've already bought the tickets. We want to take care of this before you start school again. Cancel your flight. Your dad and Julie, and Ernie and Nikki, are gonna meet you at Heathrow tomorrow so you can go on to GHANA."

"Wow," was all I could say as my armpits started to flare up. The change of plans made me uneasy. Was this some master plan to leave me in Ghana again? To leave me at Dadaba? I shuddered at the thought.

If I didn't ever set foot on Dadaba's grounds again, it would be too soon. It was one thing to tell people stories about going to school there but another thing entirely to go back. Dadaba was the place I had felt the most alone and desperate, the place I had done things I never thought I would do, like drink water with knickers floating in it, shit into a plastic bag, and bathe in a room full of naked girls like I was in some awful prison movie.

I put the phone down and told Mum the news, watching her closely to see if she looked like she had heard it before.

"That's great, Lila!" she said, her eyebrows arching in surprise even as the corners of her mouth dragged down to say she was impressed.

"We should go with her, Felicia. I need to go to Ghana and meet your sister anyway," Ronan suggested.

"What about work? Chardonnay? It's too impulsive, Ronan. And expensive. No."

"There are two incomes now, Felicia," he said, raising his index and middle fingers in a victory sign, the stone on his ring glinting in the morning light. "We are going." Just like that, Mum's resolve evaporated and she smiled that silly smile again. I knew from Dadaba that loneliness made you do desperate things, but when I saw Mum's glowing face, I prayed I wouldn't ever get so lonely I'd send my child away or forget who I was because of it.

We didn't sleep that night. Ronan stayed up packing his and Mum's things, while I helped Char pack up.

"This is so crazy that we're going!" she said as she stuffed one of her two pairs of big boots into her suitcase. "I can't wait to try that *kenkey* and sugar-water liquor you told me about."

"Those are going to burn right off your feet," I warned her.

"If it's anything like Jamaica with the mud roads, I'm going to need them."

"Whatever." I shrugged.

"You're a lucky bitch, you know that?" she said as she zipped up her case.

"You think so?"

"You got to leave London and experience something other

than the wanker Peter and Paul School. It would have been so cool if my dad sent me to school in Jamaica or somewhere like that. It's so boring over here."

"We'll see what you have to say when you see Dadaba," I said, making room for her on the bed. "Nothing lucky over there."

"That's not true. They're poor, but take away the poverty, and people there live like rich people over here. If Ghana's anything like Jamaica, people just chill with their families. They go to the beach whenever they want. They eat fresh fruit off the bushes and the trees. They don't work all the time. People over here only get to do that when they retire, innit? Who's got the better life?"

I started to say, "We do," but decided to take her last question as rhetorical and think over what Char had just said. Who knew Char was that deep? Maybe going back to Dadaba would be fun. I would get to see Brempomaa and Ivy and Hari—and Enyo. Oh, Enyo. I wondered how she was.

We slept for the few hours before we had to get up and go to the airport. We waited to meet my father, Joo-Li, and the twins on their connecting flight to Ghana. I was a little anxious about how my father would respond to Ronan and how Mum would interact with Joo-Li, but when they saw each other it was anticlimactic. No drama at all. They just shook each other's hands like strangers, then separated back into couples. It was the first time I'd seen my parents together in the flesh, not in a photograph. A flicker of sadness dragged the corners of my mouth down into a frown, but Yaw ran to hug me as Nana Yaa clutched a picture book and shouted, " 'Pussy cat! Pussy cat! Where have you been?' 'I've been to London to see the queen!' " Yaw and I giggled as Joo-Li snatched the book from Nana Yaa's hand and shushed her.

When we got on the plane I realized this was the first time

I'd flown with anyone. I was used to flying alone and getting the window seat, but now Mum wanted the window, so I was stuck in a middle seat in the middle row, having to climb over Joo-Li, the twins, and my father when I had to go to the toilet.

"Lila, will you take Yaw with you before he embarrasses us and pees on himself on this plane?" Joo-Li asked me as I got up.

54

We landed in Kumasi in the evening, like I had my first time in Ghana. Joo-Li scooped Nana Yaa onto her hip and handed Yaw to me as my father stretched to pull our carry-on luggage down from the overhead lockers. Ronan shook a snoring Chardonnay awake. Uncle Ernie and Miss Nikki had stayed in Accra but would meet us at Dadaba later in the week.

"Thank you, 'bye now," the air hostesses chorused as we stepped off the plane into the wet heat, all the women's hair curling and frizzing on contact.

The men on the ground elbowed each other as Chardonnay descended the plane's steps, ogling her thick chalk-colored legs, which went on for miles in her shorts and combat boots. "Sister, let us assist you with your bags," one of them said, helping her onto the Ghana Airways bus that waited for us.

I almost fell out laughing when Char sniffed that pungent sulphur-garlic smell that had greeted me my first day in Ghana. She leaned into the man's personal space like a police dog and instantly recoiled. "Are you wearing deodorant?"

"Oh, sister, I don't like putting chemicals under my arms," he replied.

"Well, then get you some lemon or baking soda then!"

"Chardonnay, don't be rude," Ronan rebuked her.

The same AKWAABA banner hung in the still air when the bus dropped us at the airport building. When we passed customs, the porters rushed at us with their trolleys. Nana Yaa started crying, scared. I remembered Helen, the air hostess who had taken care of me that first day, and how she had dealt with them.

"Leave us alone," I shouted at the pack, wrapping my fingers around Nana Yaa's hand. "These guys will go crazy trying to carry some bags."

"It's okay. They're just trying to do a day's work," my father said to comfort Nana Yaa before directing three of the men to take our bags.

We walked out of baggage claim as a convoy, the porters pushing our suitcases ahead of us. Auntie Irene was just outside the airport with the other waiting people, craning her neck as her eyes picked through the stream of bedraggled arrivals. My face loosened into a smile almost as silly as the grin Mum got around Ronan. Oh, Auntie. It was so good to see her, and this time I could laugh to myself at her wild weave, long fake nails, and heavily lined lips as she tottered over to hug us in too-high heels. I silenced Char with a look, though, when I saw her bite her quivering lips, trying to suppress a snicker. I was not about to have anyone laugh at Auntie Irene in front of me.

Enyo stood shy and silent behind Auntie. I pulled her to the front and threw my arms around her. "I've missed you," Enyo told the ground shyly when I released her from my embrace.

"Did you really?" I teased her.

Auntie Irene hugged me next. "Lila!" She stood back to take me in. "Wow! Look at you. *Ei!* Is this how much you've grown?" She shook her head and moved down the line to greet Joo-Li and my dad. "*Ei, Jude!* Long time."

He shrugged with a smile, their eyes saying things to each other none of us except the two of them and Mum would understand. Not that Mum was trying to understand anything. She was rocking back and forth on her heels, impatiently waiting to introduce Ronan to Auntie. She shone like the sun when her sister and fiancé finally embraced.

I threaded my arms through Enyo's and Char's and led them out to the car park, feeling comfortable, like I was home.

"Boss, where should we put the bags?" One of the porters paused at the Rover.

"There are so many of us. We can stay at a hotel before we go to my people in Apam," Joo-Li suggested before turning to my father. "Jude, I think we should take a taxi. We can't all fit."

"Nonsense." Auntie Irene unlocked the boot of the car for the porters. "There isn't much room, but we'll manage."

I wondered where we would all sleep as I squeezed into the backseat behind Enyo and Char, Mum stuffing herself in next to me. Auntie Irene's place only had two bedrooms.

"She's right, Irene. We have to split up," Mum said.

"We can take a taxi," Ronan offered, pointing to Daddy. Joo-Li didn't look happy to be left in the car with Mum and Auntie as she took the front seat and pulled the twins onto her lap.

"Okay, everybody in?" Auntie revved up the engine and music filled the car. I twisted in my seat to see Daddy and Ronan following us in a sputtering cab.

On the way to Auntie Irene's bungalow, a flashlight waved at us to stop.

Auntie Irene sucked her teeth. "Police."

"They want a bribe," I whispered to Char.

"Shhh!" Mum hissed at me as the man in uniform pointed

his light in Auntie's face. Auntie Irene rolled her window down and sighed nervously. She lowered the radio. "Yes, Officer?" The horn on the taxi behind us beeped. Char, Enyo, and I turned to see Daddy get out.

"Please, sir, those are our women," he said, exchanging a handshake and some bills with him. The policeman stuffed one hand in his pocket and waved us on with the other.

"Did your dad just give him money? Out in the open like that?" Char laughed in shock.

Joo-Li sucked her teeth. "He gave him dollars too. We haven't changed any money yet."

"These are the things I don't miss about Ghana," Mum sniffed as we started moving again.

"*Ho!* These corrupt policemen are not all Ghana is." Auntie Irene looked at us through the rearview mirror. "Lila, am I wrong?"

"Not at all."

"Bits!" I burst out of the car when we stopped in front of Auntie's bungalow and collected Bits and his furiously wagging tail into my arms.

"He missed you so much," Enyo told me as the dog softly scratched my face with his rough tongue.

"No one was giving him sausage anymore," Auntie Irene said, chuckling as she turned the car off.

"There's another dog!" Nana Yaa squealed, tumbling over to pet Moko. All we heard was a scream as Moko barked murder at her.

"The same mean little Moko." I shook my head, pulling my sister close. I started to go inside with her but remembered our things and helped Enyo and Char bring them in. In the main room, the couch and chairs had been pushed to the edges and replaced with neatly laid school mattresses. Mine, my name Magic Markered on the sides, was in the middle.

"Seriously? After eight hours in the air, we have to sleep on the floor?" Char groaned.

"You girls will be sleeping in the living room," Auntie Irene informed us. "And you won't be doing it on my couches. Lila, you'll show Chardonnay how to sleep on a school mattress, eh?" She opened the door to the room Enyo and I had shared, the fragrance of mosquito coil curling up from the glowing ember on the floor. "Joo-Li, you and Jude and the kids can be in here. Felicia, you and Ronan take my room."

"Where will you sleep?" Mum asked Auntie.

"I'll go to Fifi's."

"Where is Uncle Fifi? We didn't see him at the airport," I asked her, realizing just then that we hadn't stopped at the gate-house to greet him as usual.

"He hasn't been feeling too well, but he's anxious to see you. He was so proud when he heard you'd be writing about Ghana. Anyway, you'll see him tomorrow. Good night, everyone."

After Auntie Irene left and the adults closed their doors, I tumbled onto my old mattress. Chardonnay stepped onto the one that had been laid out for her. Her foot practically sank to the floor. "You've got to be kidding me. I can't sleep on that."

"Oh yes you can." I giggled. "Right, Enyo? And you can take a cold bucket bath too!"

"Are you serious?"

I had to laugh at the incredulous look on Char's face. Was that how my face had looked?

"Very serious," Enyo said so seriously I laughed harder and Char started laughing too. "Let me get us some coil." Enyo disappeared to produce a mosquito coil.

"For the mosquitoes," I explained.

"This place is a trip."

Within minutes, the laughter turned to loud snoring, but when I went to poke Char into a new position to quiet her snores, the exhaustion suddenly hit me and before I knew it, I was knocked out.

55

On Sunday we borrowed Uncle Fifi's car and piled into both cars for the journey to Dadaba. Villages, small towns, and miles of green bush flew past our windows as lorries and state transport buses dangerously overtook us, perhaps so we could read the Bible quotes and proverbs at their backs.

My armpits started to itch the closer we got and when Auntie Irene turned into the black gate and beeped the horn, I had rubbed my underarms raw. The watchman roused from his morning nap and cleaned his teeth with the chewing stick as he stooped to swing the gate open for us. My stomach joined the nerves in my pits, my breakfast suddenly growling, expressing the anxious energy I couldn't articulate.

It was like no time had passed. I could see myself walking the laterite paths and paranoia seized me. Was this all a ploy? Had Mum and Daddy planned this elaborate ruse with Joo-Li and Ronan and Miss Nikki and Uncle Ernie and Carly to get me back to Ghana? The irony was Enyo sat next to me, her breath catching in her throat for completely different reasons. I knew she wished she could have come to a school like Dadaba.

"This is where you went to school? I take it back, I'm glad Dad didn't send me to school in Jamaica," Char said, chuckling.

As I directed them to Addo House, my hands quivering, a glint of silver caught my eye under the burning sun. It was a massive silver water tank where the tap had been, the tap Brempomaa had woken me up to fetch water at on my first day at Dadaba. GIFT FROM OUR PARENTS was painted across it in uneven lettering. Brempomaa's parents had come through.

I saw a girl in the Ofori House print approach it with a bucket just as another girl walked in the opposite direction in a gleaming red and white Addo House uniform. Her punk haircut was high in the air, a light dusting of powder at her neck.

"Dadaba girls," I called to them through my rolled-down window, "do you know Brempomaa Fakye or Ivy Abankwah or Hari Abebreseh?"

They looked me up and down when they heard my accent. "Brempomaa?" The girl looked at her friend to see if she knew who or where Brempomaa was.

"*Sa broni.*" *The white girl.*

"Ah. Yes. The *Crifé*. She'll be at SU now."

I thought about surprising Brempomaa at chapel, but Auntie Irene said, "Lila, we should go and see your headmistress first."

I led my family up the hill to Madam's.

Madam looked the same when she thundered into her living room to greet us.

"*Ei!* Lila Adjei! You are looking like a duchess."

"Thank you so much for taking care of my daughter." My father rose to hug Madam and gave her money.

"Oh, thanks are not necessary. I am only doing what I am called to do." I turned to roll my eyes. "Have you seen your friends, Lila?"

"Not yet, Madam."

"Araba!"

Auntie Araba materialized instantly.

"Who should she send for?"

I smiled wickedly now, picturing the fear that would drip in Brempomaa, Ivy, and Hari's stomachs when they got word that Madam was calling them to her house. I rubbed my itching armpits and waited for my friends to come.

"So, Lila, how is it?" Madam asked me.

"Lila is writing a book."

Madam arched her eyebrows, suspicious. "What on?"

"About Dadaba."

Madam squared her shoulders at my answer. "Is that so?"

"Yes," I said, meeting her eyes the way I'd wanted to the day she had accepted the bribe from Auntie Irene in Uncle Fifi's living room.

"Have you seen the tank?" Madam asked me.

I nodded.

"You see things have changed considerably since you were here. I hope you will give your book the proper context."

I tuned her out as Auntie Araba walked in with my friends. I ran to hug them. Before I could reach them they were screaming my name and jumping.

"Madam, we'll be just outside."

I followed them outside and had a proper look at them. Was this how I had looked? They looked dirty but clean at the same time. It was the dust on their sandals, the whites of their prints that had yellowed from too many washes in sedimentary well water. But that defiant trace of powder was at each of their necks as they told me about how Madam kept the tank locked to ration the water. They laughed as they told me they had found a way to steal from it at night. I knew then that I would call the book I would write *Powder Necklace*.

On the drive back to Auntie Irene's I scribbled it down in the notebook Miss Nikki had given me and advised me to keep at all times, and I wrote the first draft of what became the prologue of the book I gave to Carly to submit.

When we got home, I couldn't sleep as the mosquito coil spread its heavy incense throughout the room and Enyo, Chardonnay, and I flopped onto our mats, quiet and thoughtful from the day. I thought about Mum and Dadaba and all that had happened between then and now. I still didn't understand why it all had to happen the way it did. Was it really necessary for Mum to yo-yo me about, throwing me out, then pulling me back? Why couldn't I have had a relationship with my father sooner? Why? Why? Why?

I'd probably get the answers to these questions when I didn't need them anymore. Maybe the answers weren't even the point. Maybe the point was to keep your head up—wear your powder necklace—no matter what. No matter what.

MEDASE | AKPE | THANK YOU

Holy Spirit, I couldn't have written this book without your inspiration.

Daddy, I love you for getting us Mr. Light instead of Barbie dolls—and for your commitment to making us smart women.

Essie, thank you for breaking the box and pushing me to think and write outside of it.

Kwamena, a long conversation with you makes my day. I love you.

Mommy ("who sat and watched my infant head . . ." ☺), you're my heroine.

Brew-Hammonds, Abrahams, Acquahs, Afuns, Agbodzas, Amoas, Amoonoo-Monneys, Binkas, Dankwa-Smiths, Fletchers, Ghansahs, Hammonds, Kpatakpas, Nortehs, Ntumys, Ofori-Attahs, Seddohs, Segbedzis, Sowahs . . . and everyone else in my very big beautiful family: I love you all so much!

Auntie Edith, Auntie Katherine, and Uncle Nana! You're the best.

Akua Anokye, my sister and my friend, *how* would I have gotten through Mansite without you? You and I know how we do.

Elizabeth Joté, a.k.a. the Most Banging Agent on the Planet, thank you for seeing and believing! You were and are a godsend.

Malaika Adero, my editor: *medase, akpe, oyewallado,* thank you for opening the doors and letting me in with a warm, gentle hug. Thanks, Todd Hunter!

Carole Schwindeller, the art, sales, marketing, and publicity teams, and everyone else who worked on *Powder Necklace,* thank you so much.

Brilliant KC Washington and Kseniya Melnik: thank you for patiently redlining draft after draft after draft after draft . . .

Nicole Daignault O'Malley, Stacy Soberalski, Rollie Jones, the Lawrence-Rojas clan, Sasha Dees, Kenya Hunt, Nana Akua Antwi-Ansorge, Stacey Barney, Tara Roberts, Caron Knauer, Camille Acker, Paul Malmont, Eisa Ulen, Renee Zuckerbrot, Penny Wrenn, Maya Nussbaum, Meghan Rabbitt, Alexei Afonin, Christa Mansmann, Larry Ossei-Mensah, Nana Dabanka, MelissaRoshan Perkins, Denise Simon, Suzanne Cort, Tracee Lawes, Saran Simmons, Steffany Bready, Andrea Benn, Darrelle Spears, David Grimes, Elizabeth Paige Smith, Tarah Fuller, Veronica DuPont, Natasha Kern, Barbara Baker, Michelle Sewell, Michelle Horn, Taigi Smith, Jessica Uzzan, Kehinde Akiwowo,

Adjoa Doku Blay, Francis Poku: I am so blessed to know you! Thanks for the advice, suggestions, verifications, and support, and for spurring me on in more ways than one.

Delali "Dahlin" Amoa, Dolores Amoah, Sylvia Chong: Your friendship carried me through. Sister Philippa and Sister Comfort, thank you for looking out for me! Eva Dadzie, I've stopped cuddling my backpack! Thanks for the laughs! Abena Addaquay, it meant more to me than you'll ever know when you stood up to the G-3 Girls for me that day. Evelyn Kwakye, thanks for your sweet spirit. Chonley André Butler, I wish you were here.

Monsieur Silas, Mr. Class-Peter, Mr. and Mrs. Toworfe, Ms. Kotchabrew, Mr. Lawrence Mamiya, Ms. Constance Berkley, Mr. Timothy Longman, Mr. Obika Gray, Mr. Thad Ziolkowski, Mr. William Gifford, Mr. Sidney Plotkin, Ms. Adelaide Villmoare, Mr. Andrew Davison, Mr. Henry Hinksmon, Sister Barbara Baranowski, Ms. Skiadas, Ms. June Pandolfo, Ms. Bolmarcich, Ms. Renee Hoffman, Ms. Carol Goldberg, Ms. Lynn Schiffer, Ms. Deborah Starr: You were amazing teachers.

Farida Abdul-Wahab, Patrice Floy, Lauren Taylor, Tina Gao, and the entire Girls Write Now crew: I am floored by your talent.

Mfantsiman girls: *Obra Nye Woara Bo!* Daphne Faldi and the Presentation of the B.V.M. class of 1991 crew: I'm so glad we're back in each other's lives!

Monica Halpert, Bradford Matson, Melissa Payner, Gerri Gussin, Chapin Clarke, Josh Bletterman, Danielle Gontier, Sabine Roehl, Ted Metcalfe, Mari Katsunuma, Bill Wilson, Tom Bernard, Michael Barker, Marcie Bloom, Dylan Leiner, Dori Begley, Carmelo Pirrone, Claude Grunitzky, Marjorie Miller: I have learned so much working for you. Thank you!

Uncle Abeeku, thank you for asking where my book was ever since I opened my big mouth to say I was writing one. Here it is—I hope you like it!

ABOUT THE AUTHOR

Nana Ekua Brew-Hammond has worked as a style and entertainment editor and journalist for Bluefly, AOL, *Trace* magazine, *The Village Voice*, and *Metro*, and as a Webby Award–winning interactive copywriter for Avaya, Nike, and L'Oréal. A graduate of Mfantsiman Girls' Secondary School and Vassar College, she currently lives in New York City. *Powder Necklace* is her first novel. Visit her website at www.nanaekua.com.

Powder Necklace

Nana Ekua Brew-Hammond

A Readers Club Guide

Summary

Powder Necklace is the extraordinary story of Lila, a British
teenager from a Ghanaian family whose mother abruptly sends
her away to Ghana to attend school and learn about her na-
tive country. Over the course of a year, she embarks on a wild
journey that takes her from London to Ghana to America and
eventually back to Ghana. Along the way Lila discovers her
own unique identity, learning what it means to be Ghanaian
and forming deeper roots in her family's homeland and deeper
friendships with her fellow Ghanaians than she ever dreamed
possible. After half a year of living at Dadaba, a Ghanaian
boarding school, Lila returns to London as suddenly as she left,
and she must adjust to life in England after living in such a different country. Eventually her journeys lead her to New York,
where she moves in with her estranged father and stepmother
and forms a friendship with a fellow student that unexpectedly
leads her back to Ghana, this time to write about her experience. Along the way, Lila blossoms from an obedient daughter to a willful adolescent to a self-assured young woman in a
metamorphosis that spans three continents and invaluable adventures.

Questions and Topics for Discussion

1. In *Powder Necklace* Lila undergoes both physical and mental transformations. Her haircut when she first arrived at Dadaba Girl's Secondary School is one such transformation. Although she initially mourns the loss of her hair, saying, "I started to cry for more than the hair I was losing. . . . I would look like *them*," (p. 52) Lila chooses to continue wearing her hair short after she returns from Ghana. How is her physical change indicative of an emotional one? When did this change begin to occur?

2. Like Lila's hair and the powder necklaces, there are multiple instances throughout the novel of symbolic outward appearances. What are some other examples? How are they symbolic?

3. The plaque at the entrance of Dadaba Girls' Secondary School reads: *Obra woto bobo*—"Life takes time to live" (p. 43). When Lila first arrives at Dadaba, she wonders about the meaning of the saying. What do you think the phrase means? Do you think Lila discovers its meaning by the end of the novel?

4. Discuss the symbolism of the book's title. Why do you think the author chose it?

5. When Lila first arrives at Dadaba, S'ter Penny incorrectly assumes Lila and her fellow *broni* Brempomaa are from the same country, saying, "London. America. They're all Abrokye" (p. 51). Brempomaa takes offense at the generalization, because America and England are in many ways vastly different countries with their own unique identities. By the end of the novel, how

Americanized has Lila become? Do you still consider her primarily English, or has she become more of an American-English hybrid?

6. Similarly, how do you think Lila would identify herself by the end of the novel? Do you think she considers herself more English or Ghanaian?

7. Lila's journeys take her from London to Ghana, to America, and eventually back to Ghana over a very short period of time. Along the way, her family insisted these moves were important for her to discover her roots and establish relationships. Do you think it was necessary for Lila to travel to such extremes in order to make those connections and discoveries? How did her experiences shape her?

8. In addition to struggling with issues of identity and a sense of home, Lila grapples with understanding why her life path is taking such drastic and sudden turns. For all the time she spends asking such questions, by the end of the novel Lila ultimately concludes that "Maybe the answers weren't even the point" (p. 276). Why do you think finding the answers is no longer important for Lila? Were there any unresolved questions you would have liked answers to by the end of the story?

9. One of the stark differences between Ghana and England that Lila notices when she first arrives in Africa is their treatment of religion, and she is taken aback by all the religious-themed store names. "This wasn't even religion," Lila says. "It was faith" (p. 37). What do you think she means when she says "only faith could see God" in Ghana (p. 37)? Do you agree with her?

10. None of Lila's adventures would have occurred if it hadn't been for her mother's reaction to her lying on the floor with Ev. Her mother's sudden decision to ship her daughter to Ghana sets the precedent for Lila's behavior throughout the novel, for which she gives Lila a variety of explanations, from making decisions for Lila's "own good" to needing a break from mothering Lila. What are your theories as to why Lila's mother repeatedly sent her away? Do you think she acted primarily for Lila's good or for her own?

11. After Lila arrives in New York and discovers that the secondary school she wants to attend recently took a trip to Dadaba, she starts to believe in fate and the connectivity of events. Now that you've finished the book, do you believe it was fate or coincidence that Lila wound up returning to Ghana and writing a book about her experiences? Why?

12. As Lila packs to leave Dadaba, Hari tells her to "go and tell them the truth about Africa," to which Lila responds, "Of course. . . . What am I going to say? That we drank homemade alcohol and menstrual water?" (p. 121). What do you think Hari meant by the "truth about Africa," and what is that truth if it's not the sum of daily events?

13. Lila experiences a series of intense experiences during her naturally emotional and chaotic adolescent years. How differently do you think her reactions would have been had she been forced to move later in her teenage years? Do you think she would have been as affected by her journeys?

14. Lila's father and stepmother celebrate Thanksgiving, an American holiday, by eating traditional Ghanaian dishes. Why do you think they've adopted part of an American custom—eating a special feast for Thanksgiving—but not by preparing traditional American dishes? Are there any other moments throughout the novel where cultures are combined in such a way?

Enhance Your Book Club

1. Visit the author's website: www.nanaekua.com.

2. Have book club members prepare some Ghanaian dishes to enjoy during the discussion of *Powder Necklace*.

3. Check out the author's other published works; she's written a variety of pieces, from poetry to plays.

A Conversation with Nana Ekua Brew-Hammond

Q. You've written a range of material. How does the novel-writing process differ from writing a play or short story? How is it similar?

A. For me, writing a novel is much harder than writing a play, poem, or short story mainly because the format is longer and requires undistracted extended periods of time, attention, and good friends to read your work and make sure you aren't writing a love letter to your ego.

My interest in and foray into other genres helped with the actual craft of writing the novel. I'm a big believer that all genres of writing inform each other. At the risk of oversimplification, poetry is about expressing emotion lyrically, plays are about dialogue and character development, and short stories are about plot. I called on these as I worked to develop the characters and pacing of the story.

Q. *Powder Necklace* **is loosely based on your own personal experience attending school in Ghana. How much of your story is part of Lila's?**

A. Lila's experience in Ghana is very similar to my own. When I was twelve my parents sent my siblings and me to Ghana. Because of the way the school system works over there, we couldn't all go to the same school, and I had to cut my hair—my *long, thick* hair that I LOVED flipping like a white girl. ☺ As if that weren't enough for my twelve-year-old mind to process, when I got to the school, I learned I was required to wake up at five a.m., bathe in an open bathhouse, make my bed with perfect hospital corners, perform daily chores like scrubbing a sidewalk-length patch of concrete or sweeping a large plot, hand-wash my own clothes, etc. Oh, and to make things interesting, there was a wicked water crisis going on.

But unlike Lila, my grandmother and aunt visited me pretty much every weekend, loaded down with home-cooked food and water, and my parents sent me goodies and dollars when they could. I also clung to my newfound faith. I became a born-again Christian at the beginning of my visit in Ghana, before I started school there—in that respect I was a lot like Brempomaa and Ivy—and it helped A LOT just to cry out to God in the many moments of loneliness, desperation, misery, and fear I experienced. I released Lila from her school experience after six short months as a fantasy gift to my twelve-year-old self ☺; I had to stay in Ghana for three long years!

Outside of the Ghana portion of the novel, the similarities between Lila's story and mine are more subtle. I made her British because Ghana was colonized by the British, and so a lot more of the *bronis* in Ghana were from London; I also have tons of family in London and spent a lot of time with them on summer breaks en route to New York. Lila's parents' divorce was my way of dealing with the feeling of separation from my parents. Even though I saw them each summer, I felt so disconnected from them at that time. On one summer vacation in the States we went to Disney World. Looking back on it, it was such an American moment in my life/American place to be when I was starting to feel more Ghanaian than anything else.

Finally, the feeling of being at the mercy of the adults in her life was something I felt during that time and definitely wanted to explore through Lila. Ghanaian culture is heavily into seniority. As noted in the book, any adult in your life is reverentially referred to as "Auntie" or "Uncle" whether they're a blood relation or not; seniors at school are respectfully called "Sister"; and, as a rule, "children are to be seen and not heard" (that was the constant refrain I heard growing up in the States). It was important to me to stress that though the events in your life may feel random and out of your control, if you believe that God is in control of *all* the factors in your life—even the adults—you'll see that a lot of those random moments actually had more meaning than you first realized. That very turbulent moment in my life gave me a story that helped me realize my dream of writing a published novel.

Q. Was it difficult at all to detach yourself from Lila and her journey while writing her fictional story, since you were drawing in part on your own life?

A. Yes, it was extremely difficult and at times painful to write this story because it was inspired by many real events. I started writing *Powder Necklace* as a memoir, but decided against it after workshopping it. One of the members of my writing group suggested I try writing it as a novel instead of a true story and I'm glad I took her advice.

As a memoir, I was too obsessed with the exact details and events of the story, and after a while I realized that even my best attempts would still be filtered through my own biases and perspective. Writing it as fiction freed me to explore my own beliefs in God and Ghanaian culture; the decisions the adults in my life made for me; the way I handled myself before, during and after my experience in Ghana; and how my time in Ghana impacted my identity as an American citizen.

Q. Despite how extraordinary Lila's journey is, do you think her struggles and questions about identity and fate are universal? Do you think other teenage girls can identify with her even if they haven't experienced similar situations?

A. I do think the themes explored in the book are universal—not just for girls or even teenagers. So much of our time as children and young adults is spent being talked at and over; decisions are made without our consent, etc.—meanwhile we're going through all these physical and hormonal changes, and struggling to figure out who we are independent of the people in charge of us—all while trying to please them. It's a soupy time in the life of a young person, and I think young people and older people can relate—though older people can be glad they've passed that stage. (I know I am!)

Which brings me to the question of fate; I like to think of fate as "divinely ordered steps." I think it's important for young people to know that what they're feeling isn't crazy or unusual—it's natural—but they will get through it okay; as an added bonus, all the drama they are dealing with and suffering through is fashioning them into a unique and special entity who has real value and purpose.

Q. At the novel's beginning, Lila is a child who "lived to please Mum" (p. 3) and acted according to what would make her mother happy. By the end of the book, she has become a fiercely independent thinker, making decisions for herself. Did you always plan for this emotional independence from her mother to be an essential aspect of Lila's development?

A. I didn't plan this, but I'm glad Lila evolved as she did. Part of growing up is coming to understand that loving and respecting your parents and family members does not always mean pleasing them. You have to live *your* life. Period. Full stop.

Q. At the end of *Powder Necklace* Lila ultimately decides the answers to questions she was grappling with throughout the novel are unimportant. Instead, you write that "Maybe the point was to keep your head up—wear your powder necklace—no matter what" (p. 276). Did you know when you started writing Lila's story that she would ultimately reach this conclusion? What, if any, alternate endings did you draft for Lila?

A. I didn't plan this as the ending. I toyed with ending it at Lila's mother having the baby and Lila holding the newborn in her arms and just shaking her head at all the craziness the baby didn't even know was ahead of her. In the end, I'm glad I ended the book where I did because there are some things Lila will have to grapple with for much longer before she arrives at an acceptable resolution for herself—like her parents' divorce, how her time in Ghana has shaped her, how her relationships with Enyo, Gamal, Auntie Flora, and the rest will shape her worldview, etc. I wanted the reader to walk away with being comfortable with the fact that the answers may still elude, that they aren't necessarily what's most important—what's crucial is coming out of whatever situation you're in intact.

Q. Lila has several moments of overwhelming culture shock when she first arrives in Ghana. Did you have any similar experiences when you traveled to Ghana for secondary school? If so, how long did it take you to adapt to the differences?

A. I did have several instances of culture shock in Ghana. There were the big things like poor infrastructure—dirt roads, electricity and power outages, goats and cows roaming the streets (and leaving turd presents in their wake)—and there were the subtle things like the way you address elders, or the way people treat *bronis* versus Ghanaians; and the acute class system that basically leaves poor young girls and boys no choice but to seek work as maids and houseboys in wealthier relatives' homes.

I don't know that I ever fully adapted when I was there. It helped that I learned the language while I was there; that I made some really good friends; that my family visited often; and that I knew that no matter how long I was there I would ultimately be returning to the States.

Q. **Hari tells Lila to "go and tell them the truth about Africa" (p. 121) as Lila prepares to leave for London. What do you consider to be the truth about Africa? If there was one impression about Ghana you could choose for your readers to take away from *Powder Neckace*, what would it be?**

A. I can't speak for all of Africa, or even all of Ghana, but I think the truth is that Africa is an incredibly complex place. There is a lot of poverty and as a result there is a lot of unnecessary mortality and suffering, acute classism, and corruption, but there is a lot of beauty too.

When people get old they are not ignored or edged out of society—they rather gain more respect and value in the culture. The people are incredibly industrious. The people selling wares on the roadside or under kiosk shacks are entrepreneurs who—with the proper funding—could form a powerful merchant class. The family structure is pretty airtight, one of the reasons the homelessness rate there is low. There are homeless people in Ghana but not nearly at the percentages you find in more developed nations. In spite of all the negativity that surrounds them, people, inspiringly, hold hard and fast to their faith. Also the food can't be beat!

Q. In *Powder Necklace* Lila fell into writing her book through a series of happy coincidences (or perhaps fate). What has been your own literary path? Have you always wanted to have a career in writing?

A. I've always wanted to be a writer, but being immigrants, my parents wanted me to pursue a more stable (and clichéd) path to success: doctor, lawyer, or investment banker. Even though I graduated college with a poli sci degree, I sought writing internships and interned at the *Village Voice* newspaper, and after college I skipped law school and decided to try my hand at writing. I took office jobs, but during my lunch breaks, after work, and on weekends I wrote up query letters to different magazines, which I would hand deliver.

I got a few paid writing gigs and eventually landed a dream job as an assistant editor at an international fashion magazine, where I got to write and edit professionally—and meet celebs! ☺ When funds ran too low, I started over as an intern in the acquisitions department at Sony Pictures Classics, where I got to read and review screenplays. During that time I wrote a script that was a Sundance Screenwriter's Finalist. My editorial experience and fashion background helped me land a gig as a copywriter at an interactive agency where I got to write for the NikeWomen, L'Oréal Paris, and Avaya accounts. I continued to freelance for newspapers and magazines on the side.

In the midst of all of this, I was working on *Powder Necklace*.

Q. Do you have any upcoming projects you're currently working on?

A.   Yes, I'm working on a novel that examines the themes of faith and class in a Ghanaian-American family.

Printed in the United States
By Bookmasters